The Cantor Wore Crinolines

A Liturgical Mystery

by Mark Schweizer

SJMPBOOKS

Liturgical Mysteries
by Mark Schweizer

Why do people keep dying in the little town of St. Germaine, North Carolina? It's hard to say. Maybe there's something in the water. Whatever the reason, it certainly has *nothing* to do with St. Barnabas Episcopal Church!

Murder in the choirloft. A choir-director detective.
They're not what you expect...they're even funnier!

The Alto Wore Tweed
The Baritone Wore Chiffon
The Tenor Wore Tapshoes
The Soprano Wore Falsettos
The Bass Wore Scales
The Mezzo Wore Mink
The Diva Wore Diamonds
The Organist Wore Pumps
The Countertenor Wore Garlic
The Christmas Cantata *(A St. Germaine Christmas Entertainment)*
The Treble Wore Trouble
The Cantor Wore Crinolines

ALL the books now available at
your favorite mystery bookseller or sjmpbooks.com.

"It's like Mitford meets Jurassic Park, only without the wisteria and the dinosaurs..."

Advance Praise for *The Cantor Wore Crinolines*

"I lost 15 pounds just by reading this book! In fact, I still can't keep much down."
Candy Waddle, author of "Lose 40 Lbs. the Yah-Way: A Lenten Bible Study"

"… [Schweizer's] writing is like a ballet of words, except there's no music or dancing, and the words keep smashing into each other."
Beverly Easterling, singing teacher and incidental character

"This is a book of rare insight into the human condition. So rare in fact is any insight that one may search in vain for a shred of it. This will not likely prevent the author from writing another."
Daniel Gawthrop, composer

Once I put this book down, I just couldn't pick it up again!"
Jill Brode, life coach (certification pending)

"Startlingly incoherent …"
Carol Goldsmith, TV news anchor

"Clerical underwear is not to be lightly poo-pooed. Finally the author has given ecclesiastical crinolines the respect they deserve."
The Rev'd. Erika Takacs, Priest

"Schweizer has 132 total stars on Amazon reviews. That's got to count for something."
C. DeLoach Pinter, 2013 Pulitzer Prize Committee

Plausibly ridiculous — like Puccini.
John S. Dixon, peanut broker and organist

"Do the words *Amish fatwa* mean anything to you?"
Jakob Yoder, elder, Bearded Council of Pennsyvania

"I am utterly dumbfounded when a book of this quality comes along."
Dr. Richard Shephard, Chamberlain, York Minster

"This is the Royal Flush of mysteries; the Yahtzee, the Double Pinochle, the Hi-Ho Cherry-O …"
Randy Hatteberg, business owner and incidental character

Three thumbs up!
Jimbo Swanson, book reviewer, Oak Ridge Nuclear Waste Facility

The Cantor Wore Crinolines
A Liturgical Mystery
Copyright ©2013 by Mark Schweizer

Illustrations by Jim Hunt
www.jimhuntillustration.com

Published by
SJMPBOOKS
www.sjmpbooks.com
P.O. Box 249
Tryon, NC 28782

ISBN 978-0-9844846-7-6

August, 2013

Acknowledgements
Nancy Cooper, John Dixon, Daniel Gawthrop, Betsy Goree,
Beverly Easterling, Kristen Linduff, Beth McCoy, Patricia Nakamura,
Donis Schweizer, Liz Schweizer, Margaret Secour,
and Richard Shephard

Prelude

"What's with the sport coat?" asked Meg. "I thought you were going into town for a meeting. You never wear a sport coat except on Sundays."

"It *is* a meeting, sure enough," I answered. "It's the monthly meeting of the Blue Hill Bookworms. I thought I should look professional since I am, after all, the featured author."

"The featured *what*?"

"You heard me," I said smugly. "My literary prowess has garnered me an invitation to the most exclusive book club in three counties."

"I'll say," said Meg. "Mother tried to get in a few years ago. They made her submit her reading list for the past two years and then informed her that her disposition towards romantic fiction was too pedestrian."

"Why haven't you tried to join?" I asked.

"Oh, I wanted to. They even asked me to apply. But I just couldn't do it after they blackballed Mother."

Meg was relaxing in front of the fire in her usual after-supper position on the overstuffed leather sofa. Her legs were tucked up underneath her and she had a book in her hand. Undoubtably it was something the Blue Hill Bookworms would have approved of — Molière, or Edith Wharton — or some such unreadable thing. She eyed me with that look reserved for someone who has snuck a cheesecake into the house during Lent.

"And, pray tell, why are you, Hayden Konig, the featured author?" she asked, then arched an eyebrow. "You certainly have not written a book, and your short detective stories, though mildly amusing to a certain undiscerning audience, are definitely not the stuff of fine literature. In point of fact, they are the antithesis of fine literature. The worst of the worst. You have won awards for how bad they are."

"Perhaps the *intelligentsia* of St. Germaine has discovered the layers of deep meaning lurking in my prose."

Meg laughed.

"They asked you to bring the typewriter, didn't they?" she said with a giggle.

"Well, yes. How did you know?"

5

"It's my fault," said Meg. "I admit it. I was talking with Diana and she told me the Bookworms were reading a mystery novel as a lark. Something to let their brains recover between *Finnegans Wake* by James Joyce and something or other by Virginia Woolf."

"Ah," I said.

"I might have mentioned that you had Raymond Chandler's actual typewriter, you being an eccentric millionaire detective story writer of a sort."

"So you think that they have invited me just to see the typewriter?" I walked over to my desk, sat down, and looked lovingly at the machine in front of me. It was a 1939 Underwood No. 5.

"It did occur to me," said Meg.

"Well, they did ask me read some of my best stuff," I said.

"Which means, your worst stuff."

The Underwood No. 5 had been the most popular typewriter in the world, but this was not just any Underwood No. 5. This particular typewriter had been owned by Raymond Chandler, the noir detective writer, and used to write his first four books. I'd found it listed at an online auction and paid a hefty price to buy it, have it refurbished, and get it delivered to my mountain cabin ten miles outside of St. Germaine. Now it sat on the desk in the den, basking in the glow of the green shaded banker's lamp, and tasked with channeling enough of Raymond Chandler's muse to make my efforts seem worthwhile.

"As you mentioned," I said, "I do have several sentences that have won actual awards."

"Awards for *bad* writing," said Meg. She took a sip of wine, uncurled her legs, and set the book down on the cushion next to her. "Not the same thing, but let's hear them anyway." She gave me a smile that warmed me to my toes. Her black hair, pulled back in a loose pony tail, framed a face with high cheekbones, mischievous blue-gray eyes and a delicious smile. That she could have been a model for a lingerie catalog was my good fortune. That she chose to be an accountant and a first-rate financial advisor was my good fortune as well.

"I've typed them out," I said, looking at the typewritten words dancing across the sheet of 20 lb. bond curled around the platen. There was something about seeing the actual words that gave me a thrill. I chose one of my better, award-winning sentences and read:

She'd been strangled with a rosary: not a run-of-the-mill rosary like you might get at a Catholic bookstore where Hail Marys are two for a quarter and indulgences are included on the back flap of the May issue of "Nuns and Roses" magazine, but a fancy heirloom rosary with pearls, rubies, and a solid gold cross, a rosary with attitude, the kind of rosary that said, "Get your Jehovah's Witness butt off my front porch."

"Ah, yes," said Meg. "I remember that one fondly. Another?"

Although Brandi had been named Valedictorian and the outfit for her outdoor speech carefully chosen to prove that beauty and brains could indeed mix, standing in the sudden downpour she quickly regretted her choice of attire, her sodden T-shirt now valiantly engaging in the titanic struggle between the tensile strength of cotton and Newton's first law of motion.

Meg giggled at that one. It was the most I could hope for, I decided. We'd been married for five years and I agreed with everyone else when they said that she was easily the best thing that had ever happened to me. Baxter, lying next to the fire, lifted his head at the sound, then decided that no one was offering him anything to eat, and laid his shaggy head back on his rug with as big a sigh as a Mountain Dog could muster.

"I'm sure the Bookworms will enjoy hearing your past efforts," she said. "But isn't it about time you started on a new story?"

"I was just thinking about that this afternoon as I was typing these up."

"And what did you decide?"

"Well, I was having trouble coming up with a plot."

"That," Meg enjoined, "has never stopped you before."

"Exactly," I agreed. "So I jumped right in, and guess what?"

"My guess would be that you had no problem whatsoever coming up with a so-called plot, preposterous characters, and a ridiculous title."

"Your guess would be correct," I said.

I pulled the paper containing my finest work out of the typewriter, stuck it in my computer bag, and replaced it with a different, half-filled page from the top drawer. At the top was what I knew my fans longed to see.

```
The Cantor Wore Crinolines
```

Brilliant!

Chapter 1

The Slab Café was bustling and customers were not an easy thing to come up with on a cold Saturday in the middle of January. December, sure. Everyone was out and about at Christmas time, especially in St. Germaine, a town just *made* for Christmas. With its downtown trees and shops all decorated and lit up like a Nashville Holiday Special, its churches, choirs, schools and various groups trying to outdo each other in the name of good cheer, and its fifteen hundred citizens all sweetness and light from Thanksgiving to Christmas Day, by the time December 26 rolled around it was over. Way over. Twelve Days of Christmas? Forget about it. Epiphany would get a nod from the Episcopalians at St. Barnabas; then everyone would settle into the doldrums of winter.

Yes, a bustling day in mid January was as rare as squirrel eggs.

The reason for the activity on this particular morning, as everyone knew, was an auction. At ten o'clock, on the front steps of the courthouse, three properties within walking distance of downtown St. Germaine would be offered for sale. These three houses had been forfeited to the city for nonpayment of taxes. Tax sales didn't happen often in St. Germaine, but when they did, and the properties were offered to the highest bidder, the event garnered a big crowd. Of course, in addition to the purchase price, the new owners were required to pay the lien on the property, but there was no reserve price. Theoretically, anyone could buy a house for the opening bid of one dollar.

This had never happened.

Property close to the town center generally went for a premium. That three houses were for sale on the courthouse steps on the same Saturday was unheard of, but these had all been bought by the same out-of-town investment company just before the housing crash. Now that company was out of business — bankrupt, apparently — and had defaulted on its tax obligations.

Hence all the hubbub.

Meg and I managed to get our usual seat at the back of the Slab thanks to Nancy, who had shown up early and staked it out. Three university students had apparently tried to poach the other end of the six-top, but Nancy flashed her badge, told them that the table was reserved for official police business and informed them that

Holy Grounds, the coffee house down the street, had free WiFi. They were happy with that news and all left, heads down, texting on their smart phones.

"Thanks for running my customers off," said Pete, making a face and wiping his hands on his apron as he walked up to the table. "I might have made two or three dollars off those kids by the time they'd had their third pot of coffee. One of 'em might have even ordered a bagel or something."

"Much better to have professional people hogging the table," Nancy said.

"But with you guys," continued Pete, "I'll end up losing about twenty bucks. You drink coffee by the gallon, eat everything in sight, and never pay your bill."

"You never give us a bill," Meg said in her nicest voice. "That's why we come here for breakfast."

"Don't forget," I added, "we do give you police protection and all of our good will."

"It's true," said Pete, then lowered his voice. "Don't get the country ham. I'm going to switch suppliers. The last two shipments weren't that good. I've heard some good things about the ham over in Western Kentucky. I'm going to give it a try."

"I don't know how you guys can eat that stuff," sniffed Nancy. "It's too dang salty. You're all going to stroke out."

"There was a time," chided Meg, "that you loved it."

"That time is past," said Nancy.

Nancy Parsky was second banana on the St. Germaine police force. She'd been courted for top banana status at police forces all around western North Carolina, but had declined each offer preferring, she said, to stay where she was. In St. Germaine, I was top banana, the Banana Alpha, the Banana-in-Chief.

"Glad you saved me a seat," said Dave, pulling up a chair and sitting down. "Have you guys ordered? I'll have some country ham, three eggs over easy, grits, biscuits and gravy, and a short stack. Gimme some sugar-free syrup, though. I'm on a diet."

Third banana was Dave. Dave Vance worked chiefly in the police station manning the phone and filling out reports. He seemed content with his part-time status, meager paycheck, and substantial trust fund. Dave had a badge, but didn't carry a gun. Nancy did carry a gun and had her Glock holstered on her hip. Of the three of us, she was the one that looked like a cop. Starched brown on tan uniform, badge and name tag, no nonsense attitude. You didn't mess with Nancy. I had a badge somewhere. Maybe in the office. Glove compartment? I couldn't remember. I *did* know where my pistol was. It was still in the organ bench at the church.

"Pancakes sound good for me, too," decided Meg. "In fact, I'll have exactly what Dave ordered, but with turkey sausage instead of country ham. And I'd like my eggs poached. Just two, please." Meg put a finger to her chin and thought for a moment. "Maybe skip the pancakes. And no biscuits, just toast. Whole wheat, with some apple butter. And can you substitute fried potatoes for the grits?"

"So exactly what Dave ordered ..." said Pete.

"Exactly," said Meg. "Just those little changes. Oh, and a bran muffin."

"Ditto," I said.

"Ditto to what?" asked Pete in frustration.

"Ditto to what Dave and Meg said."

"You know that I'm a registered health coach, Dave," said Nancy. "I could arrest you for crimes against nutrition.

"Maybe in New York," Dave said with a smug grin. "Or California. Not here."

Pete Moss was the owner of the Slab Café, a landmark in St. Germaine. The Slab sat on the corner of the downtown square and catered to everyone who loved an old-fashioned, downtown eatery. It had checkered red-and-white vinyl table cloths, a counter with several stools, a checkerboard floor, and all the small town ambiance anyone could ask for. If you wanted a good breakfast, a piece of pie, all the local gossip, or a good Reuben sandwich, the Slab Café was where you came. Open from six a.m. till two o'clock Monday through Saturday. These hours of operation, however, changed with Pete's whims.

"Why don't I just bring out everything we've got?" Pete snarled. We ignored him. He tended to get surly when he had to wait tables. I looked around. For a busy Saturday, the Slab seemed to be a couple of waitresses short.

"You need to get your own coffee," he said turning for the kitchen. "I'm busy."

I'd known Pete Moss for a lot of years. He'd been my college roommate. After graduation, Pete did a stint in the Army, then returned to St. Germaine, his hometown. I pursued a graduate degree in music, then one in Criminal Justice that led to my current job. Pete had been the mayor when he hired me. He wasn't the mayor any more. That post was currently held by his "significant other," Cynthia Johnsson.

Besides being the mayor of St. Germaine and a professional waitress, Cynthia was also a belly dancer — a good one — and had a belly dancer's figure. With her blonde hair and natural beauty, she was easily the best looking mayor in the state.

That they hadn't married in the seven years they'd been together wasn't much of a surprise. Pete had been married a couple of times before. Cynthia, once. Pete was an aging hippie. Sure, Cynthia had finally talked him into cutting his hair, but he still had his earring, a vestige from the early '80s. His Hawaiian shirts and sandals had given way over the past few years to warmer fare, sweatshirts and Old Friends slippers, at least during the bitterly cold months. He still embraced social causes, but with a strong eye towards the bottom line.

This had made him a good mayor and he'd stayed in the office for five terms, running mostly unopposed, and putting his stamp on the office and the town. Then he'd lost a close election to Cynthia and they'd been an item ever since.

"Where's Cynthia?" Meg asked. "I thought she'd be working on a day like this."

"She *is* working," I said, looking at my watch, "or will be in an hour. As mayor, she's in charge of the auction. She's probably over at city hall with the town clerk and the city attorney getting their ducks in a row."

"I'm going over in a bit since I'm the designated police presence," said Nancy. "As soon as I'm finished."

"Well," I said, "you look the most official, and you don't mind shooting people. There's going to be a lot of cash floating around."

With Cynthia unavailable, Pauli Girl McCollough back in nursing school after the Christmas break, and Pete grumbling in the kitchen, the only wait staff left was Noylene Fabergé-Dupont, and she was none too happy about it. Dave waved his empty coffee cup at her, then saw the look in her eyes and quickly reconsidered his position.

"Anyone else want coffee?" he asked, getting to his feet. "I'll bring the pot."

Chapter 2

The courthouse was right in the middle of the block, on the east side of the downtown square, next to the police station. The steps in front ran from the large double doors down to the sidewalk and had been cordoned off. The people were gathered on the sidewalk and in the street with the crowd overflowing into Sterling Park. Sterling Park, this time of year, was pretty bleak. The hardwoods that shaded the three-acre park were bare. The holiday decorations were gone except for a dead Christmas wreath and a couple of strings of burnt out lights dangling from the top of the gazebo. On top of that, the gazebo hadn't been painted for a couple of years and was sorely in need of a fresh coat. The grass was mostly sparse and brown. Even the snow had turned to gray slush. The hundred or so people treading what was left of the grass, waiting for the auction to begin, were quickly turning the lawn into a quagmire of muck. No one seemed worried about it. By spring, it'd be beautiful again.

Cynthia was at the top of the steps talking to Matthew Aaron, the city attorney. She had a clipboard and was busily writing. The town clerk, Monica Jones, was sitting at a small table off to the side, completing some paper work. Nancy was standing beside her, arms folded, a no-nonsense look on her face. Kathleen Carson was making her way through the crowd handing out flyers containing all the pertinent real estate facts. I looked at my copy.

Three houses were listed, along with some basic information that anyone could find by doing an on-line search — address, square footage, zoning, encumbrances, previous purchase price, tax value — accompanied by a grainy black and white image of the front of the house. I scanned the list quickly. No liens or mortgages on any of the houses. That was a surprise.

At ten o'clock sharp, Cynthia walked up to the microphone.

"Okay," she said. "Quiet, please."

The crowd settled down and waited expectantly.

Cynthia flipped through some papers on her clipboard, then settled on one and read it aloud.

"In accordance with the town charter, this auction is held by the township of St. Germaine to recover unpaid assessments. The town is foreclosing on the back taxes that are owed. If you wish to bid on any property and you haven't already registered with the clerk, you need to do so at this time. If you are from out of town, you will need to leave a certified check with the clerk in the amount of one thousand dollars. This will be returned to you in the case of an unsuccessful bid. If you're from here, we know who you are and where you live."

Laughter from the crowd, and five people made their way up to the table and stood in line while Monica took their information.

"Here are the terms of sale," continued Cynthia. "Now, pay attention, 'cause I'm not going to repeat myself. If you bid on one of these here houses, and you win, you are legally responsible for the bid. The town requires a ten percent down payment today and that payment has to be cash or certified check."

"We've heard all this before," yelled a voice. "We know how it works."

"It's freezing out here!" called another. "Get started already!"

"Just to be clear," said Cynthia, "so I don't have to throw anyone in jail: If you bid fifty thousand dollars for the house and you win, you give us a certified check for five thousand dollars or five thousand in cash right after the auction. This morning. By noon. The balance is due in thirty days. You don't pay the balance in thirty days, we keep your deposit and go again."

"What if I ain't got five thousand dollars cash?" yelled Skeeter Donalson. "Is this auction just for you rich folks?"

"Yes, Skeeter," said Cynthia. "This auction is just for us rich folks, so you go on home now."

More laughs from the crowd. Skeeter folded his arms and made a face.

"As you know," continued Cynthia, now off script, "the North Carolina company that owned these houses is bankrupt and the properties are being sold 'as is.' The city is going to make an opening bid for the amount owed in taxes, so don't go getting all mad and think we're driving the price up. We're not."

"Let's get to it," came the same voice as before. Not Skeeter. Skeeter was sulking. "*We're freezing!*"

"Finally, St. Germaine Federal Bank is open this morning," said Cynthia, "just in case any of y'all need to make a trip over there and get a certified check. Stacey Lindsey will be there until noon."

"How come we can't go into the houses?" called Helen Pigeon. "We don't know what shape they're in."

"We don't own the houses," said Cynthia, "so we can't let you in. The owners can't be located; they're probably in Brazil or somewhere. As soon as you buy it, or if no one wants it and the city buys it, we'll cut the locks off."

General mumbling across the crowd, but most everyone was nodding.

"We already got a peek inside," Annette whispered to me confidentially. "Last week. Francis is looking to get another rental property."

Francis Passaglio was an orthodontist in Boone. He and his wife, Annette, were lifelong members of St. Barnabas Episcopal Church. Annette was from old St. Germaine money but had always worked mornings in Francis' office as manager and bookkeeper. Now that the kids were grown and gone, she also kept busy as a local reporter for the St. Germaine *Tattler*. Francis was a good-looking fifty-year-old, fit and trim with salt and pepper hair and a smile that would make George Clooney blush. He was purported to have quite an eye for the ladies, although most of that was probably just grist for the St. Germaine rumor mill. One thing about Francis Passaglio: he was used to getting his way. This I knew from experience. He could be quite unpleasant.

Cynthia quieted the crowd again. "Then let's get going. The first house is on Oak Street. Lot number 317."

"Ten dollars!" yelled Skeeter.

Cynthia put her hand over her eyes and shook her head.

"The town bids twelve thousand, three hundred fifty-six dollars," said Monica from her clerk's table. "That's the outstanding tax bill."

"*What?!*" yelled Skeeter, outrage in his voice. "Are you kidding me?"

"Fifteen thousand," called Jeff Pigeon. Jeff was a chiropractor, and he and his wife, Helen, had several investment rental properties in St. Germaine. Helen taught second grade. They could be counted on to keep the bidding going, at least for a little while.

"Sixteen," countered Francis.

"Twenty," yelled Roger Beeson, manager of the Piggly Wiggly grocery store.

The bidding went higher as people decided what a house near downtown St. Germaine was worth to them. I suspected that most all these bidders were after an investment. If they could get it cheap enough, they'd turn around and sell the house, or rent it out. Rental houses were currently at a premium.

The tax assessment on the Oak Street house was $294,000. Tax assessments were always high in St. Germaine, though. Realistically, in today's market, this one might sell for two fifty or so. It was a mid-century vacation cottage, probably not recently updated, and not very big. When the bidding got to one hundred twenty, things started slowing down, and finally there were two. I didn't recognize the woman who was bidding against Jeff Pigeon. Someone from out of town, but maybe close — Boone or one of our other surrounding townships. Jeff offered one final bid at one forty, then dropped out, and Francis Passaglio jumped back in, with Annette whispering furiously in his ear. Back and forth for another five minutes, then Francis threw his hands up in disgust, turned, and walked away through the crowd. Annette followed, hissing at him all the way.

The other woman bought the cottage for $158,000. A deal probably, although the inside was a mystery. She made her way up to Monica's table and the crowd buzz started back with a vengeance.

The second house — a larger, three bedroom Victorian on Cherry Bluff Lane, about four blocks off the square — was bought for $154,000 by Jeff and Helen, obviously determined to score some property. I thought they'd overpaid. This house was in much worse shape than the one on Oak Street and would take quite a bit of money to fix up. But hey seemed to be satisfied and didn't even stay for the third offering.

The third house was on Maple Street, set on the back of the lot right next to Holy Grounds, the coffee shop. Holy Grounds was the third incarnation of the old two-story, American Foursquare house since I'd moved to St. Germaine. It was a design popular in the early 1900s consisting of four square rooms on each floor and a central hallway connecting the front and the rear of the building to take advantage of the mountain breezes in the summer. A long front porch stretched across the front and was perfect for rocking and enjoying a cup of coffee anytime of day. The house had belonged to Mrs. McCarty for as many years as anyone could remember, and then purchased by a couple from Virginia who opened a spa with adjoining coffee shop. Kylie and Bill Moffit bought it from them, closed the spa, but kept the coffee shop going.

16

On the other side of the property for sale was a law office housed in a one-story bungalow.

The house that was for sale was smaller, but more charming than either of the two beside it, with a real arts and crafts look about it. The upside was that the block was zoned for either commercial *or* residential use. The downside, if you were looking for a home, was that it was flanked by businesses on either side.

"Ten dollars," yelled Skeeter.

"The city bids eight thousand forty dollars," said Monica.

"Dadburnit!" yelled Skeeter. "Eight thousand forty-*one!*"

"This is the one?" Bud said, sidling up beside me. He already knew the answer. He was just nervous, nervous as any other twenty-two year old kid right out of college getting ready to bid on his first house.

"This is the one," I said. We'd already talked about our strategy. The house was listed on the tax rolls for $218,000. Eleven hundred square feet, two bedrooms, one bath.

"Go on," I urged, grinning.

"One hundred twenty-nine thousand dollars," Bud called out.

"*What?*" screeched Skeeter. "*Illegal!*"

"Quiet, Skeeter," said Cynthia into the mic. "I have a bid of one hundred twenty-nine thousand dollars. Is there any advance?" She looked over the crowd. People were looking frantically at their papers. The previous two houses had taken thirty minutes each to sell, the bids going up incrementally with everyone taking their time and mulling over the previous bid. Now, all of a sudden, it was put up or shut up.

* * *

Bud McCollough was the eldest son of Ardine McCollough and the older brother of Pauli Girl and Moosey. I'd known them a long time and helped the family financially when I thought they needed it ... not that Ardine would ever ask. Ardine had been a single mother for the better part of a decade now, her husband PeeDee choosing to make his home elsewhere — "elsewhere," according to some folks in town, being under a pile of rocks in some unnamed holler far up in the hills. PeeDee, by all accounts, had been an abusive husband and father and, when Ardine had had enough, she'd had enough. That was that. There were those folks in the hills

17

who didn't bother calling the law to settle family disputes. Of course, PeeDee might just have easily relocated to the Florida panhandle to start over with a new family. Hard to say.

The one thing he'd insisted on was naming his children after his third favorite thing, behind his truck and his hunting dog — that being beer. The name Bud was okay, Pauli Girl was a stretch, but Moosey (Moosehead Rheingold McCollough) got the worst of that deal. It didn't really matter in Moosey's case. By the time you knew Moosey, the name kinda fit him.

Bud, though, had always been an odd duck, but as luck would have it, a wine savant. He had a Bachelor's degree in business from Davidson and, although he hadn't graduated with any kind of distinction, he was the youngest master sommelier in the country. Ask Bud about any wine you could think of and you'd be likely to get a quick review in winespeak: a saucy Cabernet that tastes like being slapped up side of the face with a wet trout that morphs into a mermaid; a young Merlot that has all the commercial appeal of gonorrhea with notes of dung, spare ribs, horse blanket, boiled cabbage, and cardboard; a Malbec almost Episcopalian in its predictability, cream cheese and mothballs, but as haunting as a cello solo by Yo-Yo Ma; hot dog water. And he was always right.

Not only could Bud talk the talk, he had the nose, and the nose knows what the nose knows. He'd been studying wines since he'd been old enough to check books out of the library. Once he discovered interlibrary loan, there was no stopping him. He'd also been collecting wines since he was twelve, buying bottles online under several aliases, wines he was sure would mature and grow in value. I also contributed to his cellar when Christmas and his birthday rolled around, knowing that he wasn't drinking it, but stashing it for some greater purpose. I hadn't seen the stash, but Bud told me he had close to five hundred bottles — all bought for less than twenty bucks apiece. Even at face value, it was close to six thousand dollars worth of wine. Bud informed me that the market price of his cellar was closer to fifty thousand. An impressive start for a twenty-two year old vintner.

An impressive start, but not the best thing. Not the *pièce de résistance.*

This was not the first auction Bud and I had attended together. Four years ago, Bud and I went in together on some wine that Bud spotted at a farm sale. That is to say, we began our partnership. At

18

his behest, I paid ten thousand dollars for three cases — thirty-six bottles — of Chateau Petrus Pomerol, 1998. Two hundred seventy-five dollars per bottle. Ninety-two dollars per glass. The wine was cheap at that price. Meg and I had mistakenly finished three bottles before Bud pointed out (rather hysterically) that just *one* bottle of Chateau Petrus had recently sold for $3500 at auction. A year or two from now, when it reached a sufficient level of maturity, the price was likely to double. That money, close to a quarter million bucks, was what we were planning on using to open our wine shop.

All we needed was a building. A building close to downtown, within easy walking distance, and at the right price.

Okay, sure. I could buy any building we wanted, but that wasn't the point. This was Bud's deal. I was the silent partner.

* * *

"Is there any advance on one hundred twenty-nine thousand dollars?" Cynthia asked for the second time.

* * *

It's a psychological game, you see. Bud and I had talked to an acquaintance of mine in New York, an expert in buying, selling, and negotiating the best deal. He was a psychologist and had written a book about the psychology of auctions. Bud and I were happy to take some advice.

Number one: Ideally, you don't want the item you'll be bidding on to appear first on the block. The object is to get people attending the auction into a comfort zone. So they think they know how the auction will proceed. This wasn't a problem. I just asked Cynthia to auction the Maple Street property last. "Sure," she said with a shrug. Unfair? Nah.

Number two: Throw everyone a curve immediately. You don't have to go with your drop-dead highest price, but a substantial bid will freeze out most of the competition. Most auctions start low and the bids grow incrementally. Everyone wants a deal and if you can save a hundred bucks, why not? Also, the lower and slower the bidding commences, the more people get in, and once in, folks start contemplating. Hmm, they think, a hundred and fifty is still a good price for this property. I can probably turn around and sell it for one-seventy tomorrow and make twenty thousand. Not a bad day's work.

Number three: Jump in hard, jump in fast. Unless someone really wants what you're after, the chances are that they're not going to drive the price up on you for fun. If you have steel in your voice, the tendency for most people is to back off.

* * *

"Third and final asking," said Cynthia.

"One hundred and thirty thousand!" yelped Skeeter, unable to contain himself.

The crowd laughed.

"Skeeter," said Cynthia patiently, "do you have, or can you get, thirteen thousand dollars cash by noon today as your down payment?"

"No, ma'am," Skeeter said, dejectedly, looking at his feet and kicking at a pile of snow where he was standing. He looked up, fire in his eyes, "But, neither can Bud! He's poor as a church mouse!"

"Bud," said Cynthia, "do you have, or can you get, umm ..." she paused, doing the math, "twelve thousand, nine hundred dollars cash by noon today as your down payment?"

"Yes, ma'am. I have it right here."

Bud lifted his briefcase into the air and the crowd erupted in chatter.

"Sold, then!" proclaimed Cynthia. "Come on up here, Bud. That's it, everyone. Thanks for coming out."

She turned and went back into the courthouse with Matthew Aaron, leaving Monica Jones sitting at her desk finishing the paperwork. Nancy stood beside her, guarding the cash.

Chapter 3

"Don't spend too much time over there with your typewriter," Meg called from the kitchen. "Everyone will be here in an hour or so. You're the designated griller."

"Everything's all ready to go," I answered back, lifting the lid of the cigar box and fondling a *Romeo y Julieta* Cuban beauty.

"Don't you dare light that cigar. You and Pete smoke those outside. And find some decent music to put on, will you?"

I sighed and put the cigar that was about to make its way to my lips back in the box. Meg had an uncanny way of sensing a cigar about to be lit.

"What's wrong with this music?" I called back.

Meg came in from the kitchen, rested a hand clutching a butcher knife on her cocked hip and glared at me. "What's wrong with it? Just listen to it! It makes my fillings hurt."

"You don't like Bartók?"

"I don't like *that*. Not when actual people are coming over for dinner. Pick something pleasant."

"Pleasant, you say."

"No," Meg said, "I take that back. What I mean is pick something that *I* might find to be pleasant dinner music."

"How about a Johannes Ockenghem compilation. Various motets for eight voices, circa 1440?"

"No."

"Alpenhorn quartets from Gridelwald, Switzerland?"

"Nope."

"How about *Die Dreigroschenoper? The Three-Penny Opera?* A modern classic. Mack the Knife? Pirate Jenny?"

"Tempting," said Meg, "but, no. Just put on Pandora. Something fun." She disappeared with her knife.

Pandora Internet Radio was something new for Meg. We'd finally managed to get decent internet service where we lived, thanks to satellites, geosynchronous orbits, dishes, wires, routers, and fuel injectors. These were things that I didn't understand fully, even though they'd been explained patiently and with great consternation by our "Internet Installation Associate." I did know that our internet connection was now reasonably speedy. At least, speedier than dial-up, our previous option.

The reason that we were so far behind most third world countries concerning internet service was that we lived on two hundred remote acres a good ten miles from anyone else. I didn't mind much, since I came to town everyday and could check email and such. I also managed a cell phone and could text, if push came to shove. Meg came to town every day as well, but she did more internet work than I did and so appreciated the recent advances in technology. A couple of years ago, she and Bev Greene had started a nonprofit, financial counseling business for people who couldn't pay — retirees who didn't know where to go or what to do with their assets, young people starting out, even folks who hadn't filed taxes for years. She and Bev had gotten some grants and, even though Meg and I had funded the project, the whole enterprise hadn't cost much.

Not that we couldn't afford it. Before I'd met Meg, I'd had the good fortune to come up with an invention that I'd sold to the phone company for a large amount of cash. Then Meg came along and doubled my money. Then tripled it. Then lost some, but that was to be expected. Then made it back, plus a bunch. I didn't worry about it. Meg didn't much worry about it, either. She was too good.

I kept my job as Police Chief in St. Germaine because I loved it. I loved my part-time job as organist and choir director of St. Barnabas Episcopal Church as well. Usually. But St. Barnabas had been going through a rough patch concerning the clergy. A couple of the priests in the last few years had been good — excellent, in fact — but some ... well ... not so much. Part of the problem was that the good ones had moved on to higher callings. That wasn't the only reason, and it certainly wasn't the reason that I didn't have any fuzzy feelings for the recently-retired priest of St. Barnabas, Dr. Rosemary Pepperpot-Cohosh.

The thing with Pandora Radio was that you could program your own stations; then Pandora would find other stuff you'd like. Using my iPad, I clicked on one Meg had discovered: French Café Radio. Sounds of a jazz trio accompanied by a French singer filled the house.

"That's more like it," Meg called from the kitchen.

I turned my attention to the typewriter in front of me.

* * *

The Cantor Wore Crinolines

It was a dark and stormy night — the kind of night where wishful girls without prom dates ovulated pointlessly while dreaming of seven-minutes-in-heaven under the bleachers where chaperones dare not tread: a night as dark as the intentions of every adolescent male wearing a $39 rented tux from Big Bob's Land o' Tuxedos out on Highway 34 (cummerbund not included); as stormy as that song about being caught in the rain — the only song any of the boys will dance to because it's a "slow" song — the very song that Ginny Mapletoft (president of the Student Council) picked as the Prom Theme after Jake McDreamy asked her to go steady during homeroom, not that it bothered Cassandra Rollins, head cheerleader and Jake's old girlfriend, she didn't care one whit! That skank! Whatever! — that kind of night.

I took a puff on my stogy, skimmed the daily rag, and contemplated the hard ecclesiastical questions of our time. It's what I do. I'm a detective, a gumshoe, a shamus: a Licensed Liturgy Detective (LLD), with a buzzer, a roscoe, a chasuble, one of those silly hats with the pompoms, and a get-into-heaven-free card. The badge and the shooter came from the local pawn shop, the chasuble and the hat from Vestments-R-Us, and the card from the Presiding Bishop that time she was giving them away at Applebee's on the feast day of St. Yogi the Unbearable. I didn't know if the card was any good, but I wasn't taking chances. Maybe she's got some juice at the pearly gates, maybe she doesn't, but if I know one thing, I know it doesn't pay to poke the bear. And St. Yogi's Day at Applebee's is always a good deal. Two meals and doctrinal absolution for twenty bucks including appetizer? It's a deal I'll take all day. Still, I don't have much use for bishops. There's a reason they're called primates.

* * *

"Here you go, Hayden." Meg appeared next to me with a beer in her hand, then set it down on the desk next to the typewriter and read over my shoulder.

I was happy to lean back, affording her a fine view of my latest literary effort, and pick up the bottle of Cold Mountain Winter Ale. I was currently on a North Carolina beer kick.

"You can't say 'skank.' It's not polite. Take it out."

"I think it's the future participle form of skink," I said.

"You know it's not. It's a descriptive noun and you can't use it."

"Skink, skank, skunk," I said, conjugating morphemes like the true professional I was. "Skinketh, beskanked, done skunked."

"Use that in a sentence. I dare you."

"Easy," I said. "You done skunked up that potato salad."

Meg wrinkled up her nose, thought for a moment and said, "I think we've lived in the hills too long, my dear. You're beginning to make sense."

"Thank you."

"Now, take it out."

"Oh, man," I grumbled, pulling the paper out of the typewriter. "I'll have to retype the whole page. I don't see why ..."

"Hayden Konig, you love it," Meg said and gave me a kiss full on the mouth. All of a sudden I couldn't remember what I was going to say, but it was probably going to be a brilliant rejoinder of some sort. I watched her walk back to the kitchen, enjoying the view and noticing a little more sway than usual. She stopped at the door and turned back.

"What are you looking at, big boy?" she said in her best Katherine Turner voice. "If you want something, just ask."

"Well, now that you mention it ..."

"Later," she laughed. "We have people coming over."

* * *

Bratwurst Night was something special. Hot German potato salad was a necessity. Fresh rolls from Bun in the Oven, the new bakery in town. Caramelized onions, baked apples, and sauerkraut. The sauerkraut was an old family recipe, consisting of

24

a jar of good kraut with a couple spoonfuls of red currant jam mixed in to sweeten it, bacon crumbles, caraway seeds, and a dollop of goose fat. The bratwursts had to be the best: hand-stuffed into natural casings by Bavarian virgins, salted with their tears, and steamed in beer before grilling. I prefer a heavy, dark beer for steaming. Black Raven is perfect.

We never had to dress up for Bratwurst Night. That was another plus. The only person who would not be in something extremely comfortable was Kent Murphee — chiefly because he didn't own anything comfortable. I had never seen Kent when he hadn't been wearing his old tweed jacket and vest, corduroy pants, and a tie stained with whatever he happened to be working on. Since he was the Watauga County Medical Examiner, no one ever bothered to ask what those stains might be. Jennifer, the good doctor's wife, was not inclined to follow his example of quasi-formality. She was happy to dress down for the event and join the rest of us in sweatshirts and jeans.

The Murphees were the first to arrive, then Pete and Cynthia. Bev Greene and Nancy Parsky drove together and arrived as everyone else was deciding which of the colorful beers to try first.

"Or wine," Meg said to Bev, as she took her coat. "We have wine as well."

"Can we have some of that horrifically expensive stuff that Hayden and Bud bought?" asked Bev.

"No," said Meg.

Bev laughed. "A glass of Pinot Noir then."

"These are all North Carolina beers," said Pete, as he perused the selection.

"I'm embracing our mutual heritage," I answered. "Here, try this Duck-Rabbit."

"I'll have one of those Black Ravens," Kent said. "If you don't need them all to steam the brats."

"Help yourself."

"Heck of a thing about that Pepperpot woman," said Kent, popping off the cap. "You know it made the paper in Boone."

"No doubt," I growled.

"Well, she's gone now," said Meg.

"I guess the thing that made us the maddest," said Bev, "was that she thought she could get away with it. I mean, what priest in her right mind would try to funnel a hundred thousand dollars into the discretionary fund and use it to take a trip to Nicaragua?"

"It was a mission trip," Meg said. "She was on a mission."

"She sure was," said Bev. "She and that personal trainer — which, by the way, the church also paid for."

It might be said by some that Bev Greene was bitter, since she had been fired by the Reverend Dr. Rosemary Pepperpot-Cohosh from her position as church administrator within a couple months of the new priest's arrival. And that now she took a certain pleasure in seeing her fall from grace.

"It's not that I'm bitter or that I take any satisfaction in seeing Mother P's fall from grace," Bev said, then offered us all a big smile. "Well, I take that back. I am and I do. Does that make me a terrible person?"

"Yep," said Cynthia. "It really does. But I'll pray for you."

"Well, we got most of the money back," said Meg. "Except what she gave that Nicaraguan gigolo."

"She's back working at Walmart," added Bev, "or so I've heard."

I nodded. "I think that's right. Herb filed for divorce, left, and took a campus ministry position back in Iowa. I think Rosemary is up in Roanoke."

"Did Enrique go with her?" asked Nancy. "I noticed that his workout studio is closed up."

"I have no idea," I said. "I doubt it, though. A dumpy, middle-aged, ex-Lutheran, Episcopal priest from Iowa, now working as a sales associate at Walmart, might not be the catch that a young, fit, attractive ... "

"*Highly* attractive," interrupted Jennifer.

"Highly," agreed Nancy.

"... Highly attractive personal trainer with an expiring green card might want."

"She was quite smitten," said Meg. "It was true love. Agape love. She told me so right before she left."

"I'm sure it was," said Bev with a smile. "The trip to Nicaragua in October was to begin building her new church. She was sure Bishop O'Connell was going to give her the blessing of the diocese. What was she thinking?"

"She took the money down there with her?" asked Kent.

"A hundred thousand dollars in cash," said Bev. "Enrique had arranged for her to make a down payment to the builder. She was stopped when she tried to enter the country. Customs called the feds in and she was sent back to the States immediately."

Kent nodded and sipped his beer. "And Enrique?"

"He came back with her on the same plane. I guess he thought he could still make the deal work out, but once the customs officials got involved the church was contacted immediately."

"How did she get all that cash?" asked Jennifer.

Meg shrugged. "It was easy, actually, and our fault. You know that St. Barnabas has a trust fund that Gaylen set up when we got the settlement from the bank?"

"Sure," said Jennifer. "Several million bucks."

"Right," said Meg. "Well, it's set up in several accounts, one of them being a discretionary account that the priest can use. We went to computer banking a few years ago when the bank started offering online services. What we didn't realize, or even think about, was that, since Rosemary was listed as a signer on her discretionary account, she could also transfer funds between *any* of the accounts. We don't know when she discovered she could do that, or even if Señor Enrique figured it out during pillow talk after one of their 'training sessions,' but she transferred the money, withdrew the cash, and took off for Central America all within twenty-four hours. Of course, they'd been planning it for a while."

"Wow," said Pete.

"We plugged that hole pretty quickly, I can tell you," said Meg. "It won't be happening again. The clergy will have no access to anything but their own account and even then our accountant will monitor it."

"On the upside," said Bev, "our full-time interim priest arrived in town this afternoon. He'll be taking the service tomorrow morning." She turned to me and said sweetly, "Will you be attending, Hayden?"

"As you know," I answered, "I'm on sabbatical from St. Barnabas."

I had decided, after Christmas, that it was time for me to take a few months off. I'd been going to church mad, leaving church mad, and finding myself fuming every time I was within the church walls. I called my friend Edna Terra-Pocks over in Lenoir

27

and she had been happy to sub for me for three weeks during January. The music committee hadn't found anyone for February through June, but they were still looking. I, myself, wasn't looking. I was on sabbatical.

"It's only called a sabbatical when you take time off to achieve something," Bev pointed out. "Otherwise, it's called a leave of absence."

"Not really, no," I said. "Technically a sabbatical is a rest from work. A hiatus. The origin probably comes from the book of Leviticus where there is a commandment to desist from working the fields in the seventh year. In the strictest sense, a sabbatical should last an entire a year. I'm only taking six months. It's only in recent times that a sabbatical has been used to fulfill some goal, like traveling for research or doing some sort of continuing education."

"Do you have a goal?" asked Cynthia.

"You bet," I said. "I'm working on my detective story."

This announcement was greeted with a resounding chorus of groans.

* * *

I looked across my desk at Pedro LaFleur, my right hand man, a loogan, a bruno, a button, a bindlestiff with a palooka face gone to seed. He slumped heartbrokenly in his chair like a sad sack of spuds slung over the shoulder of some broken-down Idaho wharfie who'd seen too many night shifts in a city where the only second chances were left to those who managed to get out of this burghal of Unitarian Churches, Bible colleges, and unaccredited law schools.

He had a drink in his hand and a hole in his heart, a hole big enough to drive a 2013 Honda Odyssey minivan (with satellite linked navigation and a multi-angle rearview camera) down the anterior vena cava, execute a three-point-turn at the atrioventricular valve (thanks to the rearview camera), then exit the pulmonary artery without ever once scraping the Celestial Blue Metallic finish that comes standard on the EX-L. This hole was courtesy of Claire Annette Reed, the ex-girlfriend who squeaked that they should just be friends. Pedro wasn't interested. He already had a friend.

Pedro could sing, sing like a seraph on angel dust — the sweet stuff, not that junk that you get from those stinkin' cherubs down on 43rd, that junk will make your wings fall off and your halo burst into flames. He was a countertenor with high Cs to burn and, if you wanted the Allegri "Miserere" in this town, you'd better call Pedro or you'd be pushing up daisies by Easter. It was part of his deal with the Family. Da Capo Nostra.

I took a slug of hooch, cheap hooch, snapped the paper open, and looked at the clock on the wall, watching that thing hanging underneath it swing back and forth like a pendulum. Page two. Obituaries.

Suddenly there was a knock at the door. Marilyn? Nah. Marilyn was in Vegas for the week at the National Literary Device Convention.

"Come in," I called, and the door swung open.

* * *

Supper was delicious. As we ate our way through the brats and kraut, potato salad, and all the fixings, our conversation turned from St. Barnabas to other things: Cynthia's auction, Bud's purchase and our plan for the new wine shop, Pete's idea for renting out Portia the Truffle Pig to trufflers for Saturday excursions, and all the reasons why Kent and Nancy found *Bones* to be the stupidest show on television.

"Really?" said Kent, waving his hands in the air. "They expect us to believe that the Smithsonian, or *Jeffersonian,* as it's obliquely called, has a multimillion dollar crime lab that can do 3-D holographic reconstructive modeling by tapping a couple of times on the screen of an iPad, and employs five highly-trained über-scientists who are free to utilize all the resources of the government and the FBI — all to figure out the identity of a homeless guy found in a dumpster? *Really?*"

"Hang on," said Nancy. "I'll just collect some DNA from this tapeworm I found in the portable toilet and run it through our mega-database. Make sure you get a close up of the tapeworm crawling around the bottom of the crapper. Then I'll check it against all the known DNA in the entire world, and have an answer for you in a couple minutes. I'm sure we'll find a match."

"How about some dessert?" asked Meg. "We have bread pudding."

* * *

After supper, Pete and I went outside on the back deck to enjoy our cigars. Kent joined us, but eschewed our cheroots in favor of his pipe. This separating of the sexes after supper is a time-honored tradition in North Carolina. So we were rather surprised when the door opened and Nancy joined us.

"You can't come out here," said Pete. "Men only. We're smoking."

"I brought my own cigar," said Nancy, then flipped open a lighter with one hand while she rolled the end of the Cuban inside her pursed lips, wetting it.

"How does this jibe with your health coaching?" Pete asked.

"I'm a health coach, not a nut," said Nancy. "I've already eaten two brats, German potato salad, and enough bread pudding to feed an African village for a week. Besides, I've got a gun."

"Fair enough," I said, then looked at the cigar band. "You stole that one from my desk, right?"

"Sure I did," said Nancy, lighting the cigar and taking a puff. "But what're you gonna do? These Cubans are illegal in every state in the union."

The door opened again and Meg stuck her head out. "It's freezing out here," she said.

"Can't be helped," I answered. "Unless you want to let us back in the house."

"Nope," said Meg. "You'll be fine." She handed me my cell phone. "Here you go. It's Dave."

"Hi, Dave," I said into the phone. "What's up?"

"You know that house that you and Bud bought?" said Dave.

"Yeah."

30

"Well, Bud was in there looking around after his shift finished at the Piggly Wiggly. The electricity was off, so he brought a flashlight. He had a key to the place."

"Right," I said. "Cynthia gave it to him right after the auction."

"So, he called the station and, well, since I'm the cop-on-call tonight it was forwarded to my cell."

"Yeah?"

"The thing is," said Dave with a heavy sigh, "Bud found a dead body in the bedroom closet."

"You're kidding, right?"

"Nope. I'm here now."

"We're on the way."

Chapter 4

Meg elected to stay home and clean up the dishes after supper. The rest of the dinner group headed into town, since Nancy and I were heading that way anyway. Nancy dropped Bev off and headed over to Bud's new house. Kent and Jennifer wanted to stop by since it was on the way home and Kent had a professional interest in the discovery. Being the medical examiner, he'd be seeing the body eventually anyway. Jennifer decided to stay in the car with the heater running. Cynthia held that since she was the mayor, she might as well come and see what was what. Pete wanted to be deputized immediately.

"Remember when I helped you guys solve that case of the kidnapping and the double murder? I don't even know how I do it. I'm like some kind of crime-solving genius."

"I don't remember that at all," I said.

"Me neither," said Nancy.

We were standing in the living room of what looked like a small craftsman-style vacation cottage. We couldn't really tell very much about the house since we were all using flashlights. I kept two in my truck. Nancy had two as well. Dave motioned us toward a room in the back.

"In there," he said.

"Where's Bud?" I asked.

"I sent him home. That okay?"

"Fine," I said.

"He seemed sort of shell-shocked when I got here."

"I'll bet," said Cynthia.

"Anyway, the body's in the closet. It's a woman."

"Anyone we know?" Pete said, as we all followed Dave into the bedroom.

"I don't know her," said Dave. "At least, I don't think I do. It's hard to say till we get enough light back there."

"How about the ambulance?" Cynthia asked.

"On the way from Boone," said Dave. "I told them no hurry. They'll be here within the hour."

"They'll drop her off at the morgue," said Kent. "I can give her a look on Monday."

We crowded into the small bedroom and huddled around the closet door. The room was empty except for an old chest of drawers against one of the walls. The closet was framed by a couple of louvered wooden doors, both of which were standing open. The beams of our flashlights all found the body at the same time.

It was a middle-aged woman. She was sitting on the floor with her back against the side wall of the closet. Her legs were stretched straight in front of her, her feet splayed to either side. Her hands were folded in her lap and her eyes were closed. She was wearing a woolen dress that looked a little big for her, a scarf, and shoes with a short heel. Church clothes.

"She's been dead for a couple of days at least," said Kent, putting his face close to the dead woman's face, sniffing, and peering closely with his flashlight. He put a hand on her abdomen. "Probably longer. It's been below freezing for what, two weeks or so? With no electricity on in here, it's like a freezer. Hardly any decomp at all, but that's to be expected since she's solid as a rock."

"It's been winter since way before Christmas," I said. "We've had a few days up in the forties, but even so, the temperature in here might not have climbed high enough to thaw her out."

Kent nodded. "Yep. Once she was frozen solid, it'd take a few days to thaw her out. Think about a twenty-pound turkey. That takes a day or so at room temperature. She looks to be maybe a hundred forty pounds. So, even if she thawed a bit during the day, every night she'd freeze back up."

"Anyone recognize her?" asked Dave. "I don't."

"Yeah," I said. "It's Darla Kildair. She didn't live here, but she cut hair over at Noylene's Beautifery until last year. Then she and Goldi Fawn Birtwhistle had a fight and Darla opened her own shop down around back of Dr. Ken's Gun Emporium on Old Chambers. He gave her that basement space. Not easy to find unless you know where it is, although there's a sign for it on the highway. Darla's Hair Down Under."

"So that's what that is," said Dave. "I had no idea."

"Well, I'll be darned," said Nancy, shining her light right into the woman's face.

"That's not Darla," exclaimed Cynthia with astonishment. "I saw Darla at Thanksgiving when I went over there for a haircut. This woman is older."

"Pretty sure that's her," I said.

"What you're seeing is some desiccation," said Kent. "That's to be expected, even with the freezing. When a body loses fluid, the aging process appears more pronounced."

"Her hair's different, too," said Pete. "Didn't she used to have blonde hair?"

"It was sort of auburn," said Cynthia. "Now it's almost black and a lot shorter. I guess it's her though, now that I look closely."

"Oh, Darla," said Pete thoughtfully, "what has brought thee to this terrible end? A bad haircut?"

"That's not funny," sniffed Cynthia. "She was a nice person."

"Sorry," said Pete.

"I don't imagine," said Nancy, "that she wandered into a locked-up house, walked into the closet, and died of natural causes."

"I don't imagine she did," I said.

"Lookee here," said Kent, flashing his light on one side of her face, then the other. "She's just got the one earring. The other one's missing."

I pointed at Pete and Cynthia and said, "You two keep quiet about that earring. That's a clue, so don't spread it around."

"We won't," said Cynthia.

"What earring?" added Pete.

Kent stood up from his crouching position. "I can't tell you any more till I have a chance to take a closer look. Naturally, liver temp won't do any good and I may never be able to give you a time of death."

"Those *Bones* guys over at the Jeffersonian could do it," Nancy said. "They'd just get a frozen blowfly larvae out of her ear, do a holographic 3-D analysis of the larvae's intestines, and then figure out she died on January 13th at 1:32 a.m."

"They'd also have the crime solved by the third commercial break," growled Kent. "So, you'd better get cracking!"

Chapter 5

My plan had been to avoid church and I managed to do just that for exactly one Sunday. The second Sunday of my sabbatical was the first Sunday of Epiphany and Meg prevailed on me to attend. I remember because Kimberly Walnut, St. Barnabas' Christian Formation Director, had managed to dress three of the ushers as kings and send them down the aisle to the opening hymn, *We Three Kings*. Epiphany (January 6th) fell on a Thursday, but January 9th was close enough. The Burger King crowns were a nice touch, bright gold cardboard with just a whiff of fries. Easter would be late this year, Ash Wednesday still more than a month away. Now, a week later, here I was again.

Edna Terra-Pocks was at the organ in the choir loft in the back of the church. Most churches are not set up like this, preferring to have their choirs in the front. There was some discussion about repositioning the choir after St. Barnabas had burnt to the ground a few years ago, but it was decided to build the church back just as it was, with the exceptions of all the behind-the-scenes improvements: a state-of-the-art sound system with plug-ins for the hearing-impaired; topnotch security including cameras in the nurseries that Moms could log into and watch their darlings during the service on their smart phones; wireless internet throughout the building; radon and carbon dioxide detectors; in short, everything the modern church might need to worship the Creator in beauty and holiness.

I sat in the back, last pew, on the end by the door. Meg was up in the loft with the others, the choir having already warmed up, rehearsed their music, vested, and now waiting for the service to begin. A stricter director might have quieted them down a bit. As it was, it sounded like they were having a frat party up there. I supposed that Edna was tired of battling with them, and since this was her last Sunday as my sabbatical replacement, she was now marking time as far as choir discipline was concerned. The congregation wasn't anywhere near as noisy, although there was a good crowd. I thought about going up the stairs in the narthex and shushing them. Nah.

The large crowd was due mainly to the appearance of our new interim priest. Any time St. Barnabas had a new priest show up, interim, supply, or regular, the pews were always full for a few weeks. In the dead of winter the crowd also varied depending on the weather. Today was overcast and cold, but not bitterly so. Too cold to work outside, or to take a long walk in the mountains. A good day for church.

Bev had told me that the new interim priest was an Anglo-Catholic. Something new for St. Barnabas. Bev knew this because she was on the search committee for the new full-time rector. Their first job was to find an interim priest and they'd done that rather quickly.

St. Barnabas had never been what anyone might characterize as "high church." We weren't low by any means, just somewhere in the middle, and the music had always been pretty good. We followed the prayer book, sang the psalms, and enjoyed great hymns, singing them lustily and with good courage. We had days when high church seemed appropriate, and on those days the incense and chanting abounded. But since our last priest, church had become much more "howdy" than I was used to. There was a lot of superfluous chatting between the priest and congregation, bad show tunes couched as worship songs, cutesy children's moments that had begun to wear thin, and a casualness that I, quite frankly, found off-putting. This is just me, of course. As Meg often points out, I am the president of the Liturgical Curmudgeon Society.

I blamed all this on the Rev. Dr. Rosemary Pepperpot-Cohosh, or Mother P, as she liked to be called. She was cut from a different cloth: a midwestern, Lutheran cloth — calico perhaps, or corn-dyed muslin — but it wasn't her fault. Not really. There were some folks who liked an informal church service and since she was of that bent herself she certainly didn't mind "blending" the service to cater to their enthusiasm. No, it wasn't *entirely* her fault, but I didn't mind blaming her.

I was thinking that an Anglo-Catholic priest might be just the ticket. So, on this, the Second Sunday of Epiphany, I had come to church to see what St. Barnabas had gotten itself into. Granted, there wouldn't be any immediate change in the warp and woof of the liturgical fabric. We'd be draped in calico for a while yet, but an interim priest sometimes stayed for a year and *sometimes* they decided they liked it so much they applied to make the position permanent.

36

I'd programmed the music for January before I'd taken my leave for six months, so I wasn't surprised to hear the choir sing (and quite well!) *Almighty and Everlasting God* by Orlando Gibbons as an introit. That was just about as snooty as the priest was likely to get, given the current atmosphere. Mother P had encouraged Kimberly Walnut to become a deacon and Kimberly Walnut had completed the process just before Christmas. I stayed out of it. About a year earlier, the two women had come to an understanding of the style of liturgy they could both embrace. This no longer included a processional during the opening hymn (too much trouble to get everyone lined up), no incense on high and holy feast days (Mother P claimed allergies), no acolytes (too hard to get the kids to show up), no chanting of any part of the service (too much practice required), no singing the Psalm (too boring), and nothing else that, in my opinion, might take a bit of effort. That's me being a curmudgeon again.

I was watching the priest. He'd been advised about the current practices of the congregation, but I could tell he was uncomfortable. Bev informed me that once he'd told the search committee he was happy to chant the service, he was in. It didn't hurt that the search committee included Bev, Joyce Cooper, Mark Wells, Bob Solomon, Georgia Wester, Fred May, and Francis Passaglio — all but Francis and Joyce, members of the choir. Joyce was ready for a change and Francis didn't care much one way or the other.

The rest of the service was par for the course. No surprises, except maybe for the new priest. Kimberly Walnut presided over a particularly doleful Children's Moment. The kids were bored, had been bored for months, and now couldn't be bothered to make any cute comments. They sat on the steps with their chins in their hands, no expression at all on their little faces. Bored, bored, bored.

"Does anyone know what this is?" asked Kimberly Walnut, holding up a big plastic fish.

No answer.

"It's a fish, isn't it? Jesus made fisherfolk his disciples. Does anyone know why Jesus called them 'Fishers of Men?'"

No answer, although one little girl managed a beautiful eye roll. Bored.

"Does anyone want to sing the *Fishers of Men* song with me that we learned in Sunday School?"

37

They did not. Not even when Kimberly Walnut started the song, then leapt in with wild gesticulations, waving the plastic fish in a bizarre swimming motion.

I will make you fishers of men,
fishers of men, fishers of men.
I will make you fishers of men,
If you follow Me.

The children didn't move. Not a bit. All nine of them, ages four to seven, sat on the steps of the chancel, unsmiling, unspeaking, unimpressed by Kimberly Walnut and seemingly tired of being put on display for the congregation's amusement. They waited till she finished her song, then, without being prompted, got silently to their feet, and walked sadly down the aisle to Children's Church with their heads down. Bored.

It was almost worse than the old days when they reigned terror on whichever priest dared to call them forward during the service.

The choir sang well, though: a lovely anthem, *Trust in the Lord* by Dan Gawthrop and a beautiful little Mozart communion motet. The rest of the music was good. The hymns were well-played and sung, and the sopranos added a descant on the last one they'd had in their pockets for years.

The sermon was fine. This guy was a fairly good preacher.

He didn't chant any of the service, but I expected that it wouldn't be long before he'd make some changes.

Edna kicked into her postlude, the Widor *Toccata*, since it was her last Sunday for a while. She always played it on her last Sunday for a while, even though she now had to don her sports bra to manage it. "Sure, it's uncomfortable," she told me, "but people expect it. It's my signature tune. Now I just strap the girls down and let 'er rip!"

* * *

We went over to the Ginger Cat for lunch. It was Meg's favorite place to eat in town because they had a great chef (this I'd been told on numerous occasions) and they always had a lunch special. The restaurant sat on the northwest corner of the town square, prime real estate in St. Germaine. Next to the Ginger Cat, across Main

Street, was Noylene's Beautifery: an Oasis of Beauty, and Eden Books. The Bear and Brew, serving great pizza and beer, was just a block down Main, away from town. St. Barnabas dominated the west side of the square. There were many other shops and offices lining the perimeter of Sterling Park.

Annie Cooke, the owner of the Ginger Cat, met us when we entered. Ruby, Meg's mom, had skipped church and gotten there early. Lucky for us. The small shop in the front of the restaurant was jammed with parishioners who all had the same idea. They were perusing the local jams and jellies, pickles and sauces, handmade quilts, gewgaws and gimcracks, that made up the inventory. Annie pointed us to the table Ruby had staked out.

"Good afternoon," said Ruby, smiling when she saw us. Ruby looked like Meg, or vice versa. An older version, sure, but the same beautiful features, delightful smile, and twinkling blue-gray eyes. Where Meg's hair was mostly black, Ruby's had become a lustrous silver.

"I see you skipped church," I said to her. "Or else you bailed out during the Children's Moment."

"Nope. I skipped. Sometimes there's no greater joy than skipping church."

"A fact that Hayden well knows," said Meg, "although he did manage to make it today."

"I wanted to see the new priest," I said.

"And?" said Ruby.

I shrugged. "He was fine. The sermon was good. Kimberly Walnut was awful, as usual — something about how a plastic fish was like Jesus. I wasn't really paying attention. Then, she got lost during the prayers of the people and forgot the offertory sentence."

"I'm sure no one noticed," said Meg, perusing the menu. Meg always perused the menu, but neither Ruby nor I knew why she bothered. It was a forgone fact that Meg would order the special, no matter what it was. She might change it a bit to suit her taste, but Meg never ordered off the menu.

"Probably no one did notice," I agreed.

"Remember that time last Advent when you played the *Gloria* instead of the *Kyrie*?" said Meg. "No one's perfect."

"It was wrong in the bulletin," I said, "but your point is well taken. I retract all disparaging comments about Kimberly Walnut. She ministers to the sick and the dying, she succors and comforts

39

those in need. She is truly a gem among deacons. We're lucky to have her."

"Are you kidding?" said Meg, incredulously. "She does none of that! She's awful. She's as nutty as this warm green bean salad with toasted cashews and Corsican acorns." She tapped a page in her menu. "Which, by the way, is what I'm having for lunch."

"*What?*" said Ruby. "That's not the special!"

"You don't know me," said Meg, her eyebrows raised. "I am unpredictable. I might do anything."

Our waiter appeared at the table and filled our water glasses.

"Hi, Wallace," said Meg, smiling at the college-aged kid. "How's school going?"

"Fine, Mrs. Konig. I have a full schedule, plus choir and orchestra, so I'm staying busy, I can tell you. What can I get you to drink?"

"I'll have sweet tea," Meg said.

"Same for me," Ruby added.

"Make that three," I said, "and we're probably ready to order."

"Great," Wallace said, pulling a pad from his apron pocket. "Would you like to hear about our spec ... ?"

"I'll have the warm green bean and cashew salad," interrupted Meg. "With those other acorny things. That's what I want. It's right there on the menu."

"Umm, yes, ma'am," said Wallace, "but our special today is a lightly grilled tuna with shaved fennel dressed in herb oils and a spicy marinade. It's served with a fresh garden salad."

"I'll have that," said Ruby. "The special."

Meg's shoulders slumped. "Okay, I'll have that, too."

"Ditto," I said with a laugh.

Wallace said, "I can substitute the warm green bean salad for the garden salad if you'd like," and Meg brightened immediately.

"Thank you. Just a small salad, though," she said.

"Of course," said Wallace, writing everything down.

We'd almost finished our salads when I saw Nancy and Dave come in the front door of the restaurant and look around. They spotted us and quickly made their way back to the table.

"Sorry to interrupt your lunch, Chief," Nancy said, "but you gotta come right now."

Dave nodded his agreement.

"What's up?" I said. "You find something in the house?" I knew that both of them had been over at Bud's new house first thing this morning.

"We didn't find anything at the house on Maple Street," said Dave, then lowered his voice, "but we just got a call from a woman named Rachel Walt. She's a real estate agent in Banner Elk."

"Yeah?" I said. Nancy looked as though she was standing guard, hands on her hips, checking out the patrons at the other tables to make sure no one was overtly eavesdropping.

"She bought one of those houses yesterday," continued Dave. "The first one that sold, the one on Oak Street."

"I remember."

He lowered his voice and bent low over the table. "She just called. There's a dead body in one of the closets."

"*What?!*" blurted Meg.

"Shh," said Dave. "Keep your voice down, will you?"

"Are you serious?" whispered Ruby. "Another body?"

"Oh, yeah," answered Dave. "We haven't been over there yet. We were at Bud's house when I got the call on my cell. Nancy said you'd be over here eating lunch."

"Well, it *is* Sunday," said Meg, then turned to me. "You go on. I'll settle the bill. Give me a call when you get a chance and let me know what's going on."

Chapter 6

We walked the two blocks from downtown to the corner of Oak and Greenaway. 317 Oak Street was an address that had some history to it. The house number hadn't resonated with me during the auction, but as we walked up, all of us recognized it as the old Cemetery Cottage, so called because of the five tombstones set deep on the back of the property. These overgrown markers were from the 1860s and, even though there had been some talk about moving the remains to a more suitable grave yard — either Mountainview Cemetery or Wormy Acres, nothing had been settled and the owners had been content to let the dead lie undisturbed.

The house was a nondescript 1920s vacation house, probably originally with no insulation, no electricity, and no plumbing, that had been converted sometime in its life to four-season living. It looked much like every other house on this block of Oak Street, small and set on a long, narrow lot. There was a raised front porch, and the young woman I'd seen yesterday was standing next to the front door, wringing her hands.

"Oh, my God!" she said when she was sure we were within earshot. "You've got to do something!"

"Yes, ma'am," I said as we climbed the steps. "We will. Let's go inside and you can tell us what happened."

She led us through the front door and into a small living room. I'd been right about one thing. Nothing had been updated in this house for several decades. Maybe since the 70s.

"I'm Rachel Walt. I bought this house yesterday. You know, at the auction."

The young woman was in her late twenties or early thirties, very pretty. She was wearing a calf-length stylish winter coat and a fur hat. Her hands were stuck deep in her pockets. She was shivering, but probably not only from the cold.

"I was there," I said. "Nancy was, too."

"I remember you," said Nancy.

"I'm a realtor in Banner Elk. I live there. I saw this auction come up and did some homework and figured that if I could get a property at a good price, I could flip it and make a nice profit."

"I thought you got it at a good price," I said.

"That's what I thought, too. Then I find out there are a bunch of bodies buried in the back yard."

"I wouldn't worry about that," said Nancy. "This is the Cemetery Cottage. Everyone in town knows about it. It isn't going to hurt the value any."

"No," said the agent, "but I'm dang sure that dead one in the back closet will."

"Would you show us?" I asked.

Rachel Walt gave a shudder. "I guess. She's right back here."

She led us down a short, paneled hallway and through a door on the left. We entered a rather long, narrow bedroom by the looks of it, although there was no furniture. At the near end of the room was a closet and the door was standing open.

"Right there," she said and pointed toward the dark entrance.

As at Bud's house, the power to this one had been turned off at some point, but we'd brought our flashlights. In addition, there was sunlight coming in the two windows of the bedroom. This woman, like the last one, was propped up against the side wall of the closet, legs stretched out in front of her, hands folded neatly in her lap. Her eyes were closed, but her face was drawn and she looked to be shriveled. Dried up. She was wearing a skirt and a blouse and her feet were in what looked to be expensive shoes. Nice clothes. Church clothes.

"Amy Ventura," said Nancy, shining her flashlight in the woman's face.

"Yep," I said.

"Who's that?" asked Rachel. "Who's Amy Ventura?"

"She lives up on Tinkler's Knob," Nancy said. "Makes a living as a grant writer. Works from home. I think she freelances all over, but I know she's done some work for the Wings of Eagles Foundation and Big Sisters in Boone."

"How do you know?" asked Dave.

"I'm on their boards," said Nancy. "You know, Dave, it wouldn't hurt you to get out and do a little community work every now and then."

"She also works for the St. Germaine Town Council," I said. "Cynthia knows her."

"Huh," Dave grunted.

"Did you already call the ambulance?" I asked Dave.

He shook his head, pulled out his cell phone and tapped it a few times. "I was hoping we really wouldn't need one," he said, then walked out of the bedroom into the hallway to talk.

"I'll call Kent and give him a heads-up," said Nancy, "when we're finished here."

"So, tell me what happened," I said to Rachel. "How exactly did you find her?"

Rachel thought for a moment and made a face. "I came here right after church. I go to Arbor Dale Presbyterian in Banner Elk. I drove up, unlocked the door, and came in. I was looking around. You know, going into all the rooms as one does. At the auction yesterday, someone — I don't remember who ... a woman I think — said to me, 'I see you bought the old Cemetery Cottage.' Then, when I didn't know what she meant, said that there was a graveyard at the back of the property. So I was getting ready to go out there next when I opened the door to that closet and there she was."

"Did you touch anything?" I asked.

"Of course not. Well, the door knob, I guess. I dialed 911 and they patched me through to Officer Dave out there. Then you guys all walked up. What's the deal? You don't have a police car?"

I ignored her.

"Nope," said Nancy. "We're just bumpkins, not like your fancy police force in Banner Elk."

Rachel's face flushed. "Sorry," she muttered. "I didn't mean anything."

"We're going to have to keep you out of the house for a couple of days," I said. "Just till we figure out what happened to Amy Ventura. We'll need your contact information."

"I understand," said Rachel. She handed me one of her business cards. "Just let me know when you're finished. And if you ever need a good realtor ... "

"You'll be the first one I call," I lied.

Rachel Walt walked out of the room and we listened to the front door open, then close with a bang. Dave came back into the room.

"The bus is on the way," he said.

"Good," I said. "Now call the electric company and get the power turned on here and in Bud's house, too. Today. Don't take any excuses. If they have to send someone out, get them to do it, but I'm reasonably sure they only need to press a button somewhere."

Dave nodded and turned his attention back to his cell.

I took Nancy's arm and steered her back to Amy, then squatted and pointed at her left ear. "Missing earring," I said softly, then stood up. "We've got to call Jeff and Helen Pigeon and get into that house they bought yesterday."

Nancy looked confused for a moment, then understanding crept across her face. "You don't think ...?"

"I hope not."

Chapter 7

Helen Pigeon informed us that Jeff wasn't home — he'd gone to a Sunday School men's retreat and wouldn't be back until after supper — but she would be glad to come and meet us. Ten minutes later, Nancy and I were waiting on the covered porch of a Victorian-style house on Cherry Bluff Lane. We'd walked over since our vehicles were still downtown and the address was only three blocks away.

"I checked on the next of kin for Darla Kildair this morning," Nancy told me as we walked. "I couldn't find anyone. No husband, no family that I could locate. She was married once but divorced back in 1996."

"How about Amy? You know if she's married? Any kids?"

Nancy shook her head. "I don't know. I knew who she was because I've sat in a few board meetings with her, but I didn't know her well."

Helen drove up, parked on the street, and joined us on the front porch of the house a minute later.

"What's going on?" she asked.

"Afternoon, Helen," I said. "We just need to look inside. There's been a problem with the other two houses that were sold yesterday."

"What kind of problem?" Helen was fumbling with a ring of keys, trying to find the one that fit. "Dang it! Jeff put the key on this ring with our other ones. We have three other houses that we rent out."

"Yeah," I said, ignoring her question. "Jeff told me that."

"I haven't even gone in yet. Right after the auction, Jeff took off for that retreat and I was in Hickory yesterday. I didn't get back until last night and the electricity isn't turned on, so I didn't bother to come over. Then, church this morning ..."

She found a key that worked and the door swung open. She led the way in.

"Helen," I said, "why don't you wait outside? We just need to do some checking."

"Why can't I come in?"

"It'd be better if you waited on the porch."

Helen scooched around me and made for the living room. "Oh, I won't be any bother. Why don't I just look around as long as I'm here?"

"Helen," growled Nancy, "get on the porch and stay there or I'll handcuff you to the railing."

"Well!" said Helen in a highly offended tone. "Well, I *never!*"

"We won't be long," I said. "You can go on back home if you'd like. We'll be happy to lock up after we're finished."

"I certainly will not! I'm going to wait right here until you tell me what's going on."

"Suit yourself," said Nancy, glaring at her. "But you step inside this door again before we give you the okay and I'll take you to jail." Nancy liked to play "bad cop."

"You don't have a jail," sniffed Helen, "but I'll stay on the porch."

Nancy and I went straight for the bedrooms. In the second one we checked, we found the body — this one with a purse clutched in her hands. She was stretched out in the closet like the others and wearing a stylish pant suit. Our flashlights revealed a middle-aged woman, medium length salt-and-pepper hair, eyes closed.

"Do you know her?" I asked.

"Nope," said Nancy.

I had my phone out and was getting ready to call Dave. Before I'd punched in the number, the lights in the bedroom came on.

"Huh," I said. "Dave's on the ball. I didn't even tell him to get this house turned on as well as the other one."

"Yeah," said Nancy, "he's a smart guy." This was high praise from Nancy. In the old days, Dave had had quite the crush on Lieutenant Nancy Parsky. She tolerated it, then rather enjoyed it, then they'd become a couple briefly, then the infatuation had worn off and Dave had found other romantic interests. He was currently seeing his old fiancée, Collette Bowers, who lived in Wilkesboro, about an hour away. Nancy had nothing but contempt for Collette, but, as far as I could tell, she and Dave had found middle ground and were good friends.

There was a closet light, but it hadn't been left on. I flipped the switch and an old fluorescent bulb sputtered to life. I squatted down beside Nancy.

Nancy had her latex gloves on and the purse out of the woman's hands. She rifled through it, then pulled out an overstuffed wallet and opened it.

"Crystal Latimore," Nancy said, reading the driver's license. "5427 Highway 105 in Linville. The picture matches." She thumbed

47

through the wallet. "Credit cards, a St. Germaine Library card, insurance card, some receipts. Usual stuff. All with her name on it."

"What's going on?" said a voice behind us. Helen's voice. She was standing in the doorway of the bedroom. "All the lights came on! Did you find something?"

Nancy stood up angrily and when she did Helen spotted the woman's legs stretched out straight across the closet floor.

"Oh, my *GOD!*" she screeched. "Is that a dead person?"

"Helen Pigeon," Nancy said, fury in her voice, "you're under arrest for being a pain in the ... "

"Hang on," I said. "She was bound to find out in a few minutes anyway."

"I don't care," said Nancy. "I'm going to cuff her."

"Who is it?" asked Helen, ignoring Nancy and sidling into the room for a better look. "Anyone we know? A woman? Has she been murdered?" She tried peeking around my shoulder to get a better look.

I got to my feet. "We don't know, Helen," I said. "All we know right now is that she's dead."

"That's Crystal!" shrieked Helen, seeing the woman's face. "Crystal Latimore! Wait a minute ..." Helen's eyes narrowed in consternation, then realization dawned and they grew wide. "Wait ... just ... one ... minute. There were dead bodies in the other two houses, weren't there?"

"Can I arrest her *now*?" asked Nancy in disgust.

Helen suddenly looked very uncomfortable, not green exactly, but maybe half way there. "I'm feeling sort of ... umm ... you know. May I go into the hall for a minute?"

"Sure," I said. "You take your time."

Crystal was as frozen as the other two corpses. Nancy, kneeling next to the body, pulled her shoulder length hair away from her face, one side, then the other, then looked up at me and nodded. A missing earring. She let the hair drop back to her shoulders.

"I'm okay, now," said Helen, coming back into the room. "I don't know what came over me. I'm usually fine around dead people."

Nancy and I gave her a look we reserved for lunatics.

"What I mean is," said Helen with a nervous laugh, "that, you know, when I have to go to a funeral or something, the dead body doesn't bother me. I'm happy to stand and chat all day!"

48

Nancy and I exchanged glances.

Helen fluttered her hands, then bleated nervously, "No, not with the dead person. I know that the dead person can't chat or even hear what I'm saying, but what I mean is that I'm happy to talk to other people hanging around the dead person, but not the dead person because that would be a ghost and I don't believe in ghos ..."

"I get it," I said, interrupting, then stepped back. Nancy stood and moved aside as well.

I said, "How do you know Crystal Latimore?"

Now that I was out of the way, Helen stared down at the body. "She goes to our church. You know, Mountain Grace Fellowship at Price Park."

"Do you know if she's married?" I asked.

"I don't think so," said Helen, still staring. "At least, if she is, I've never met her husband. Of course, he might just not come to church."

"Kids?" I asked.

Helen shook her head. "No, but they might be grown and living somewhere else. She's in her forties, I guess."

"Forty-five, according to her license," said Nancy. She took out her phone. "I'll call Dave and have him send the ambulance over here when they're done at Oak Street."

"I *knew* it!" said Helen, her face lighting up with a certain excitement.

"Helen," I said, "you are now going home and we're locking this house up. You're not saying anything about this to anyone, because we have to notify the next of kin. It would be very unchristian of you to spread this news before we've done so. You understand?"

Helen's visage became somber immediately. "I understand, Hayden. May I tell Jeff at least?"

"Yes, but you give him the same warning. We have to try to get hold of Crystal's family."

"Poor Crystal," Helen said, then turned and walked out of the bedroom.

"She'll be on the phone the second she hits her front door," said Nancy.

Chapter 8

The ambulance showed up and took the bodies of the women over to the morgue. I called Kent Murphee, told him what was going on and made an appointment to meet him the next afternoon. By the time I returned home, it was well after dark and I was beat.

Baxter spent most of his days outside roaming the two hundred acres we called home and was waiting for me when I drove up. He gave a few barks at the old pickup truck, welcoming barks since he'd known this truck since he was a pup-in-arms and since this old 1962 Chevy truck makes a very specific sound coming down the hill to the cabin. I greeted him fondly, opened the back door of the house, and he bounced in ahead of me. He slid to a stop on the kitchen tile, then looked at me in expectation. I gave him some dog chow and his shaggy head disappeared into the bowl.

I looked into the living room for the other member of our household and spotted him right away, sitting quietly on the mantle just beneath the giant elk head mount. Archimedes. Baxter was a pet, but Archimedes wasn't. It's hard to keep an owl as a pet unless you lock it in a cage. Archimedes came and went as he pleased through an electric window in the kitchen, but he spent most of the winter in the house, perched on the mantle or on the head of the stuffed buffalo. He might have been part of the decor until he leapt into the air and glided silently through the house. He was a wild creature but was happy to visit, and we in turn were happy to have him. To thank him for his friendship, Meg and I supplemented his diet with mice, baby squirrels, and chipmunks — frozen, and vacuum packed, and all sent to me by Kent Murphee. I didn't ask where he got them. Archimedes didn't need the supplements. At least, I didn't think so. He was a fine hunter and we often saw him outside in his favorite tree, happily tearing apart some poor animal he'd caught.

I opened the refrigerator, found the coffee can in the back with "Archimedes" scrawled across it, and pulled out a freshly thawed chipmunk. I thought the owl was asleep, but when I turned back around there he was, standing on the counter right beside me. I never heard a thing. He took the cold chipmunk from my hand with one talon, then gave two hops to the window, waited for it to slide open, and, when it did, took one more hop and disappeared silently into the night.

Nancy, Dave, and I had gone through all three houses again, looking for any kind of clues as to how the bodies got there. Nothing. We checked for fingerprints on the closet doors. Nothing usable. Nancy took a few DNA swabs, but that was a long shot. Long shot, nothing. It was a moon shot, and we all knew it. We looked for blood, searched the houses top to bottom looking for a murder scene, looked for signs of a break in, and scoured the grounds as long as there was light. Nothing. The three bodies just seemed to have been dropped off: placed carefully in the closets and left there.

I was happy to stop thinking about it for a little while. Meg had decided to stay at her mother's house in town, and whenever she did that I lit up a cigar. She'd know, but she said she enjoyed the smell as long as smoke wasn't wafting through the house while she was there. She didn't like to breathe it. Fair enough.

I got myself a BottleTree Imperial Red Ale, then walked over and turned on the stereo. Then I sat down at the typewriter, lit up a cigar, and prepared to give my burgeoning story my best shot. I was positive that I did my best writing while listening to choral music. Meg wasn't so sure. She certainly didn't appreciate the madrigals of Carlo Gesualdo. But Meg wasn't here.

Gesualdo, Italian Prince of Venosa in the latter half of the sixteenth century, is known — as I remembered from my classes in music history — both for his intensely expressive music that uses a chromatic language not heard again till the twentieth century and for his murderous temper. Coming home early from a hunting trip, he surprised his wife *in flagrante delicto* with the Duke of Andria, and murdered them both in the bed, stabbing them multiple times while shouting, "They're not dead yet!" Then he shot the duke in the head for good measure and dressed him in his wife's clothes. This was enough to get him started writing madrigals. It would be enough to get anyone started.

Listening to Gesualdo madrigals was an acquired taste, like Skeeter's homemade Possum-shine, or Stinking Bishop cheese. Or maybe like enjoying the wordplay of a multilayered detective story with no discernible plot.

The woman swept in like a mezzo aria: her middle-aged melody anticipated by the accompanying strains of a lush, overripe, dewberry-scented décolletage. She surveyed the office, gave Pedro the once-over, then dropped her gaze on me like a feed sack full of alto-meal. Her lips were fleshy and wanting in that kind of way that lips get after eating Hunan spicy beef with Szechuan peppers, extra hot, with enough monosodium glutamate to exacerbate water retention and cause lips to be plump as a couple of roundworms. I thought about lunch.

* * *

That's a keeper, I thought. Meg will appreciate the subtlety of my description. I finished my beer, puffed on my stogy, and listened to the wailing coming from the stereo. I might have to rethink the Gesualdo thing. I was fairly sure I used to like it, but maybe that was the pretentiousness of youth. I probably enjoyed Gesualdo the way the Blue Hill Bookworms enjoyed reading *Magic Mountain* by Thomas Mann.

* * *

"My name is Anne Dante. I need a detective," she blarbled in a voice halfway between warbling and blubbering. She could have been blubbleing, though. I wasn't sure. I was never sure with these mezzos. Most of them were as easy as opening a jar of pickles, not one closed so tight that a woman would get a hernia trying to open it, although I've never heard about any woman this happened to — I guess it could, but doctors don't ask them to cough so how would they know — but one already opened and the lid left slightly askew so that the pickle flavor gets all into the leftover lasagna even though you put it in one of those plastic containers, which is also easy, but not as easy as most mezzos.

"I need a detective," she belugled again, in case anyone had forgotten where we were in the narrative since the previous sentence was relatively long but contained a certain literary device called "adumbrating," which is a vague foreshadowing of events to come and is, if not actually relevant, at least apropos to the plot in an upcoming chapter that the reader hasn't gotten to yet. "I need someone I can trust."

Pedro took a swig of his drink, swished it around in his mouth, made a face like an Episcopal priest who'd been slipped a three-dollar wine during communion, then gulped it down, and went straight for an aphorism.

"Life is short."

Suddenly, a shot rang out.

* * *

The doorbell rang, then I heard the kitchen door open and Pete call out, "You home?"

"In the living room," I called back. "Grab a couple of beers out of the fridge, will you?"

I tossed the empty bottle into the wastebasket, on top of quite a few sheets of unbegun detective stories. Then I pulled my current opus out of the typewriter, placed it in a manila folder, and slipped it into the top drawer of the desk. I clicked off the lamp and stood up just as Pete came in.

"What in God's name is that caterwauling coming from the stereo?" Pete said.

"Just ... nothing," I said, deciding to turn it off and put on some Leon Redbone, my favorite jazz and blues singer. It took me about a minute to switch the music over and by the time I was finished, Pete had settled himself onto the sofa, drunk half of his beer, and looked to be almost asleep.

"Did you ever read *Magic Mountain* when you were in college?" I asked.

"I sure visited it a few times," Pete answered with a grin. "It was the '70s."

"Thomas Mann," I said.

"I know who wrote it," said Pete. "I read it in some English class. Part of it anyway. I was supposed to read the whole thing and write a paper. German existentialism. I'm pretty sure it was the worst book I never finished."

"Full of symbolism and deep meaning?"

"Full of something," said Pete, taking another draw on his bottle. "Are you struggling with the meaning of art and of life again?"

"Always," I said. "Perhaps I shall find it by drinking another beer."

"Couldn't hurt," said Pete. "You know, if you ever reach total artistic enlightenment while drinking beer, I'll bet it comes shooting out your nose."

"Probably," I agreed. "You want one of these cigars?"

"Nah. I'm trying to cut down. No cigars after nine. That's my new rule."

"Why the late visit? What's up?"

"Well, Cynthia told me that Meg was staying with her mom tonight, and then we heard over at the Slab that you'd found three dead bodies inside those three houses auctioned yesterday. All murdered."

CNN had nothing on the St. Germaine grapevine. "You came to check on my well being?" I asked.

"Nah," said Pete. "Cynthia told me to come out and see what was going on. She's the mayor, you know."

"Yep. And you are her paramour."

"The power behind the throne," said Pete. "The puppet-master."

"I'll mention that to Cynthia when I see her."

"Don't you dare." Pete finished his beer and walked to the kitchen for another. "Now spill it. What's the dope?"

"The grapevine is right, as usual," I called after him. "Three dead bodies. We spent all afternoon going through the houses. Didn't find anything."

Pete came back into the living room. "You know who they all are?"

"Yes, we do," I said. "You'd better write this down for Cynthia. You're never going to remember it."

"Well, gimme a sheet of paper. I'll take some notes."

"There's one on the desk and a pen in the drawer."

I waited for Pete to settle onto the sofa again, this time with pen and paper in hand. He picked a book up off the coffee table to write on.

"Darla Kildair, Amy Ventura, and Crystal Latimore," I said.

"Amy? You're kidding!" said Pete, his shoulders slumping. "Oh, man. Really? Amy Ventura?"

"All middle-aged women, all single and living alone, we think. Darla was well-known in St. Germaine, since she worked at Noylene's Beautifery for a number of years, then opened her own shop. Amy Ventura didn't live here but worked for the town council. She also had clients in Boone and other places. Crystal Latimore lived in Linville and Helen Pigeon knew her from church. She did have a St. Germaine Library card. I don't know what she did for a living. Not yet."

"So they had no connection that you know of," Pete said, scribbling away.

I smiled. "Pete, you sound like a detective. Or maybe a reporter."

"Just getting the facts right. Cynthia is going to grill me like a pork chop when I get home."

"We know there's a connection. There's *obviously* a connection. We just don't know what it is yet. We also don't know how they died and won't until Kent gets hold of them tomorrow morning. I suspect they were all put in the houses around the same time, but maybe not. We've had freezing weather for weeks and they could have been there since before Christmas or anytime after."

Pete quit taking notes and brightened. "You know, this probably puts us back on top."

"How so?"

"We haven't had any murders for almost two years. Now three right in a row. I'll bet we get our title of 'Murder Capital of North Carolina' back again."

"We certainly will not," I said. "North Carolina had about five hundred homicides last year, most of those in the cities."

"*Per capita*, I mean," said Pete. "I'll bet we're up there *per capita*."

"I doubt it. Besides, I'm not sure that's an advertising slogan we want to use. *St. Germaine — Come for the shopping, Stay for your funeral.*"

"Well, maybe not," conceded Pete. "It wouldn't fit on the sign anyway."

Chapter 9

I got to the station at eight o'clock Monday morning, determined to spend the day doing my best detecting. Three dead bodies was not something we wanted on our plate for very long. St. Germaine had had a spate of murders during the past ten years, but to our credit, and unlike the big cities with higher crime rates, none of our murders went unsolved.

I was the first one to arrive. Nancy usually checked in around 8:30. Dave, on donut patrol, was probably down at Bun in the Oven bakery right now talking Diana Evarts out of a dozen day-old crullers. As far as Nancy and I could tell, Dave lived on donuts during the week. I put on the coffee pot and had just settled into the chair in my office when I heard the front door open and the accompanying buzzer go off.

"Hayden?" called a familiar voice. Georgia Wester's voice.

"In here," I called back, getting to my feet. "Coming."

Georgia Wester owned Eden Books on the Square. She was also in the choir at St. Barnabas and, more importantly, the newly-elected Senior Warden.

"Father Dressler would like to see you when you have a few minutes," she said.

"The new priest?"

"Yep. I had a meeting with him at seven-thirty this morning so he could tell me what's what."

"I'm on sabbatical," I said. "You want some coffee? It's fresh."

"No, thanks. He says he knows you're on sabbatical, but since you're still a member of the staff and in town he'd like to see you sometime today. Just call Marilyn and she'll schedule you in."

"Well, tell him I'm busy."

"I did. He says, and I quote, 'Let the dead bury their own dead. We go and proclaim the kingdom of God.' What does that mean?"

I growled. "It means that he heard about the three murders and decided to quote scripture at me."

"*Three murders?*" gasped Georgia.

"I'm surprised you haven't heard. Everyone else has."

"When did *that* happen?"

"We don't know. Sometime in the last month, we're guessing. We'll know more this afternoon." I didn't see any harm in releasing sketchy information. Maybe someone had seen someone else coming or going from one of the empty houses.

"Who was killed? Anyone we know?"

"Probably. You knew Darla Kildair, of course, since Noylene's Beautifery was right next door to the book store."

"*Darla!*" Georgia said. "Oh, *no!* I had an appointment at her new shop right after Christmas — Darla's Hair Down Under — but when I showed up, there was a note on the door saying that she was sorry, but she'd be gone for a few weeks. Then I heard at the Beautifery that she had to go take care of her mother."

"We went by her shop, but there wasn't a note. It was just locked up. You don't know what happened to the note, by any chance?"

"No idea," said Georgia, now thinking hard. "Maybe hand written. Not something from a computer printer."

"Okay," I said.

"Who else?" asked Georgia, dread now evident in her voice.

"Two other women. Amy Ventura, and Crystal Latimore, neither one from St. Germaine."

"Amy? I knew Amy," Georgia said sadly. "She was a good person. I don't know the other name."

"Crystal was from Linville," I said. "We'll find out more about her this morning."

"This is just depressing," said Georgia.

"Are you going back over to the church?"

"I have to open up the shop."

"Well, I'll see if I can get over there some time today. But, only to get you off the hook."

"Thank you. I appreciate that."

Georgia turned to leave just as Dave came in the door carrying his usual box of at least a dozen donuts.

"Morning, Georgia," he chirped. "Care for a Cream-filled Delight?"

"No, thanks," said Georgia and left without another word.

Dave watched her go and said, "Wow. She seems really depressed."

"She knew Darla and Amy," I said. "I guess a lot more people knew Amy than I'd thought, even though she didn't live here."

"I guess," Dave agreed. "Has Nancy called in?"

"I figured she'd be here at 8:30."

"Nope. She went over to Linville early this morning to see about Crystal Latimore. She was meeting someone at the courthouse."

I nodded. "I might as well go over to the church and meet the new priest."

"I thought you were on sabbatical."

"Yes, I am, but I have been duly summoned and I am nothing if not amenable to the whims of the clergy. Then I'm meeting Meg for breakfast. If Nancy comes back, you guys come on over to the Slab."

"Will do," said Dave.

"Also, would you get a key from Dr. Ken to Darla's shop? He's the landlord. We'll check it, but I'm not hopeful."

"All due diligence," said Dave through a mouth half-filled with a jelly donut.

* * *

I walked into Marilyn's office and she looked frazzled. Marilyn was unflappable and didn't usually look frazzled until Thursday afternoon.

"You look frazzled," I said, stating the obvious. "It's only Monday morning."

She glared at me. "You can't go in," she whispered. "You don't have an *appointment!*"

"That's okay," I said with a shrug. "No problem. I can come back. Who's in there with him now?"

"*No one!*" Marilyn hissed under her breath. "No one. But you ... don't ... have ... an ... *appointment!* He was very clear about scheduling *appointments!*"

"Oh. An *appointment.* Why didn't you say so? Shall I schedule one then?"

"If you like." Marilyn's left eye twitched. "He has a free half-hour at one o'clock."

"I'm sorry," I said very loudly, loud enough to be heard through the closed door of the priest's office. "As you know, I'm on sabbatical. I can't make it today at one. I'll try to schedule an appointment next week sometime."

The door to the priest's office opened suddenly and the newest clergy member of St. Barnabas stood there in a full-length, black cassock. He had a dark-red band cincture around his waist and the white clerical collar was prominent at his throat. He offered me a warm, moist hand and I took it. He didn't let it go, but squeezed it meaningfully, like he was milking a cow.

"Hayden, how very nice to meet you," he said. "I've heard so much about our illustrious police captain and organist. I have just a few minutes between appointments, but perhaps we can chat for a moment. I'm Father Dressler."

"Good to meet you, too," I said, letting him usher me by the hand into his *sanctum sanctorum*.

He released my hand, and I managed to wipe it unobtrusively on the back of my barn jacket while he walked around the desk and sat in the large leather chair bought by one of his supercilious predecessors. I didn't bother to remove my jacket. I wouldn't be in his office that long.

Bev hadn't told me much about this new priest and I hadn't met him before today. He was younger than he'd appeared when I'd seen him yesterday from the back of the nave, and I hadn't gone up for communion. I judged him to be in his mid-forties, although his short hair was graying. He had a strong chin and a slightly hooked nose, but smallish, quick, dark eyes that were rather unsettling. I was reminded of nothing so much as a rodent in a clerical costume. Still, you can't judge a book by its cover.

"Have a seat," he said and gestured to the smaller armchair across from his desk.

I sat down and said, "I really can't stay long. I just came by to say hello and introduce myself."

"Thank you very much for that," said the priest. He picked up a mug of something hot that was on his desk, blew across the top, and took a sip. "Would you like some black tea? I find it invigorating."

"No, thanks. I do have a question, though. Do you always dress in your cassock?"

"Not on my days off, certainly," he replied, "but whenever I'm doing the Lord's work. Do you approve?"

I nodded. "Absolutely."

"That was a well-attended service yesterday. There are certainly some things that I'd do differently." He waited for me to respond, then added, "I saw you sitting in the back."

"Yes, I would probably have done some things differently as well."

59

"Such as?"

"Well, that's really up to you, isn't it?" I said. "I'm on sabbatical."

"So I heard. That was Mrs. Terra-Pock's last Sunday, wasn't it?"

"Yes, it was. I believe she has other commitments starting this week. Just after Christmas I gave the music committee a list of names of some organists who might be available." I stood up. "It's good to meet you, but I really have to get back to the station."

"I'll get right to the point then," said Father Dressler. "You are to come back to work immediately. I'm afraid your sabbatical has been cancelled."

I laughed out loud and he looked shocked.

"I'm sorry, did I say something funny?"

"Really," I said, "thanks for asking, but I'm rather busy."

"I ... I don't think you understand," sputtered Father Dressler.

"I've got to go. It's been a real pleasure, Father."

I opened the door and exited into the church office. Marilyn was at her desk, obviously privy to the commandment she knew would be coming down from on high. She would have also known my reply. "Have a nice day, Hayden," she said, then smiled an ornery grin and turned back to her computer without another word.

* * *

"Hayden!" Pete called out as I came into the Slab. "What's the news?"

"No news since last night," I said.

The café wasn't full. It was Monday morning. The six a.m. crowd had come and gone. The next wave arrived at eight. By nine, we had the place almost to ourselves. Meg was at our table and Cynthia was sitting next to her. Two empty tables over, sat Billy and Elaine Hixon. Billy had a lawn service company, but at the end of a cold January didn't have much work for a month or so. He and his crew did a bit of clean up around the various properties he contracted with, but these were his down months. Come summer, though, he'd be putting in twelve hour days just to keep up. Elaine kept the books for Billy and also sang in the choir at St. B.

"I heard you found eight dead bodies," said Billy. "Cult murders, all found with parakeets in their mouths."

60

"It was only six," corrected Elaine. "And I heard it was some sort of sex club."

Noylene, who was taking the coffee pot around to the two tables, shook her head in disbelief. "Sex club?" she said. "Parakeets? What some people will come up with! It was poor Darla in that closet."

"Darla?" said Elaine. "*Your* Darla?"

"Yep," said Noylene. "My poor Darla."

I sat down at the table with Meg and Cynthia, and Noylene appeared beside me and filled my coffee cup.

Billy said, "I thought you and Darla had a big ol' fight."

"That wasn't me," said Noylene. "Me and Darla got along just fine. That was that crazy Goldi Fawn Birtwhistle. Darla never did like Goldi Fawn. Said that Goldi Fawn stole her favorite scissors — you know, the pair with the comb built right in — and Goldi Fawn comes back that Darla poached one of her best customers and, even if she did 'borrow' the scissors, it was a fair trade. Then Darla says that Goldi Fawn is a lunatic for believing in all that Christian Astrology stuff and she shouldn't be giving Satanic readings in a God-fearing House of Beauty, and Goldi Fawn says that she'd be happy to give Darla a reading and tell her the exact date when she'd be going straight to hell."

"Wow," said Pete. "Sorry I missed that."

"Yep," said Noylene with a sad shake of her head. "Then Darla went at her with a styling wand. All this during a busy Thursday afternoon when we're having our special on blue rinse. The place was packed, I can tell you."

Blue-Rinse Thursday, as anyone in St. Germaine could tell you, was Noylene's busiest day of the month. It only happened on the third Thursday, but on that day every chair in the Beautifery was booked from eight till eight. Noylene had specials now and again, as everyone knew. You could get into the Dip-n-Tan for half off if you timed it right and got the coupon out of the *Tattler*. College students could get a five-dollar haircut on Wednesday morning. If you were lucky (or unlucky) enough to be singled out by the Carolina Neighborly Commission on Beauty — known locally as CarNCOB — and given a citation, you received a fifty-percent discount at any one of the sixteen beauty and stylist shops to which the members of CarNCOB belonged, including Noylene's. The members of CarNCOB spent most Saturdays outside the Walmart

Supercenters handing out citations to those offenders who chose to wear spandex leggings with high heels and tank tops.

Noylene Fabergé-Dupont-McTavish had started the Beautifery and had managed to build the enterprise into a thriving small town business. She was now a wealthy woman by mountain standards, and her last marriage — to Brother Hog (yes, *THE* Brother Hog, nationally known evangelist) — had resulted in a bouncing baby boy named Rahab. Despite her success, Noylene still worked at the Beautifery four afternoons a week, granting her gift of beauty to those less fortunate than herself. She also put in a couple of mornings at the Slab helping out.

"Whatchu want for breakfast?" Noylene asked me, snapping her gum like it was punctuation.

"Ah, surprise me."

"I'll just get you what the girls are having."

"That'd be great, thanks."

Pete pulled his apron off over his head, then pulled out a chair and sat down. "So, nothing new?"

"Not yet. I did get to meet the new priest."

"What did you think?" said Meg.

"Well, he informed me that my sabbatical had been cancelled and that I was to report back to work immediately."

Cynthia, who'd been taking a sip of coffee, spit it back into the cup with a muffled laugh.

"Really?" she said.

"Yep."

"Hayden," said Meg, "you weren't rude to him, were you? You know how you get."

"I was not rude in the least. I just told him I couldn't. I told him I was busy."

Pete's old cowbell banged against the glass door, signaling another customer. We glanced up and saw Nancy come in. She shed her jacket, hung it on one of the hooks by the door, then came over to the table.

"Good morning," said Meg brightly.

"Good morning," echoed Cynthia.

"What's wrong?" I asked, more used to reading Nancy's temperaments.

"Nothing's wrong, I guess." Nancy dragged a chair from an adjoining table up to the corner and sat down. "Just no luck. I've been checking on Crystal Latimore and trying to find out if these women had anything in common. There's got to be a common thread somewhere."

"I agree. Did you find anything?"

"Nothing of note." Nancy flipped open her note pad. "Crystal Latimore worked as a court advocate in Boone. She lived in Linville and owned her own house, although there's still a mortgage on it. Divorced, no kids. Forty-five years old. A very active member of Mountain Grace Fellowship Church. She had a St. Germaine Library card, but since the library doesn't open until ten, I don't know for sure if she used it a lot. I'll check it out, though. We'll have to look through her house."

"Maybe they all have the library in common," suggested Cynthia.

"Maybe," I said.

"Nah," said Noylene. "Darla wouldn't a been caught dead in a library. She said the last book she read was *Jonathan Livingston Seagull* and it was so bad it put her off reading forever. She wouldn't even pick up a *People* magazine like everyone else did when she had a break. To tell you the truth, I think she was probably dixelsticks."

"Or," said Pete, "dyslexic."

"Or that," sniffed Noylene.

"All the women were single ... right?" asked Meg.

"All single," said Nancy, "but that seems to be the only connection. Amy was a grant writer and worked from home. Darla cut hair ... "

"She was a purveyor of beauty," corrected Noylene.

"Sure," said Nancy. "Darla was a purveyor of beauty and worked at her own shop. Crystal was a court advocate and worked out of the courthouse in Boone. Nothing in common. Hair: different. Weight: different. Body shape: all average, nothing outstanding. Crystal and Darla both went to church, but not the same one. Amy didn't go. There has got to be a connection we haven't found yet, of course."

"Like what?" asked Meg.

"Anything," said Nancy. "Their chiropractor, for example."

"The same prescription drug store," I added. "A Christmas party they all went to. A concert series they had tickets to. A lawyer they all used for something. It could be anything really."

"I see what you mean," said Meg.

"So what you're saying," said Cynthia, "is that you have no clues whatsoever."

"Oh, we have clues, all right," I said. "Piles of them. We just don't know what they mean. I'm thinking that Kent Murphee will shed some light on the crimes. I'll be going to see him after lunch."

Chapter 10

After breakfast I walked down Maple Street to see Bud. It was still cold, below freezing, in fact, but nothing new for January. Bud had told me that it was his plan to give his two-week notice at the Pig as soon as we were sure we'd gotten the house, and when I'd called him the night before, he said that Roger said, thanks for the notice, but Bud was free to leave. Roger had a couple of other employment applications already.

I walked past the St. Barnabas garden, the flower shop and Holy Grounds Coffee Shop to Bud's new house. There didn't look to be much activity on this Monday morning. Bud's old Gremlin was parked in the driveway. There wasn't any parking for customers on the property, but there was ample parking on both sides of the street. Neither of us thought that would be a deterrent to business.

I opened the front door, went in to the living room, and called for Bud.

"In here," he answered from the kitchen. "I'm cleaning out the fridge."

I followed his voice and found him, head and shoulders buried inside the 1972 vintage Frigidaire, in avocado green. He had a giant, plastic, contractor-sized garbage bag beside him and it was already half full.

"Bud, what are you doing?"

"I'm cleaning this thing out. It's been sitting here for probably a year or so."

"Three years," I said, "and we're not saving it. It's going to the dump."

Bud pulled his head out of the fridge and gave me a quizzical look.

"All this stuff," I added, "is going to the dump. The stove, that microwave on the counter, all of it, including the kitchen sink. This is a total redo."

Bud looked shocked. "You mean we'll redo the whole kitchen?"

I smiled. "Nope. I mean we'll redo the whole house. I have an architect coming by in fifteen minutes. You have some drawings of the house, right?"

"Sure. Right there in my briefcase."

"Then you're going to meet with her and tell her what you want. Her name is Jessica Adeline. This is a wine shop now, not a house. We need a galley kitchen, but we don't need all this space."

"A tasting room?" Buds face was alight with possibilities. "We'll still need a stove to cook hors d'oeuvres. And we'll need shelves and racks. And wine glasses. And bottle openers. And a long counter for checking out. We could put a walk-in refrigerator in the back bedroom for chilling. And the basement will be perfect for our cellar."

"You design it, Bud," I said. "You and the architect. You could get rid of these walls, open this whole space up." I looked around the room, then added, "Don't forget bathrooms. His and hers. And your office."

"Oh, man!" said Bud, rubbing his hands together in delight. "This is gonna be *great!*"

"I wouldn't mind seeing the plans when you're done. Our contractor is ready to start Thursday, so don't be too long in the designing. We can make changes as we go if we see something won't work, but not many, so sit down with the architect and put some thought into this."

"I will!" Bud said, then grew somber. "What about that lady I found in the closet?"

"We're working on it. You know that two other women were found in the other two houses?"

"Yeah. I heard."

"It's nothing for you to worry about. You concentrate on this."

"I will. Thanks."

* * *

Dr. Kent Murphee was dressed in exactly the same clothes when I walked into his office on Monday afternoon as he was wearing on Friday night. His pipe was clenched in his teeth.

"Sit down," he said, gesturing to the uncomfortable chair in front of his desk. "How about a wee scotch?"

"Well, seeing as it's Monday, I wouldn't mind."

Kent pulled open one of the drawers of his desk and came up with two glasses and a bottle of Highland Park, 21-year-old scotch. "I'm afraid I don't have any ice handy," he said.

"No problem here. Isn't that the bottle I gave you for Christmas?"

"Nancy delivered me a case, courtesy of the St. Germaine Police Department," Kent replied with a smile, concentrating on pouring exactly two fingers into each glass. "This is bottle number two. I have to make it last all year, but I'm happy to share as long as you don't get greedy."

We sipped our whiskey, then I said, "Okay, give me the scoop. How did these three women meet their ends?"

"I can't tell you for sure how they *all* died. I can tell you how the one we found on Friday night died."

"Darla Kildair."

"Right. The others are still frozen. They may be thawed out by tomorrow evening, but I'd rather take it slowly and keep them refrigerated. We don't want them at room temperature."

"I get it."

"Darla died of a heart attack."

"That doesn't seem right."

"My suspicion is that I will discover, in due course, that they all died of heart attacks. Highly unlikely that they'd all die of heart attacks and be placed in separate houses in the same positions."

"All owned by the bank," I added.

"As I said, highly unlikely."

"Poison, then?" I asked.

"Maybe. If so, I can't detect it and I looked for markers for the common ones: potassium chloride, calcium gluconate, renin, the usual stuff. Of course, these are undetectable after a short time, as the body absorbs the chemicals, but sometimes they do leave traces — elevated levels of sodium, for example. I didn't find any of that. She was wearing contact lenses, if you're interested. And she had a pin in her ankle, but that injury is probably six or seven years old."

"Should I be interested?"

"Nah."

"So, heart attack."

"I also looked for needle marks. None that I could see, but since the body had dehydrated quite a bit, those marks may be indiscernible now. Unless you have a specific poison that I should test for, the chances are not good that I can find it. Even then, it may be a moot point. Sorry I can't be of more help."

"You know, the scientists at the Jeffersonian would just re-hydrate the body by soaking it in a solution of diluted turkey broth, then run it through the 3-D CAT scan, and discover the needle mark placed inside the belly button piercing."

"Get out," said Kent.

"Let me know what you find out on the other two when they thaw, will you?"

"You'll be my first call."

Chapter 11

"The choir would like to know if you'd be interested in coming back for two weeks," Meg said.

We were relaxing in the living room after a long Monday. Snow was drifting down from the cold, overcast sky. The dog was asleep on his rug in front of the fire, the owl was dozing on the mantle, Bach was on the stereo, and my wife was curled on the couch with her iPad, reading something or other. I was flexing my fingers in anticipation of a flurry of belletristic creativity. All was right with the world.

"Nope," I said. "Not remotely interested."

"The choir has deputized me and instructed me to provide certain favors in acknowledgment of a positive response."

This caught my attention. "Certain favors?"

"Indeed," said Meg, blushing, but not looking up from her tablet.

"And these favors would be ...?"

"Above and beyond."

Now my attention was rapt. "Above and beyond, you say. Above is pretty high and beyond is quite a long way."

"It is," Meg said with a giggle. "It's the terrible price that I, as a choir member, am willing to pay to get you back, even for a couple of weeks."

"Hang on," I said. "Who authorized this brokering of favors?"

"The president of the choir."

"That would be you."

"After everyone realized that Edna was leaving and we didn't have anyone else, we were all trying to come up with suggestions."

"That was the best one?" I asked.

"Well, the choir suggested that I tempt you with a Reuben sandwich. I came up with this on my own."

"I don't know ... What about my detective story?"

"You could pass it out on Wednesday during rehearsal."

"I was just getting used to sleeping in on Sundays."

Meg stood up and pulled something small and lacy from underneath one of the sofa cushions. "I guess I might as well take this back to the store then. I think it's too small anyway. I was going to go get ready for bed and see if it fit, but I suppose that, since it's so cold out, I'll just pull out my flannel footie pajamas, roll my hair, and slather on some facial cream."

"Two weeks? That's it?"

Meg gave me a smile that I felt all the way to my socks. "Two weeks."

"Above and beyond?"

"Oh, my. You have no idea." Meg put her iPad on the couch, turned slowly and slank, actually *slank,* toward the bedroom. Slowly. Suggestively. Libidinously. She turned at the door and looked back. "What do you say?"

"Yes," I managed, with a gulp. "I say, yes. You have found and exploited my one weakness."

"One caveat," she said. "You tell the choir it was the Reuben sandwich."

"*And* I want a Reuben sandwich."

Meg laughed out loud and disappeared behind the door, then stuck her head out and said, "Give me fifteen minutes."

After staring after her for a good two of those minutes, I turned my attention to the typewriter. I might get a few paragraphs finished now that I had some real inspiration. I wondered if this was the way Raymond Chandler worked.

* * *

A shot rang out, a man screamed in a high-pitched lady-voice but you could tell it was a man, a small dog howled, and somewhere a woman named Ginger wept openly but she didn't know why but it turns out that she was mildly psychic and the long lost sister of Anne Dante, more about this later.

"That's the quickest anyone's been shot in one of your stories," Pedro quipped. "She only got about a dozen words out."

"Enough for a clue to her murderer."

"Maybe," said Pedro. "You think you're that good?"

I bent down to look at the cold body, although she hadn't been dead that long, but it was a really cold night, her minidress bunched angrily around her waist, her leopard-print blouse rudely unbuttoned — then ran my finger across the hoarfrost clinging to her fishnet stockings and wondered briefly about the origin of the strange meteorological term and whether it was a clue worth considering.

"Well, since you have the gun in your hand and it's smoking and there's a bullet hole in Miss Dante, I might have this one wrapped up by lunchtime."

"I didn't do it," said Pedro, slipping the gat into his shorts.

I was sure there was a clue here somewhere. Something was gnawing at me like those bedbugs I got at the Hymn Society retreat.

* * *

Fifteen minutes later, I flipped off the old banker's light and called it a night ... as far as my writing was concerned.

Chapter 12

I walked into Marilyn's office and announced myself too loudly, then said, "I don't have an appointment, but maybe I can see Father Dressler if he's not too busy."

The door to the rector's office opened quickly and Father Dressler stepped into Marilyn's alcove.

"Good morning, Hayden. I have a few moments. Won't you come in?"

"Sure," I said, and followed him through the door. He shut it behind me, gestured me into one of the small chairs in front of his desk, then walked around and eased into his grand, leather throne. Officious-looking books lined the cases behind him, most of them bound in leather and carefully arranged. The top of his desk was cleared: no papers, no pens, no pictures or knick knacks.

"How may I help you?" he said, then adjusted his cassock, folded his hands and rested them on the desktop.

"I told Meg that I'd be happy to help St. Barnabas out for a couple of weeks. Just until you can find someone to fill in while I'm on sabbatical."

He steepled his fingers and tapped his chin a few times. "I have just called someone whom I know will be an excellent replacement, but he won't be here until a week from Sunday. So, if you could fill in until he arrives, we would certainly appreciate it."

"Great," I said, happy that Meg wouldn't be coercing me into extending my two-week offer. "Is it anyone I know?"

"I doubt it," sniffed Father Dressler. "He's a *serious* musician. I know him from my former parish."

"Well, I do know a lot of folks. What's his name?"

"The *Chevalier* Lance Fleagle. He's coming down from Niagara Falls."

"Chevalier?"

"Yes. He and I are both members of the Order of St. Clementine, the Canadian Priory."

"That's interesting," I said, deciding that a little small talk was in order. "I know nothing about the Order of St. Clementine. Is it like the Elk Club or one of those other service organizations?"

"Absolutely not. Nothing at all like the Elks. The Order of St. Clementine is inspired by the statutes which defined the Fraternal Society founded by Ladislaus the Posthumous in 1441. Many, though not all, of us have military service in our backgrounds."

"And do you?"

"Well, ... no. But all of us are pledged to uphold the chivalric virtues." He started ticking them off, one finger at a time. "Prowess, courage, honesty, faith, generosity ... "

"I understand," I said. "So, why do we call this fellow 'Chevalier'? Has he been knighted by the queen or something?"

"Each member may use the title if he chooses. It is one of the benefits of membership and membership, I might add, is *very* selective. You have to be nominated by an existing Knight or Dame of the order."

"Sort of like a Kentucky Colonel, then."

He huffed in exasperation. "Nothing at *all* like that." He made a terrible face as though I wasn't comprehending the seriousness of his organization. "Can you honestly say that you've never heard of the Order of St. Clementine? What kind of backwater town did I come to?"

"One that's never heard of chevaliers, obviously," I said. "But, okay, I'm with you. When's your boy coming in?"

"He's hardly a boy. He's thirty-two years old with a master's degree from Oberlin. A *master's* degree."

"A master's degree, you say. Wow. But *when*?"

"I think he'll be able to start a week from Sunday."

"That's great," I said. "Then I'll be happy to take the rehearsals on the next two Wednesdays and the service this Sunday."

He nodded at me, then said, "I'd like to make some changes to the service. Minor changes for now."

"How can I help?"

"First, I'd like to switch to the Rite One service. As you know, it's much more formal. Traditional language, solemn prayers."

"Verily, it is thine own prerogative," I said, smiling at my own joke. He didn't seem to get it, or maybe his sense of humor had taken the morning off for prayers and mortification. I continued, "It might be a nice change for a while. I don't know how the congregation will react to that change being permanent."

He ignored the comment. "We won't need the *Gloria*. The *Trisagion* will do."

73

"Okay."

"We won't be having a children's sermon. I've already spoken with Kimberly Walnut."

"Fine with me," I said.

"For now, we'll skip the *Angelus* at the end of the service — I'll add it at a later date — but I'll certainly want the Psalm sung. Can the choir do Anglican Chant?"

"They're out of practice, but it shouldn't be hard to get them back in shape."

"I myself will be chanting the entire service, including the collects. I won't need a pitch from the organ. I have perfect pitch, you see. The Chevalier has already given me the Perfect Pitch test and I passed in the ninety-eighth percentile. The Chevalier was quite pleased."

"Excellent. I'll check that off my list of things to worry about."

"I understand Benny Dawkins is a member of this parish. I was quite excited to hear that."

"He is," I said, "but Rosemary Pepperpot-Cohosh was not fond of smoke, so Benny hasn't censed at St. Barnabas for the better part of two years. That doesn't mean he's out of practice. He has invitations and jobs almost every week."

"I think he's easily the best thurifer in the United States right now," said Father Dressler. "Maybe in the world! I saw him at St. Mary's in New York last year during the Greater New England Thurible Invitational." The priest closed his eyes and took on a visage of utter rapture. "He came down the aisle utilizing a simple double-hanging glide step — almost comical in its simplicity, but elegant beyond belief — then, as he passed the pew octave, launched into one of the most enchanting and decorative rosette quillions I've laid eyes on. I tell you, after that, people flung themselves down, face first, in the center aisle, such was their reverence."

"I'm sorry I missed that one," I said. "Benny has told me that Smokey Mary's is the best venue in the country. I've seen some stunning examples of his art over the years. I remember one time ..."

"He won hands down," interrupted Father Dressler, waving a dismissive hand at me. "No surprise there. And that little girl! His protégé. What is her name?"

"Addie Buss. She's no slouch with the thurible either."

"She was *extraordinary!*" he bubbled. "She only got fifth place, but you can just feel the talent ready to burst forth. The thurible was an extension of her beautiful soul. So pure and innocent, childlike, yet profound beyond her years. The chains sparkled as they flew through the candlelight, and the smoke moved like it had a will of its own. But no one there could look away from her face. In another few years, she'll be ready to ascend to the throne!"

"I suspect so," I said with a smile. I was glad at least that this priest had an appreciation for the fine art of the thurifer. The clergy I'd worked with lately had more in common with Tallulah Bankhead than the Archbishop of Canterbury when it came to swinging an incense pot in a church service: *Dahling, your dress is divine, but your purse is on fire.*

"Marilyn has his phone number," I said. "Addie's as well. I'm sure you can get in touch with one of them."

"Well, that should do it then. I shall pick the hymns, of course. You will choose the anthems and the Psalm chant, but let me look at them. Rite One service music. Is there a setting the congregation knows?"

"Yes," I said. "The Healey Willan setting. I don't think we've used it for two or three years, but everyone probably still knows it."

"It will do for now," Father Dressler announced. "Once the Chevalier arrives, we'll learn some Gregorian settings as well."

"Oh, fun," I said, my lightly veiled sarcasm apparent.

He glared at me for a long moment, then said, "That will be all."

I turned to go, then remembered something I'd meant to ask. "Father Dressler, I'm afraid I don't even know your first name."

"Gallus Dressler," he said. "My first name is Gallus. I took that name when I became a priest, but I would prefer you call me Father Dressler."

* * *

Darla Kildair's rented apartment was attached to the back of her beauty shop and all of it was located in the basement of Dr. Ken's Gun Emporium. The Gun Emporium was a fine establishment where one could purchase one's choice of fine

75

weaponry and ammunition suitable for every need: hunting, recreational shooting, home protection, or stockpiling for the apocalypse. Dr. Ken also carried archery and other hunting supplies, a large supply of bear urine, camouflage outfits, beaver musk, orange hunting vests and hats, earplugs — anything the modern gun owner might find useful. The store faced the highway and there was parking for about ten cars in front of the barred, plate-glass windows. It appeared from the street to be a low, squat, cinderblock building, but it was built on a hillside and was, as many buildings were here in the mountains, two stories tall. We got the key from Dr. Ken and drove around the side of the Emporium and down the steep hill to the entrance of the beauty shop. Darla's Hair Down Under.

Darla had given Dr. Ken her rent in advance and was paid up through the end of February. We opened the glass storm door, which was unlocked, used the keys on the metal door, walked in and flipped on the lights. There were no windows, but the lighting seemed to be good, and the metal door could be left open for some daylight to come into the room.

The shop was clean. There was one station — one beautician's chair bolted to the floor in front of a sink. There was one large mirror on the wall. All the cutting and styling implements seemed to be in their place: various scissors, combs, bottles of hair goop. Nothing lying about. The floor had been swept, the trash, emptied. Against the far wall were two chairs for waiting customers and a little table with a small stack of used magazines. It was neat. Done-for-the-weekend neat.

"Her apartment is back here, I guess," said Nancy, heading for the rear of the shop. There was a free-standing, folding, room divider zigzagging across the shop about halfway back. Nancy went around it and said, "There's a bathroom here, too. For the customers."

I followed her to the back of the shop, then opened the door to the apartment. It was unlocked. We stepped into what would be considered the living room but was also probably the dining room and the bedroom as well. There was some light coming in from a small, barred window high on one of the walls, the bars probably put in by Dr. Ken at some point when he was using the downstairs to store his inventory. Nancy found the light switch quickly.

76

The small kitchen, part of the larger room we were in, contained a stove, a refrigerator, a microwave, and a sink. The counter space was limited and was placed against the wall between the appliances. The room itself had a sofa, a cheap entertainment center with a flat screen TV, and a small dining table with two chairs. There was a tattered throw rug in the middle of the linoleum floor. Personal items were placed around the room to give it a homey feel — pictures in frames, a silk floral arrangement, an afghan draped over the back of the sofa. All very neat. There were no dishes in the sink. Nothing out of place. Nancy opened the door to the closet.

"It's a big closet," she said. "Her dresser is in here, too." I heard the drawers open and close, then Nancy said, "Everything's folded and stashed in its own drawer. Clothes all hung up. There are a couple of pillows and some blankets on the upper shelf."

I opened the bathroom door. There was a shower, a vanity sink, and a toilet. Nothing much, nothing special. A mirrored medicine cabinet hung on the wall over the sink. I opened it and went through the usual stuff one might find: a contact case and lens rinse; some over-the-counter medicines; a retainer in a plastic case; some antacid; and a bottle of pills labeled "Premarin."

"Nancy," I called, "she's got a bottle of Premarin pills. Do you know what it's for?"

"Yeah," came the answer. "It's estrogen. That's a pretty common prescription for women aged forty-five."

Under the sink was a bunch of hair products, makeup and such. I called to Nancy again and had her come in to give everything a closer look since I was out of my element. I also had her take a picture with her cell phone of the contents of both the vanity cabinet and the medicine cabinet.

"Normal stuff," pronounced Nancy. "Nothing out of the ordinary. She sleep on the couch, you think?"

"Maybe it's a sofa bed."

It was, and a minute later Nancy and I opened it up. The mattress had sheets already on, the blanket and the pillows in the closet.

"Looks like she just went away for the weekend," Nancy said. "Cleaned everything up and left."

"It does, doesn't it?"

* * *

Darla's old, gray Toyota Corolla was parked in the lot outside her shop. It was locked. Nancy used her slim jim, more properly known as a lockout tool, to pop the door lock, then opened the trunk. We looked through the car carefully. In the glovebox was the usual stuff — registration, inspection certificate, insurance card and her Toyota handbook. There were a couple of gas receipts stuffed into the ash tray. Underneath the front seat was an old cardboard coffee cup and some other trash. The back seat contained a Polartech sweatshirt and a box of hair products; the trunk, a set of jumper cables, two beat-up umbrellas and a couple of old plastic grocery bags. Nothing, really. Nancy dusted for some prints, but we weren't hopeful.

* * *

After lunch Nancy and I drove up to Linville to meet Capt. Boog Mitchell at Crystal Latimore's house. We arrived before he did, but took time to walk around the little mountain bungalow. It was a well-kept yard, a little lawn, but mostly natural landscaping with some laurel, rhododendrons, small evergreens, and dormant azaleas. The weather had changed dramatically and quickly, as it did so often here in the mountains. What had started out as a cold sunny day was now looking like a cold, overcast, wintry day, and the clouds were starting to spit. A police car drove up and parked behind my truck in the driveway.

"Good to see you guys again," said Boog, getting out and zipping his leather jacket. "Sorry about the reason, though. I knew Crystal. She was a nice lady."

"I didn't know her," I said, "but I'm sorry, too. Can you tell us anything about her?"

"Well, I knew her, but not well," admitted Boog. "Divorced, I think. She was active around town. Showed up at events, on a couple of committees, that sort of thing. I knew her from the Library Council. My wife's on that as well, and Crystal has been to the house a few times for meetings."

"She had a St. Germaine library card," said Nancy. "Any reason you might know of?"

78

"Sure," said Boog. "Our library has been closed since August. We got a big bequest and the town is redoing the whole thing. It should be quite a showplace when it's finished. That's mainly what the Library Council has been meeting about. Anyway, I suppose she wanted to check out some books or something."

"Makes sense," said Nancy. "I checked at our library and she used her card quite a bit."

"I wonder," said Boog, "if this shouldn't be *our* case. If she was murdered here, it's certainly our jurisdiction even if the body was dumped over in St. Germaine."

"Absolutely right," I said. "You are welcome to it. With my compliments."

"Yeah, I thought you'd say that. Tell you what, if we do find out that Crystal was killed in Linville, I'll take it off your hands. Otherwise, you just let me know what we can do to help."

Just then a panel van arrived and parked on the street in front of the house. The lettering on the side of the van identified it as belonging to Cooter's Locks 'N Such. A grizzled, old man in blue overalls, a stocking cap and an over-insulated ski jacket got out, opened the sliding door, picked up a toolbox and trudged down the stone walkway to the front door.

"Hey, Boog," he grumbled, then set his toolbox on the front stoop, got out a set of picks and started to work.

"Hey, Cooter," answered Boog.

"You using lever picks?" asked Nancy.

"Yeah," said Cooter, squinting hard at the dead bolt he was working. "I'm gonna need that tension wrench, too."

"Here you go," said Nancy, handing him what he needed. Nancy was good at locks, but had left her own set of picks at home. Her slim jim didn't work on house locks.

"Thanks," grunted Cooter, taking the wrench without looking away from his task and, in another minute or so, the front door of the house swung open.

Cooter stood up, held out his hand to Boog and said, "That'll be thirty-five dolla'."

"Write up an invoice and take it to the station," said Boog. "Sheesh, Cooter, you know how this works by now."

"Yeah," grumbled Cooter, packing his tools up. "I gotta wait for another danged month before I get my money."

"Here you go," I said, pulling out my money clip. I peeled off fifty dollars and handed it to him. "I want a receipt before you leave. St. Germaine P.D. The extra fifteen bucks is to re-key the lock and give me two copies."

Cooter looked me in the eye and gave me a nod. "Sure. Thanks." He trudged back down the walk to get more tools and his receipt book.

"Did you find any next of kin?" I asked Boog as we walked into the hallway behind the front door and found the light switches.

"No. We couldn't find an address on the ex-husband. His name is Kevin Latimore, but he hasn't lived in Linville for at least eight years. The last address we had was in Landrum, South Carolina, but the phone number was not his. The directory in Landrum doesn't have him either. Maybe Crystal had his number in the house. Maybe her parents are still alive. She was only, what, in her forties?"

"Forty-five," said Nancy. "So her parents could possibly be in their late sixties or early seventies."

"We need an address book, or computer, or something," I said. "Hopefully, there's one here somewhere."

Nancy, Boog, and I went through the house. We didn't find an address book and we didn't find a computer. We did find a cable modem, a wireless router, and a WiFi printer. An obvious setup for a laptop, but no laptop. As a court advocate, Crystal probably carried her laptop with her daily.

"Here's your keys," called Cooter. "I'm leaving them on this here dining table."

"Thanks," I called back from the kitchen.

The rest of her house was neat as a pin. Nothing out of place, although there were dirty dishes in the dishwasher. There was a small load of laundry still in the dryer. The trash can in the kitchen, however, was empty, as was the small one in the bathroom. Everything seemed to be in order. In the bedroom, the bed was made and next to it on the side table was an open book, face down marking the page. The cover said *The Devil in the White City*. I picked it up and turned it over, then flipped to the front. St. Germaine Public Library.

"Nothing here," said Nancy, rifling through the closet. Boog was rifling through the dresser but came up empty as well. After an hour of going through the house, we called it quits and left. I gave Boog one of the keys and Nancy put the other one on her key ring.

Crystal's late model Chevy Trailblazer was sitting on the street. Nancy popped it open and we gave it a thorough going over, but found nothing. We said our farewells, promised to stay in touch concerning the case, and headed up to Tinkler's Knob.

We made a quick stop in St. Germaine since it was on the way, and Nancy got her own set of lock picks out. Tinkler's Knob was way out in the county and would have been the county sheriff's jurisdiction, but I'd already called him and he really didn't want to bother driving all the way out there since I was going anyway. He wasn't anxious to have a murder on his plate.

Amy Ventura's house was a log cabin. Not an old one like mine built of two-hundred-year-old, hand-hewn chestnut logs, but one of the new round-log kits that were popular about twenty years ago. The logs had an orangish stain and they were topped with a green tin roof. A narrow, covered front porch stretched the length of the house and two large windows were positioned on either side of the wooden front door. There was no garage or carport, and the driveway, as well as the road up to Tinkler's Knob, was unpaved. Amy's Jeep Wrangler was sitting in the drive. It wasn't locked. The cabin seemed to be in good repair, even though some settling was evidenced in the cracks in the chinking. Not an expensive house, but comfortable, probably.

Nancy went to work on the door while I walked up to check the mailbox. I found an electric bill and two circulars from Dollar General. Nancy had the door open by the time I made it back to the front porch.

"We're up in the middle of nowhere," I said, and checked my phone. "No cell service."

"She worked from home," Nancy said. "A grant writer. There has to be satellite internet and probably TV as well."

"Yeah. I just got that satellite internet service. It's great."

We spent the next hour or so going through Amy's house and, by the time we were finished, the sun had dropped down behind the hills and an early dusk was upon us. Nancy was right about the satellite setup, but again, no laptop. Amy was less of a housekeeper. The bed was unmade, there were dishes in the sink, and a laundry basket full of dirty clothes waiting to go into the washing machine, but everything was fairly tidy and clean. Her vacuum cleaner had been left in the living room, plugged in, and several of the lights in the house had been left on.

Nothing in the Jeep.

We were no further along than we'd been when the day had started.

Well, maybe a little.

Chapter 13

"I think we have a good layout," said Bud. "I brought a drawing with me."

"Well, let's see it then," I said, clearing a space on the table.

"Absolutely," said Meg.

We'd decided to meet at the Slab and review the plans for the wine shop. Bud had already met with the architect and I had spoken with the contractor, but neither Meg nor I had seen any plans yet. Bud unrolled the drawing and spread it out. It wasn't a detailed rendition, but was a contractor's drawing showing walls, outlets, bathrooms, fixtures, and the like. A floor plan.

"Here's where the shelves go," said Bud, pointing to the main room. "All along the walls and two in the center with plenty of room to get around. There's a bar here and shelves behind that as well. We'll use that for tastings. Here's a sink and a big rack for wine glasses. Now, this is the kitchen ... "

Bud went on excitedly for about thirty minutes, showing us where each vintage would be kept and why, where the stools would go, the stairs to the basement wine cellar, his office, the shipping room, the new kitchen, cash register, everything.

"Wow," said Meg when he was finished. "This is quite impressive."

"Thanks." He looked over at me for approval.

"Good job, Bud! I think we're on our way. Roberto will be there tomorrow morning to get started. I want you to be there, too."

"I met with him yesterday. He's bringing his crew, and I called and arranged to have the dumpster dropped off at seven. I'll be there first thing."

"Good deal."

"I'm heading back to the house," he said, rolling his drawing back up and snapping a rubber band around it. "I'm still gonna clean up a bit. It'll save some time tomorrow."

"Have fun," said Meg. "We're really proud of you, Bud."

"Indeed we are."

* * *

Buxtehooter's was a pipe-organ bar with something to prove. It was a classy joint, not like those other pipe-organ bars downtown - The PipeRack, Celeste's, and the Bearded Gamba, to name a few. Buxtehooter's had all the panache those dives forgot and a velvet rope besides - the rope to keep the Southern Baptists from sneaking in. Yeah, they said they were only coming in to pass out some Bible tracts and shepherd these sinners back on the path to righteousness, but they spent a little too much time up at the bar, especially on wet-dirndl night. Who could blame 'em? The waitresses at Buxtehooter's were blonde, pigtailed Tyrolean dolls. They could sing like Moravians, shimmy like Methodists, and pour suds like Lutherans, all of which made them very attractive to the Southern Baptists, the ones that managed to slip past Big Lucille.

Pedro and I grabbed our table in the back and listened to one of the girls standing on the bar warble a Geisslerlieder — something unintelligible in Medieval German — while some of the more fervent patrons had formed a flagellant dance line and were gaily beating themselves around the floor with golf umbrellas.

"Guten Abend!" said the waitress who suddenly appeared at the table. "My name is Klingel. What can I get you boys?" She smiled a smile that could make Wagner order a matzah ball.

"Gimme a pitcher of Schweinestinke extra-dark," said Pedro.

"Ja, ja," tinkled Klingel.

"Same for me," I said and stuffed a sawbuck into the top of Klingel's dirndl. She was a looker all right, but it was Pedro she was giving the eye to. I thought about taking my sawbuck back.

"You're a peach," I said, shooting her a look and thinking she really was much like a peach, except for her not being a fuzzy three-inch fruit of the genus Prunus produced by a tree with pink blossoms and that she had internal organs and could talk, so not really.

"You gonna fill me in?" I asked Pedro, as Klingel chingled away.

"I told you," said Pedro. "It wasn't me. I didn't do it."

"Hmmm," I pondered. "I believe you, but this is gonna come back on us. I mean, we can prop up the body in Marilyn's chair for a while. I don't think anyone will notice. But then Marilyn's coming back from Vegas."

"Yeah," agreed Pedro. "Anne Dante's gonna be ripe as a peach in a week."

"And if you didn't do it, then who did, and why?" I rankled sleuthily, summing up my work for the day.

"I think it has to do with groundhogs," Pedro said. "There was an article in the paper this morning on the religion page along with her picture. You'd have recognized her if you'd gotten past the obituaries."

"I was getting there. I had to see who was dead, didn't I?"

Something was bothering me and it suddenly hit me ... hit me like a huge squishy bug that smacks into your teeth when you're riding your motorcycle, and bothering me like one of its legs that lodges behind a molar and you flick at it with your tongue but can't get it out without flossing.

Anne Dante's name was in the obituaries. I'd read it. But she hadn't been killed yet.

* * *

The choir members were all in their chairs when I walked up the narrow stairs and entered the choir loft. "Welcome back!" said Mark Wells, the first one to see me standing in the doorway. This was followed by a chorus of welcomes that made me feel downright humble. I'd come up earlier in the afternoon and put music and my new detective story on each chair.

"I'm glad you're back, too," said Marjorie. "I don't get this story, though. As usual, it's beneath me."

"You mean, *beyond* you," said Martha Hatteberg, one of the altos. Marjorie sat on the edge of the alto section for appearances, but sang the tenor part most of the time. On the other side of her sat Martha's husband, Randy, and Bert Coley, a police officer in Boone.

"I know what I said," sniffed Marjorie. At age seventy-plus, she was the eldest in the choir and had vowed to drop down to the bass part when the tenor line became too high for her to manage.

"I like the part about the squishy bug," said Sheila DeMoss.

Tiff St. James raised her hand like the dutiful student she was. "Excuse me, but this title says *The Cantor Wore Crinolines*. What the heck are crinolines?" Tiff was our unpaid choir intern from the music department at Appalachian State.

Marjorie guffawed. "You don't know what crinolines are? You poor, deprived child. I remember when I had to wear them for my confirmation."

"Well, what are they?" asked Tiff again.

"Petticoats, dear. Horrible, stiff petticoats. They hold your dress out like one of those Southern Belles in *Gone With the Wind*."

"I had to wear them when I was a girl," said Martha. "Hated 'em. In the old days, some of them had hoops. Not mine, though. I'm not quite that old. Marjorie's probably had hoops made out of whalebone."

"They did not!" barked Marjorie.

"Originally," said Bert Coley, reading while his fingers scrolled across his Smartphone, "crinoline was a French fabric made by weaving horsehair with another fabric. Very stiff. Then it came to mean the actual petticoats that offered shape to women's dresses. You'll be gratified to know that crinolines, as a fashion statement, are now making a comeback in bridal attire."

"I *am* gratified to know that," said Elaine, then asked me, "Now, why are you writing about crinolines?"

"An author's genius is often not recognized during his own lifetime," I said, finally making my way through the choir and down to the organ console.

"That's true," said Rebecca Watts, the town librarian and acknowledged literary expert. "Take Emily Dickinson, for example. Or Edgar Allan Poe."

"Or Jesus," said Goldi Fawn Birtwhistle, a soprano-turned-alto who had just recently decided that Marjorie might be right and that her high Gs were reminiscent of a swan being gutted alive and roasted on a spit. She had sadly traded all her solo accompaniment tracks for ones in a lower key.

All the altos were accounted for except for Dr. Ian Burch, PhD, our countertenor with a cherished doctorate in early music, who was on a two-week tour of France with the Appalachian Rauschpfeife Consort.

Also present was a full complement of sopranos, including Bev, Georgia, Elaine, and Rhiza Walker. Four basses and three tenors filled out the choir. Eighteen singers and all the parts covered.

"I heard the new priest has already found your replacement," said Phil Camp.

"My *sabbatical* replacement," I said. "I'm only off until the end of June."

"Well, who is it?" asked Phil. "Anyone we know?"

"No one you know," I said. "If I remember correctly, Father Dressler told me he has a master's degree from Oberlin. He'll whip you guys into shape in no time flat."

"What's his name?" asked Bob Solomon. The basses all sat in the back row under the life-sized, stained glass image of St. Barnabas himself.

"Umm ... hang on ... " I hunted around in my jacket pocket for the slip of paper on which I'd written the name of Father Dressler's organist. "Here it is. The Chevalier Lance Fleagle."

"The Chevalier?" said Marjorie. "Jesus, Mary and Joseph!"

"Apparently, he's a knight," I continued. "He would like to be referred to as 'The Chevalier.'"

"Well, if that don't shellac the beetle to the brisket!" said Marjorie. "A real knight?"

"Named Lancelot, no less," I said, "but he won't be here until a week from Sunday, so you're stuck with me until then. Now, I've put some new music on your chairs, so let's give it a look. Our interim priest is an Anglo-Catholic, so we'll be changing some things about the service."

"An Anglo-Catholic?" said Goldi Fawn. "What's that?"

Meg said, "As choir president, I've done my due diligence on the subject and am now prepared to offer a report." She pulled a piece of paper out of her choir folder, stood up, and put on her reading glasses.

"Lay it on us," said Steve DeMoss from the bass section.

"The term 'Anglo-Catholic' describes people, beliefs and practices within Anglicanism which affirm the Catholic heritage and identity of the various Anglican churches, rather than the churches' Protestant heritage. In this 'Catholic' revival, Anglicans began again to embrace the rituals of the ancient church with renewed enthusiasm for the gift of the Sacraments, recognizing that a biblically-informed, Gospel-centered church need not be at odds with the Catholic tradition and is strengthened by the expression of God's love in both Word and Sacraments."

"That sounds okay to me," said Sheila. "I don't know about this knight thing, though."

"So, we're going Catholic?" asked Tiff. "My mom isn't going to like that one bit. She's a Southern Baptist. She's got enough of a problem with me singing with you Whiskeypalians."

"Aw, c'mon," laughed Bert. "We don't drink whiskey *that* much."

"Speak for yourself," muttered Marjorie.

"I'm sure we're not going Catholic," said Meg. "Just slanting a little toward that part of our heritage." She looked at her paper again. "There's also some historical stuff here about the Oxford Movement in 1833 and the Caroline Divines in the seventeenth century."

"Feel free to skip that part," said Bob Solomon.

"Do we have to start chantin' the rosary? That's what I wanna know," said Goldi Fawn. "I ain't gonna chant the rosary!"

Meg shrugged and looked over at me.

"I'm sure you won't have to," I said, "and, even if it does sneak into the service now and then, it's nothing to worry about." Then I added, "I think you'll all enjoy this experience. You'll all be glad to know that the choir will be singing the Psalm. We haven't done that for going on two years."

General nods of agreement across the choir.

"Father Dressler likes good music. He likes high mass. Acolytes, crucifers. Benny Dawkins will be back in business. We're going back to snooty."

More smiles and nods.

"How 'bout me singing with my CD accompaniment?" asked Goldi Fawn, a sad resignation evident in her voice. "I just bought all new tracks, but now I guess that's out." Goldi Fawn had been lobbying hard since Christmas to get her "Special Music" placed in the communion slot. As long as I was riding the pine, she knew that wasn't going to happen, but since I'd been taking a break, she figured she had a good shot at it. With Deacon Kimberly Walnut in charge for the past three weeks, Goldi figured it was only a matter of time.

88

"Nope," I said. "No CD accompaniments. We're also going to Rite One."

There were general groans across the choir. The language and liturgy of Rite One, as compared with our usual Rite Two, was much more formal. More than that, the music that we knew for Rite One wasn't especially popular with the choir.

"I expect," I said, "that once the Chevalier starts rehearsing, you all will be doing communion and mass settings by the great composers, — Mozart, Palestrina, William Byrd, and the like."

"We can't learn all that stuff," said Marjorie. "Too many black notes. As you know, I'm not usually prejudiced, but I like my notes white."

"No more congregational singing?" asked Bev.

"Well, hymns, certainly," I said. "Probably not the mass settings."

"Who hired this priest anyway?" Mark Wells said.

"He's just our interim," said Fred May, his voice full of its usual optimism. Fred was an upbeat, glass-half-full kind of guy. "It'll do us good to get a new perspective on worship. Anyway, *you* were on the committee that picked him."

"Huh," said Mark. "I must have missed that meeting."

* * *

We learned the Psalm for Sunday, went through the anthems for the next two weeks including Hassler's *Come, Sing Unto the Lord, Surely the Light is Sweet* by Carson Cooman, and Roland Martin's setting of the George Herbert poem, *Love Bade Me Welcome*. All very different, all lovely. It was good to be back with these folks, making music. We worked on *Love Bade Me Welcome* the previous fall but hadn't polished it before Advent rolled around, and it had been shelved in favor of more seasonal choices. Now the choir picked it back up quickly. I had thought that they could do the piece after the Chevalier arrived, but changed my mind once I heard them sing it, and rescheduled the anthem for communion this Sunday. The two other pieces were familiar to the choir and brushing them up wasn't going to be a problem. We worked on some notes and phrasing, and I ranted about diction for a few minutes —the usual stuff choir directors do — and, when we sang through it again forty minutes later, it was ready to go.

"Love bade me welcome, yet my soul drew back," sang the choir.

"I love this anthem," said Rhiza, when we'd finished. "How come we didn't sing it before Christmas?"

"We didn't sing it nearly this well, as you may recall."

"I know why exactly," said Elaine. "We were working on it when that crazy Rosemary Pepperpot-Cohosh was having her affair with the yoga guy. It threw us all into a tizzy."

"Yes, that was it," agreed Meg. "Remember? Rosemary quoted the poem during the sermon, right after she confessed her sin to the congregation and announced she was leaving after Christmas. We couldn't sing it right after that."

"Well, I'm glad it hasn't been forever tainted by *that* woman," said Elaine venomously. "And, while we're on the subject, why on earth would she make a big production of confessing to the congregation anyway? Where is her sense of decorum? She should have just packed up and left in the middle of the night like any normal hussy."

"Some people just need the attention," said Marjorie.

"Oh, she was plenty shrewd," said Mark Wells. "Since she confessed and asked our forgiveness, we didn't feel like we could fire her sorry butt, not right before Christmas. She bought herself another month's salary and time to go find herself a job at the Walmart store."

Martha jumped in. "You remember the 4th of July weekend that she decided to decorate the altar with American flags and fireworks? Then Kimberly Walnut nudged that string of black cats into the altar candle during communion and the whole thing went up like ... well ... like the Fourth of July?"

"That was hilarious!" said Bob Solomon. "Best communion service ever!"

"It was *not!*" said Bev. "We had to call the fire department. It cost several hundred dollars just to clean up the mess, not to mention the altar cloth that was ruined!" Bev was still fuming. The altar cloth had been given to St. Barnabas by her grandmother and was one of the few things that had escaped the great fire that claimed the church just a few years ago. Luckily, it was at the dry cleaners when the church had burned. This time, though, dry cleaning wouldn't help.

"Roman candles," laughed Bob, unmindful of Bev's wrath. "Spinners, a couple of sparkling fountains. It was great!"

"Well," growled Bev, "I'd like to stick one of those Roman candles right up ... "

"How about the *Trampoline Mass*?" hooted Randy. "Who ever thought *that* was a good idea?"

"And the liturgical dancers during Holy Week?" said Georgia.

"Liturgical dancers are quite common," I said. "Sometimes it can be a very meaningful ..."

"*Tap dancers*?" said Georgia. "Tapping to Pergolesi's *Stabat Mater* during the stripping of the altar?"

"They were wearing purple outfits, at least," offered Meg.

"These things happen," I said, interrupting the stream of derision aimed at Mother P, "and I'm sure we're all very sorry for any bad feelings, but it's time to press on. Move ahead. Besides, we need to look at this service music. We haven't sung it for a few years."

Chapter 14

"His name is what?" said Meg.

"Gallus," I said. "His name is Gallus Dressler. He never introduced himself other than 'Father Dressler' so I went ahead and asked him. He informed me that was the name he took when he entered the priesthood. I don't know his given name."

"I guess it wasn't in the bulletin, was it?" said Bev. "It was on his C.V."

"I didn't see it," answered Meg. "I would have remembered that."

"Gallus. That's Latin, isn't it?" asked Ruby.

"Yes, it is," I said. "He's probably leaning more toward Rome than he led the search committee to believe. Not that I mind."

"Doesn't *gallus* mean 'chicken'?" asked Ruby.

"I looked it up," I said, "and it means 'comb.' Hence the common chicken is the *gallus domesticus*. I don't know why he'd choose to be named after a chicken. The composer Jacob Handl was sometimes known as Gallus, maybe because Handl is a derivative of Hahn, German for rooster."

"Well, he's our chicken now," said Meg. "As an interim anyway. Maybe the committee will find someone permanent in a hurry."

I'd been invited over to Ruby's house for lunch, an invitation I always took advantage of. Meg was already here, and she'd brought Bev since they'd been working this morning over at the financial counseling office. I was used to being the only male invited to these amusements and, although I was happy to answer questions when posed, mostly I had learned to shut up and eat. These questions were usually posed at the beginning of the meal so that the ladies could get down to some serious gossip without feeling that I had to be included.

Meg asked me, "Did the contractor show up this morning?"

"Bright and early, and Bud was there to meet him. Apparently, we also have plumbing problems, specifically to do with the septic tank."

"Roots in the lines?" said Meg. "It's an old house."

"I hope that's all it is. Anyway, the septic tank guy is coming out this afternoon. Harm Pooter. I used him when I built the cabin."

"Any news on the dead women?" asked Bev.

"Nothing new. I'll hear something from Kent today I expect. The other two bodies are probably thawed by now."

"Would you like your *gallus domesticus* salad on a sandwich or just on a plate?" said Ruby. "You can get your own chips. They're on the counter."

"Sandwich, please," I answered.

"You know," said Ruby, sitting down beside me at the kitchen table once I'd gotten my glass of tea and found my chair, "there's something funny going on."

"To what hilarity are you referring?" I said.

"To the murder hilarity, which is not hilarity at all," said Ruby, giving me a stern look.

"Right," I agreed. "What's the funny part?"

Meg and Bev joined us at the table and Meg placed my plate in front of me. Chicken salad on dark rye with a little mayo, chips, and a pickle. Perfect!

"The funny part is this," said Ruby. "You know the Blue Hill Bookworms?"

"The book club? Yeah."

"Did Meg tell you how they blackballed me?" asked Ruby.

I shrugged. "She did mention how they found your choice of literature a little too ... um ... shall we say, 'prosaic,' for their taste."

"*Bourgeois* is the word they used," said Ruby. "All because of a few romance novels that were in my reading list. I could have left them off, but I was trying to be honest and show my 'lighter' side."

"I think it's just awful," said Meg. "Those snobs!"

"Oh, I wasn't the only one they snubbed," continued Ruby. "There was Wynette Winslow, Roweena Purvis, Annette Passaglio ... hmm ... maybe a couple of others. They only entertain new members once a year — in February."

"Very exclusive," I said.

Ruby rolled her eyes. "Anyway, the Blue Hill Bookworms have a website and a blog. Annette showed me. They post about books they're reading and write tremendously dull reviews about even duller books. Apparently anyone can get on and read, but you're not allowed to post or comment unless you're a member."

I nodded understanding since my mouth was full, and managed a grunt.

"So, since I'd been refused membership, I decided to log on and see what high and mighty tome the Bookworms were reading and if it was any good."

I swallowed and said, "Just to keep pace with the local literary illuminati."

"Exactly," said Ruby. "So I went to their blog and it turns out that they're reading trash."

"Trash?" said Meg. "What kind of trash?"

"Well, not trash exactly, but certainly not high art. They finished *Madame Bovary* just after Christmas and their next big meeting isn't until next month. I guess they don't meet in January. They've decided to start Ayn Rand's *The Fountainhead* in February. I've read it. I'm not a big fan."

"That probably wouldn't be considered 'trash' though," said Bev.

"No, it wouldn't. But in between, to 'cleanse the palate' as the website says, they're reading a murder mystery. It's called *See Your Shadow* by Kitty Holly. It's just fluff. A cozy. I'm sorry I called it trash. It's not trashy. Not like that *Fifty Shades of Grey*."

"*Mother!*" said Meg. "You read *that*?"

"Well, of course I did, dear," said Ruby. "It was a bestseller, after all. Anyway, I downloaded the murder mystery onto my Kindle since it was only a dollar and read it yesterday afternoon. You know, just to keep up with those book snobs."

"Okay," I said, having no idea where this was going.

Ruby continued. "It seems that there are four separate murders in this mystery. The victims are all women. A publicist, a lawyer, a hair dresser, and a minister."

That got my attention.

"The bodies are all discovered in closets. They're all sitting up, hands in their laps, and they're all wearing nice clothes. Church clothes. It turns out that they were all in the same prayer group, but we don't find that out until the end."

"Oh, my God!" whispered Bev.

Meg looked at her mother, horrified.

"I'm sorry," Ruby said to me. "Meg gave me the particulars of the murders. I haven't told anyone else."

"It's common knowledge at this point," I said. "I'm sure Helen Pigeon has given Annette an eyewitness account for the *Tattler's* Friday edition."

"The *modus operandi* is not exactly the same," said Ruby with a satisfied smile, "but I do believe that those Blue Hill Bookworms might have some explaining to do."

***

I met Nancy at the station and, once she got onto the website, we had the names of the Blue Hill Bookworms along with a brief autobiography of each. Thank you, social media. Nancy gleaned the information and condensed it. Most of it was probably useless, but it was somewhere to start.

The Bookworms had eight active members.

- Rachel Barstow – home gardener, herbalist, sells at the Farmer's Market; has quite a *Pinterest* following; historical mysteries, political satire, and existentialist fiction listed as favorites.
- Alison Jaeger – doctor; plays the piano; enjoys baking; has a wide, eclectic reading list.
- Stephanie Bilton – part-time personal assistant; married with children and pets, including chickens, a dog, and ferrets; grows asparagus as a hobby; an excellent cook and frequently provides dinner for the group; favorite reading: metahistorical romantic fiction.
- Catherine Duncan – secretary in the music department at Appalachian State; married; sings in a community and church choir; aficionado of offbeat Latin American and Spanish novels.
- Sara Black – pharmacist; married with children; enjoys riding horses; favorite books: ergodic literature, especially Milorad Pavic's *Landscape Painted With Tea.*
- Annabel Stratton – marital counselor; a member of the *Sugar Mountain Cloggers*, a clogging group that meets weekly for dances; enjoys Dickens, Bulwer-Lytton, and other Victorian writers.
- Sarah Aspinall – personal injury lawyer; keeper of the Bookworms' reading list; compiles quizzes on the books they've read; prefers dark comedy and medical thrillers.
- Diana Evarts – baker; owner of Bun in the Oven bakery; widow; part-time ASU history department thesis and dissertation proofreader; sings in the community choir with Catherine Duncan; likes Russian novels and biographies.

I'd met all the members when they'd extended me the invitation to address their book club, but of the eight, I only really knew three of them: Diana, Sara Black, and Catherine. Nancy knew those three as well, plus Rachel and Alison. The other three we didn't know, but, since Diana was right across the street at her bakery, we decided to start there.

Nancy reviewed her list as we walked across the park.

"What the heck is ergodic literature?" she asked.

"I have no earthly idea, and *I'm* a famous author."

Nancy ignored that comment. "Stephanie Bilton," she said, tapping the name on the paper. "Who needs a personal assistant? Maybe some hotshot in a big city, but around here?"

"I dunno," I said. "We shall ask her. I'm also curious why anyone would grow asparagus as a hobby."

"Is this one of those clues where we find out that the flowers of the asparagus plant are poison if you pluck them just prior to pollination and this is the exact poison that killed the three ladies? Then I discover a surreptitious motive and save the day?"

"I certainly hope so," I said with a smile. "Then I take all the credit and we'll be finished by lunch."

The bakery was on Main Street, two doors down from St. Barnabas. It had been a CPA's office until Larry Wenger had retired. Then Diana Evarts had moved in and opened the bakery. Diana had been selling cupcakes out of her kitchen for a couple of years and had more business than she could handle. It was time for her to make the move to a permanent establishment. She rented the storefront from Pete Moss, who had collected several downtown properties over the years. Pete also helped her out by finding good, used equipment including ovens, stoves, mixers, and anything else a bakery might need. Pete had connections.

Diana not only made delicious cupcakes, but her menu now included donuts, breads, cookies, desserts of every kind, wedding and birthday cakes, and whatever else anyone might need or want from a baker. When she was settled in, she brought Jacki Flowers on board. Jacki specialized in cake decoration and immediately saw the advantage in the partnership. Now they were as busy as woodchucks in April.

The front door opened with an obnoxious buzz, notifying the two ladies in the back of the store that there were customers present. I much preferred Pete's old-timey cowbell clanging against the glass door of the Slab, but *suum cuique.* To each his own. I noticed that, since lunchtime, Latin phrases learned in my youth were coming back to me, probably thanks to *gallus domesticus.* I certainly didn't mind. *Catapultam habeo. Nisi pecuniam omnem mihi dabis, ad caput tuum saxum immane mittam.*

Diana came out of the kitchen cleaning her hands on a towel. She was wearing an apron that was dusted with flour, along with other evidence of the creative culinary art process. She had dark, short hair and gave us a warm smile when she recognized us.

"Good afternoon, Chief. Nancy. I was expecting Dave."

"Dave?" said Nancy.

"He always comes in after lunch to get a dozen day-olds. Actually, he gets them before they're a day old. They're left over from this morning. Shall I get them for you?" She slid open the back of the glass case that separated us. We could see on the shelves all manner of confectionary. Cakes, and cookies, and cupcakes. Pastries and loaves of bread. Lemon squares, brownies, and eclairs. My mouth watered just looking at everything.

"We're not here for Dave's donuts," said Nancy. "We need to ask you about your book club."

"The Bookworms?" said Diana. "What about it?"

Jacki came out of the back, cleaning her hands, just as Diana had a minute earlier. "What's up?" she asked. Jacki was shorter than Diana, and just as attractive.

"We need to talk to Diana," said Nancy. "Police business."

"Oh," said Jacki. "Shall I leave, then?"

"If you don't mind," I said. "We'll be finished in just a few minutes."

Jacki undid her apron strings, then took off the apron and put in on the counter. "I'll go get a cup of coffee."

"Thanks," I said.

She walked out of the front door and, with a furtive look back at us, headed toward the Holy Grounds Coffee Shop.

Diana looked very nervous. "So ... what's up?" she managed.

"The book you've been reading," I said.

"*Madame Bovary?*"

"Nope. The new one. *See Your Shadow.*"

"I haven't finished it, yet. Rachel sent it around and thought it would be a good break from the heavy stuff."

"How much of it have you read?" asked Nancy.

"Maybe the first hundred pages or so. It's not very long. I guess I'm about half-finished with it."

"Has anyone died yet?" said Nancy. "In the book, I mean."

She thought for a moment, then said, "Three bodies, so far. It's not a very highbrow book, you know. It's just, well … "

"Fluff?" I said.

"Exactly," said Diana. "Fluff."

"I'm going to read it tonight," I said. "You say that it was Rachel who recommended it?"

"Yes. Rachel Barstow. We're all free to recommend things, and we had a few weeks in between the big reads we'd decided on earlier in the year. Rachel said she read this one last summer at the beach and liked it. So we all voted to read it. It was a lark, really. I think most of the girls decided to do it to make fun of Rachel at the next meeting. She can be such a book snob sometimes."

"So, do you think most members of the book club have finished it?"

"I really doubt it," said Diana. "We don't meet until next week, and it's so … fluffy, that they won't bother with it until a couple of days before the meeting. If it was something substantial, they'd all be into the middle of it by now."

"So you think that Rachel might be the only one who's read it all the way through."

"That would be my guess, but, I may be totally wrong. The only reason I started it is because I have some proofreading to do next week and won't have time to wolf it down in a couple of sittings." She paused for a moment, had a thought, then said, "You might check the Bookworms' blog. I haven't been on it this week, but sometimes the girls post things about what they're currently reading. No spoilers, though."

"What's the blog address?" asked Nancy, pulling a pen and pad out of her breast pocket. She had the web address, of course — we'd already been all through the blog, but this was part of our show. She diligently wrote the information in the pad, flipped it shut and returned it to her pocket.

"Thanks, Diana," I said. "I'd really like to meet with your book club again. I need to get some information. Do you think you can get everyone together before your scheduled meeting? It'd be easier than tracking all of you down one at a time."

"You bet. I'll call everyone and see if we can get together tomorrow for lunch. I don't think we can do it tonight. A couple of us have community choir practice, and I think Annabel has clogging."

"Thanks," I said. "Tomorrow will be fine. As many of you as can make it."

"Did you want to take these day-olds over to Dave?"

"Sure," said Nancy, taking the box from Diana, "but Dave will have to pay for them."

"Oh, there's no charge for day-olds. Not for our city's finest."

* * *

"I found something," said Kent.

"Something important?"

"Would I call if it wasn't important?"

"Fair enough," I said. "What did you find? A different cause of death than we thought?"

"Nope. Heart attacks, all three. No trace of any kind of poison that I can find. That doesn't mean they weren't poisoned. It just means I can't find it. It also means we can't prove it."

"Let's go, for now, on the assumption that they were poisoned. It would be a very strange coincidence if three middle-aged women all died of heart attacks in random closets on their way to church."

"I agree," said Kent.

"So what is it that you found?"

"I noticed when doing the autopsy on Amy Ventura that she had some swelling of the soft palate. I took some tissue samples but they're inconclusive. Still, the swelling was pronounced."

"Maybe a sinus infection or something?" I said.

"I sincerely doubt it. If it was, then Crystal Latimore and Darla Kildair both had the same sinus infection. No, this was something else. Not only was there swelling, but there were small lesions evident on the tissue. Almost like welts."

"Huh," I said.

"After I found the swelling, I checked the other two victims and sure enough, all three women had the same symptom. It was less pronounced on Crystal, but it was there."

"You're thinking it was a reaction to the poison."

99

"That is my theory," said Kent. "The interesting thing about this would be the type of poison. I did find about fifty kinds of poison that swell the soft palate, either as a side effect or as the main consequence. Everything from black hellebore to iodine."

"Why would it be a main consequence? You mean that the poison was *intended* to swell the soft palate?"

"Well, if the palate swells enough, it will cut off the airway and, depending on the severity, can easily cause a heart attack."

"Can't you check for that?" I asked. "Suffocation, I mean."

"I checked for petechial hemorrhaging. None evident. So I'm thinking that it was a side effect. The fact that the swelling is still visible is the strange thing. That and the lesions. I'll keep checking on the fifty poisons on the list and I have a call in to a friend of mine in Washington. She's quite a connoisseur of poisons. If it's one of these, she'll know about it."

"How about asparagus flowers?" I asked.

"Huh?" said Kent, confused.

"Asparagus flowers. I have it on good authority they're highly poisonous."

"Don't be ridiculous."

* * *

Bud was standing out in front of the new wine shop with his brother Moosey and Harm Pooter when I walked up. It was cold. Bud was wearing a ski jacket, a scarf, and a stocking cap. Harm was in the traditional winter garb of the outdoor laborer: insulated coveralls, a work jacket, and heavy boots. He had a baseball cap pulled down low, but it didn't do much to shield his ears and they had turned a lovely shade of red just about matching his nose. Moosey was dressed in as many layers as his mother, Ardine, could make him put on. He wore gloves, something the other two had shunned, and his hat had earflaps that at least attempted to keep his head warm. He was sitting proudly at the wheel of a used, gas-powered, four-wheel drive golf cart.

"We've got groundhogs," said Bud sadly.

My face showed my confusion. "Huh?"

"We got groundhogs," said Moosey, grinning with delight. At age eleven, almost twelve, Moosey hadn't changed much since he was a little kid. He still had his infectious smile, his untamed mop

100

of straw posing as hair, and his ears that protruded just a tad too far into space. He still sported the same wire-rimmed glasses, blue jeans, and red, high-topped Keds. He might give up those Keds in adulthood. Or maybe not.

"You got groundemhogs, sure 'nough," said Harm Pooter. "Never seen a worse case."

"What's with the cart?" I asked, forgetting for a moment about the groundhogs.

"It's my idea," said Bud. "We're offering free delivery within a mile radius of downtown. Moosey is the delivery boy."

"For five dollars an hour plus tips," said Moosey proudly. "Bernadette's gonna help. Bud says I don't even need a license to drive this around town."

"Depends," I said. "Is it street legal?"

The golf cart was dark green and had only two seats, but was equipped with a small cargo bed on the back. It was about four feet wide and had a hardshell canopy covering the whole thing, a full windshield, but no windows.

"It's not street legal," said Bud, "but I made sure that it's street *allowed*. I checked with Mayor Johnsson. We have a town ordinance that says golf carts are welcome in the community of St. Germaine. No drivers license needed. No registration, no tag, no headlights, none of that stuff. We can't go on any highways, though, and we have to stay inside the city limits. That's why we only deliver within a mile."

"You've got it all sorted out," I said. "Sounds good. Any rules about underage delivery boys or girls?"

"No, sir!" said Bud with a grin. "I checked about that, too." He looked sheepishly at his feet and said, "I sort of told Bill Crowell that you'd pay him for the cart. I have a receipt inside."

"No problem," I said. "It's a good idea."

"Now about these varmints," said Harm, "you got a botheration of groundemhogs."

Harmonious and Tommy Pooter were the two septic tank guys in town and they made a good living. Not a profession I would have chosen, but an honorable, if odiferous, way to make ends meet. Harmonious Pooter's Robo-Rooters was a well-known local business and the bright lavender van parked in front of anyone's house always announced who was having problems with their plumbing. Pooter's (as it was known) was a member of the

Chamber of Commerce, gave liberally to the scout programs and churches, could always be counted on for a donation to almost any cause, provided free services to the library and any number of other worthy organizations, and yet the owners were hardly ever invited to any of the gatherings that the rest of St. Germaine's business community frequented. There was a reason for this and the reason was obvious.

"Where's Tommy?" I asked.

"He's got another call," said Harm. He didn't offer me his hand. Years of having no one shake it had conditioned him to keep them both stuck deep into the pockets of his insulated overalls. "You got a whole passel of them hogs. They're in the busted clay sewage pipe and have dug clean through all the field lines."

"Well," I said. "That's a new one on me. I would have thought that this time of year they'd all be hibernating."

"They were hibernating," said Harm, "till I dug 'em up. Then they weren't."

"How many are there?"

"I counted four that I seen, including a young pup, so there are probably more pups down there somewhere. There could be dozens. And that's not your only problem."

"Yeah?"

"I brought the little backhoe and dug down to the tank to clean it out …"

"And?"

"And you don't got no septic tank," said Harm. "What you got is a refrigerator. Looks to me to be a 1950 Northstar. Cherry red. My grandma had her one of them. She liked it right well." He reminisced thoughtfully for a moment and smiled at the memory. "Looks like they sunk it in the ground and run the sewer pipe in through the top."

"Oh, man," I said, glancing at Bud. He had a sick look on his face.

"What are our options?" I asked.

"I was you," said Harm, "I'd keep my mouth shut, cover the fridge up with concrete, exterminate them groundemhogs, and hook up to the city sewer. You gotta pay the water bill anyway. Cost you maybe a couple of thousand by the time you get the permits, run the pipe, and all."

"Sage advice," I said.

"You're not gonna kill them groundhogs, are you?" asked Moosey, horrified at the prospect.

"They ain't no good to nobody," said Harm, wiping a sleeved arm across his nose. "All they do is dig stuff up. You can eat a young one, though. Tastes right good barbecued."

"Can't we take 'em out of here?" asked Moosey. "We can let them go in the woods. Maybe I can keep a pup, if there is one." Moosey was always happy to have a new pet. He and the rest of the McColloughs lived out in Coondog Holler, far away from anyone who might care what kind of critters Moosey brought home. "Penny Trice has a little groundhog," he said. "His name is Pig Whistle. She's also got a possum named Possum Joe, and a turtle, and a hamster, and a mousey thing with a long nose. Oh, and a chicken."

"Good to know," I said. "I'll call Gwen Jackson and see if she has some live traps she can bring over. We'll trap them if we can, but the ones we can't get will have to be destroyed. They'll start tearing up other people's yards and then we'll be in trouble."

Moosey nodded thoughtfully. For a twelve-year-old kid, he was pretty savvy. "I understand. I'm thinking I'll name mine Ginger."

Harm shook his head in amazement. Saving groundhogs? He'd obviously never heard of such a thing. He said, "You want me and Tommy to come on out and take care of 'em, we'll do it no charge. There's one of them pups, there's prob'ly a dozen. Them younguns is right tasty if you cook 'em right." He smacked his lips at the prospect.

"I'll probably take you up on that, Harm, but give us a couple of days," I said. Then I turned to Bud. "Would you tell Roberto that we're hooking up to the city sewer line? Tell him we'll need some concrete dumped on that refrigerator in the back yard, then have him cover it up."

"Yessir," said Bud. "I'll take care of it."

Chapter 15

Ecclesiastica Rodentia: the newest wrinkle in the polyester leisure suit of the common liturgy. The Fraternity of Insane Bishops was behind it, of course. I'd gotten the memo last week, read it, then put it in the bathroom on top of the stack of the other memos from the F.I.B. where I found them to be useful in the end.

The bishops had decided to merge Groundhog Day with Candlemas. Why not? They both fell on February 2nd and Candlemas needed a boost. As a feast day it ranked slightly behind Septuagesima in popularity, and the groundhog was getting more press popping out of his hole than You-Know-Who.

St. Groundlemas was revisionist theology at its finest and the Council wasn't above creating a few ancient narratives to make it all work. Now, according to the "newly discovered" texts, the Groundhog appeared on Candlemas to give his blessing to The Presentation at the Temple. Sure. Why not? They even had some hymns ready: Hail the Day that Sees Him Rise, O Sacred Hog Now Grounded, and The Snow Lay on the Groundhog. I figured that, before it was over, Lazarus would come forth, see his shadow, and predict six more weeks of Advent.

I took a slurp of my Schweinestinke and noticed we had company. She was parked next to Pedro, and he was already dancing his eyes at her — a suggestive allemande or maybe a trollopy hornpipe — but her gaze was on me and I met it with the intensity of a vegan baritone in the meat aisle of the Piggly Wiggly. Her long fingers slid slippily on her champagne glass and her eyelashes fluttered independently, as if they had a mind of their own and weren't being wiggled by an infestation of eyelash mites.

"My name is Kitty," she purred cuddlingly. "You boys looking for a good time?"

I didn't trust her. Groundhogs didn't mix with cats. Not in my book.

Pedro coughed up a hairball.

* * *

Nancy, Dave, and I were at the Slab on Friday morning having breakfast when Cynthia walked up and dropped a copy of the *Tattler* in the middle of the table.

"You made the front page," she said. "Again."

"No doubt," said Nancy. "If we can't make the front page of a weekly rag with three dead bodies, something's wrong."

"They've had almost a whole week to put the story together," said Dave.

Cynthia pulled up a chair and joined us. Pete wasn't far behind. The Slab wasn't doing much business and Noylene had the two other customers well in hand. They had their food and full cups of coffee, and they were now digging in. We had our coffee, but were still waiting for our food orders to come out of the kitchen. Nancy picked up the paper and read the headline.

"Foreclosed Properties Cloak Gristly Murders."

"Good headline," said Dave appreciatively, taking a sip of coffee. "Descriptive, concise, makes you want to read further. I especially want to learn about the gristle. Was it 'death by gristle?' Or maybe there was gristle lying around after the fact."

"The article has Annette's byline," said Nancy, ignoring Dave and skimming the page. "The headline's better than the article." She tossed the paper back onto the table.

Dave picked it up and read, "Three women were found dead in each of the three houses auctioned last Saturday on the steps of the courthouse. Foul play is suspected. The three dead women, who seemed to have no connection, were identified as Darla Kildair of St. Germaine, Amy Ventura of Tinkler's Knob, and Crystal Latimore of Linville. According to an eyewitness at the scene of the discovery ..."

"That would be Helen Pigeon," said Nancy.

"Yeah, probably," agreed Dave, then continued. "According to an eyewitness at the scene of the discovery, Crystal Latimore was dressed in a classic, double-breasted, cutaway, linen blend pant suit (in taupe) from Donna Vinci. Wood buttons and flared legs provided a classic accent. Her coral, scoop-necked blouse was a silk blend which lent exquisite softness and drape to the otherwise conventional outfit."

"A murder fashion show?" I said.

"Hang on," Pete said. "How did Helen know all that?"

"Don't be silly, sweetie," said Cynthia. "Helen knew all that five seconds after seeing her."

"The detectives at the scene acknowledged that all the women were found in the same circumstances. It is not known whether the missing earring was common to all three victims."

"Helen is a loudmouth," growled Nancy. "I knew I should have arrested her."

"The conclusion of this reporter is that Crystal would have been the best dressed of the three. Crystal was known for her sense of style and, as a court advocate, she was occasionally seen on Channel 3 News discussing crime statistics and trends."

"Really?" I said. "I never saw her on TV."

"Now that I think about it," said Cynthia, "I seem to remember that. Didn't she come on and talk about domestic violence and stuff whenever there was a particularly awful case in the news? It's been years, though."

I shrugged.

Dave read on. "The three houses were purchased by Bud McCollough of St. Germaine, Rachel Walt of Banner Elk, and Jeff and Helen Pigeon, also of St. Germaine. It was thought that Police Chief Hayden Konig was a silent partner in the bidding of the house bought by Bud McCollough, although Mayor Cynthia Johnsson denied that this was the case."

"Heh, heh," snickered Pete. "Culpable deniability."

"I denied it," said Cynthia, "because Bud handed me a satchel full of cash and said it was his."

"It was," I said. "Some of his share of the wine loot."

"That stuff that sells for ten grand a bottle?" asked Dave.

"More like seven, I think, but that's the stuff. You want to buy a couple bottles?"

"Tempting," said Dave, "but I think I'll wait till I win the lottery."

Noylene came out of the kitchen with plates full of food stacked neatly up each arm, maneuvered around the table, and expertly placed each order in front of us. We all thanked her, passed the coffee pot around, and dug in.

Dave started on a stack of pancakes topped with two fried eggs. He took a couple of bites, then added extra syrup, and looked back at the article in the paper. "Blah, blah, blah ... addresses, then some stuff about Darla's fight with Noylene."

"That warn't no fight!" said Noylene, who had walked back behind the counter. "I told Annette that it warn't me that made her leave. Darla got sideways with Goldi Fawn Birtwhistle and I couldn't have them two duking it out on Blue-Rinse Thursday. I asked them to shake hands and make up, but Darla grabbed her styling tools and stormed out of there like I'd just told her that double coupons don't work in February."

"Says here," said Dave, grinning, "that you fired her and she had to make ends meet by doing makeovers down at the bus station in Boone."

"*What?!*" screeched Noylene. "That Annette! I'll show her! Next time she's in to the Dip-N-Tan, I'm going to turn her so orange the rabbits will think there's a hundred and eighty pound carrot walking around town!"

"Hang on," laughed Dave. "Much as I'd like to see that, I was just kidding."

Noylene glared at him and stormed off into the kitchen.

"Did you read the mystery?" Nancy asked me.

"I did," I said. "It wasn't very good."

"What mystery is that?" asked Pete.

"*See Your Shadow* by Kitty Holly. It may hold clues to the murder."

"Really?" said Cynthia. "Do tell."

"There are four murders in the book," I said. "A lawyer, a book publicist, a hair dresser, and a minister."

"Yeah?" said Cynthia.

"They're all women. In the book they're all middle-aged, except the lawyer who is just out of law school. They're all single and their bodies are all found in closets of houses that are for sale. Empty houses."

"Wow," said Cynthia.

"They all belong to the same Sunday School," added Nancy. "And they had all been to a Sunday School party which is why they were dressed up. We don't find that out until the end, though. "

"Seems like a copy-cat killer," said Pete. "Or at least a copy-book killer. Who did it in the book?"

"The police chief," said Nancy with a smile.

"I'm fairly sure that I didn't do it," I said.

"He wasn't even a character," said Nancy, disgust evident her voice. "Kitty Holly brought him in at the last minute to tie things up. Then, to top it all off, the one decent clue was the earring all the victims were missing. Know what it was?"

"What?" said Cynthia. "Don't keep us all in suspense."

"The police chief's mother wouldn't let him wear an earring to the prom. She was a Sunday School teacher. How lame is that? Kitty Holly throws all this into the confession that the chief blurts out right before he throws himself in front of a church bus."

"*Deus ex machina*," said Dave.

"Huh?" said Cynthia.

"*Deus ex machina*. I was an English major, you know."

"Okay," said Pete. "Impress us."

"*Deus ex machina* is a literary device whereby a seemingly unsolvable problem is suddenly and abruptly resolved with the contrived and unexpected intervention of some new event, character, ability, or object. Critics claim that it's usually done when the author has painted himself into a corner or has a deadline looming. Of course, it can be used for comedic effect as well."

"The end of the *Three Penny Opera* for example," I said.

"Exactly," said Dave. "*War of the Worlds, As You Like It ...* there are many examples."

"So, did you glean any other clues from the book?" asked Cynthia.

"Not really," said Nancy. "These women were poisoned at the Sunday School party. Our three victims didn't attend the same church. In fact, Darla didn't even attend."

"How about the poison?" asked Dave.

"The poison in the book was succinylcholine," Nancy said. "Kent's checking on it this morning. It causes respiratory paralysis and the victim usually dies of a heart attack."

"According to the internet," I said, "it's mostly used in hospitals to allow the insertion of a breathing tube into a patient who is still conscious."

"Had our three dead women been in the hospital lately?" asked Cynthia.

"Not that we know of," I said. "We'll check on that this morning. It may be the connection we're looking for, though."

"A lawyer, a publicist, a hair dresser, and a minister," said Pete. "Not exactly the same. We have a trial advocate, a grant writer, and a hair dresser."

"Still, it's pretty close," said Dave.

"One thing that bothers me," I said. "We have three of the four murders that happen in *See Your Shadow* happening here in St. Germaine. There's still one to go."

Nancy nodded and said, "Or maybe we just haven't found her yet."

"It's a minister," said Cynthia. "We don't have a woman minister in St. Germaine."

"We have a woman deacon, though," I said. "Kimberly Walnut."

Chapter 16

The Blue Hill Bookworms were meeting at the Bear and Brew. I had presumed that, considering their highfalutin pedigree, they'd be tasting watercress mini-sandwiches and drinking tea — pinkie fingers extended — at the Ginger Cat. They weren't. When I found them, they were gathered around a table with a large *Panda Spinacis* pizza in the center: mozzarella, spinach, and shiitake mushrooms. The concession to the lack of ambiance in the Bear and Brew was their choice to drink champagne, rather than order one of the brews on tap. In reality, the Bear and Brew had plenty of ambiance, just of a different sort. Where the Ginger Cat was an upscale eatery serving pretentious, bite-sized portions of things, like Oysters Gerard with carrot mousse, the Bear and Brew was modeled after an old feed store and served gigantic pizzas, a few other Italian dishes, and twenty-seven beers on tap.

"Champagne?" I said as I walked up to the table. "Why champagne?"

"We always have champagne," said Diana. "It's a Bookworm tradition. We bring it ourselves, if the restaurant doesn't have any."

"We used to go to the Ginger Cat," said Sara Black, "but Annie decided to charge us a fifteen dollar corking fee, and that was the end of that."

"Too bad, too," said Catherine Duncan. "I really liked the carrot mousse."

"No one likes carrot mousse," said a woman I recognized, but couldn't put a name to. She introduced herself. "I'm Rachel Barstow, Hayden. Nice to see you again."

I took the hand she extended and shook it. "Nice to see you again, too. All of you."

"I'm Annabel Stratton," said the curly haired blonde woman to Rachel's right, and the other women I didn't really know introduced themselves as well: Alison Jaeger, Sarah Aspinall, and Stephanie Bilton. Eight total.

"Stephanie," I said, shaking her hand. "You're the personal assistant, right?"

"Used to be," she said with a shrug. "There's not much call for it anymore. Now I'm working for an insurance agent."

"We're all here," said Diana. "Except for the newest member. She won't be invested until our meeting in May."

"Who is it?" I asked.

"Oh, we can't reveal that," said Diana. "It's very hush-hush."

"Top secret," said Stephanie.

"We could tell you, but then we'd have to kill you," joked Rachel, then put her hand over her mouth. "Oh, my God! I didn't mean that. We'd never kill anyone!"

"You did tell Ruby Farthing that she *wasn't* getting in, though."

"Sure," said Stephanie. "We have to tell the ones who *aren't* getting in. That's only polite."

The waitress showed up at the table, took my drink order and went to get my pint of Thunderstruck Coffee Porter, a seasonal brew that I'd never tried. The ladies were attacking the pizza and I, with expert maneuvering, managed to get a slice without losing any digits.

"It's no wonder you all eat like you're starved," I said, counting my fingers. "It's probably that miniature food you eat at the Ginger Cat. Man does not live by carrot mousse."

"It's true," said Sarah Aspinall. "We really should come over here for our meetings."

"Don't be silly," said Alison. "This isn't an *official* function. We could never be seen having our meetings here. Maybe at Virginia's Tea House, but not in a beer and pizza joint."

"I agree with Alison," said Annabel. "We do have a reputation to maintain."

"Which is why I'm surprised that you're reading a third-rate murder mystery," I said. "A cozy, no less."

All the women except Diana blanched.

Stephanie leaned across the table and whispered, "Who told you that?"

Diana caught my eye and gave me a panicked look.

Rachel said, also in a hushed tone, "We are *not* reading any such thing!" Alison agreed by shaking her head.

My beer arrived at the table and I took a sip. Good. A robust porter with some hints of chocolate, mild hops, and a glimmering of coffee. "Here's the thing," I said. "It's on your blog. Your whole reading list is on the blog, along with all your reviews, comments, and everything else."

The ladies looked confused and Sara B said, "Sure, but that blog is private. You can't read it unless you're a member. You have to log in."

"No, you don't," I said. "I went right to it. Bluehillbookworms/blogspot.com."

"Are you *kidding*?" said Annabel. She glared at Stephanie. "Sure, you can get onto the Bookworms' site, but our blog is private, *right*?"

Stephanie looked uncomfortable and squirmed in her seat. "Well, it used to be, but then I updated it and couldn't get the privacy settings to work right. I *thought* it was private, but then we never had to log in anymore. Didn't you notice?"

"*What?*" said Sarah A. "I just thought my browser had saved the password as a cookie or something. You mean everyone has been reading our blog?"

"Not everyone," I said, between bites of my pizza. "I'm sure there are many people in the world who don't really care what you're reading."

"You know what I mean," said Sarah A, glumly. "Can everyone post comments as well?"

"No," said Stephanie. "Thankfully, you still have to log in to do that."

"This is awful," said Catherine. "I wonder how many people have read our private posts?"

"I can tell you that I know at least three people who have been on your blog site," I said. "Myself, Lieutenant Nancy Parsky, and Ruby Farthing."

"Ruby's been reading it?" said Stephanie. "Oh, *no!* She knows we've been reading that trashy beach mystery!"

"Yes, she does," I said, "and she was quite appalled. She told me that she found the Bookworms' taste in literature to be totally bourgeois. Or maybe she said 'banal.' I don't quite remember, but you get the drift. She said she's considering joining the faculty wives' book club over at Lenoir-Rhyne University."

"She said that?" asked Catherine, thoughtfully. "Oh, my. Maybe we should reconsider her application."

"I *do* think we should reconsider," said Diana. "We haven't announced our new member yet. We might want to rethink our choice."

"Whatever," I said. "That's not what I asked you here to talk about."

"Oh," said Diana. "Sure. The murders."

"Indeed." I looked around the table. "You know about the similarities?"

Diana said, "It didn't take long to figure it out, Hayden. It's all anyone has been talking about all week. I finished the book last night and called the Bookworms, and ... well ... it was obvious why you wanted to talk with us."

"How many of you have finished the book?" I asked.

All the women raised their hands and Sara B said, "We all finished it last night after Diana called us and told us what was happening."

"I read it last summer," said Stephanie.

"Then you know that these three killings are copies of the ones that took place in *See Your Shadow*."

Everyone nodded.

"Have any of you seen the *Tattler* this morning?" I asked.

No one had, or admitted they had.

"Well," I said, "quite frankly, this book makes you all suspects."

"*What?*" said Sarah A. "Why?"

"Because, as far as we can tell, up to this point, you eight are the only ones who have had occasion to read this book. You all, Nancy and I, and Ruby — and Ruby is my mother-in-law and therefore above reproach."

"Really? Above reproach?" said Rachel.

"Absolutely. Oh, she might have murder in her heart, but I can't see a seventy-year-old woman, no matter how spry, hauling three corpses into dark, locked houses."

"You do have a point," said Alison, who'd been mostly quiet till now. "Ruby's not a big woman. She's tall certainly, but fairly thin."

"So that leaves you eight," I said, counting them off around the table. "Eight prime suspects."

"Well, then," said Catherine, "have you come up with a motive? In the mystery, the victims were all members of the same Sunday School class. Is it the same with these three?"

"No."

"What about the victims?" said Diana. "In the book, the victims were a personal injury lawyer, a book publicist, a hair dresser, and a priest."

"A minister, to be precise," I said. "Almost the same as here, or close enough."

"How about the minister?" asked Sara B.

"We haven't found another victim, but we also don't have the resources or probable cause to search every vacant house in St. Germaine. Many of these are vacation homes. The three houses where the women were found had all been owned by the same corporation and were all up for auction on the same day. That's a connection we can't ignore. Also, we don't have a timeline on any of the murders. With this cold we've been having, the medical examiner can't give us any reasonable time of death."

"Well, it had to be after January 12th," said Catherine. "That's when we decided to read the book and put it up on the blog."

"Good to know," I said.

"How about the missing earring?" asked Stephanie. "Is that part of it?"

"I'd rather not say."

"We'll take that as a 'yes.'"

"What are the names again?" asked Alison. "I remember Crystal Latimore, because I knew her. She was a patient of mine a few years ago, but I haven't seen her for some time. She might have found a new doctor, but I don't think so. I would have sent her records over and I don't remember signing off on that."

"Darla Kildair and Amy Ventura were the other two," I said. "Do any of the rest of you know these women?"

"Sure," said Rachel. "I knew Amy and Darla."

"I knew Crystal," said Stephanie. "Not the other two, though."

I took a count and discovered that all the Bookworms knew at least one of the victims, none knew all three. Or rather, none admitted knowing all three.

"How about a female member of the clergy?" I asked. "Do any of you know one?"

Silence, then Diana said, "Does Kimberly Walnut count?"

"Yes, she does."

No one else admitted knowing one, so I turned to Sara B and said, "Tell me about ergodic literature."

"Sure," she replied. "Espen Aarseth coined the term in his book, *Cybertext, Perspectives on Ergodic Literature.* In ergodic literature, nontrivial effort is required to allow the reader to traverse the text. If ergodic literature is to make sense as a concept, there must also be non-ergodic literature, where the effort to traverse the text is trivial, with no extranoemic responsibilities placed on the reader except — for example — eye movement and the arbitrary turning of pages."

"Great," I said. "I have no earthly idea what that means."

"Neither do any of us," said Diana. "We pretend it's all about subtexts."

"It's not," said Sara B, her exasperation evident. "We all read *Landscape Painted With Tea*. I've gone over this with you a hundred times!"

"Okay, okay," I said. "Would you ladies like to see my latest story?" I was feeling pretty darn good about my efforts lately, and I wouldn't mind the Bookworms cheering me on. "I happen to have a few copies. Eight copies."

"Absolutely," said Stephanie.

I passed the pages around and finished the last slice of the *Panda Spinacis* as they were reading it. It was only about 2600 words at this point, but represented some of my finest writing to date.

* * *

"Care for a pickle?" Kitty offered, opening the jar on the table easily with her giant man-hands. Something was odd about this one. Maybe it was the dark hair on her knuckles, maybe it was the Adam's apple jutting from her throat, like she'd swallowed one of those painted pet turtles without chewing, maybe it was the three-day stubble on her upper lip, but my gut told me this dame would be trouble. I usually listened to my gut when it was yacking. It was my only friend.

Kitty gronked a gherkin in one bite, then leaned in with a crooked finger, motioning us to do the same.

"I'm undercover," Kitty growled lowly. "The real name is Holly. Holly Tosis. Perhaps you've heard of me."

He reached into his camisole, came out with a cheap business card, and slid it across the table.

The name was as familiar as that Praise Chorus that you could never remember, but left you feeling sort of nauseous and made you want to go wash your hands to get the praise off. Then, leaning in, I smelled his breath and it all came rushing back to me. 'Hollywood Tosis' it said on his flimsy card, shoofly from the East Side. Not much in the way of a snoop, but cheap as a pair of disposable underpants.

"You probably know my sister Ginger."

"Ginger Vitas?" I interrogued.

Pedro snorted into his beer. Everyone who knew Ginger Vitas knew her in the Biblical sense, both Old and New Testament, with a little bit of the Gnostic Gospels thrown in for fun. She was a good-time girl and as easy as C Major.

"That's enough of that!" snapped Holly, mad as a snapper, which is why he snapped, probably.

I lowered my usually euphonious tone to a whisper. "So tell me, Holly, what's with the petticoats?"

"I'm working for the Anglo-Catholics. They want nothing to do with this St. Groundlemas. Not enough mysticism. This groundhog merger is bad for business."

"And?" I said expectantly. Getting the whole story out of Holly Tosis was like pulling teeth, and not teeth from someone who wants all his teeth pulled because he found out that the government was giving away free teeth, but rather someone who is having all his teeth pulled because his breath is so bad it would make sewer rats take up dental hygiene, and that brought us back to Holly.

"They all wear this stuff. Those Anglo-Catholics have already forgotten more about snoot than the Roman Catholics ever knew! Choir ruffs, crinolines, seven layers of robes, silly hats, incense, smoke and abalone ... you name it, they've got it."

"Does this have anything to do with Anne Dante?"

"Of course it does! She was involved up to her pretty little scapulars. In fact, she was supposed to broker a deal with Jimmy the Snip to get the two front paws of Punxsutawney Phil and bring them back for the reliquary."

"So what's with that wig, makeup, and eyeshadow?" Pedro asked.

"Well," said Holly with a smile as coy as a pond full of giant goldfish, "a fella's gotta look nice."

* * *

"Wow," said Sarah A. "You've got some ... uh ... real good writing going on."

Alison slowly nodded her agreement, then said, "Holly Tosis, Ginger Vitas. A dentally superb cast of characters."

Rachel added, "And many metaphors and similes which are the writer's hammer and tongs."

"I've really got to get back to work," said Stephanie, and they all popped to their feet. "Thanks for lunch, Hayden."

"Huh?" I managed, but they were all scurrying for the exit.

"I told them you were paying for lunch," Diana said, the last to leave.

"That's not what I meant. I'm happy to pay for lunch. I was hoping to get a little constructive criticism from the group."

"I'm sure that our criticism wouldn't sway your style one way or the other," Diana said over her shoulder as she headed quickly for the front door. It swung open, then closed, and I heard laughter on the sidewalk in front of the Bear and Brew. Mocking laughter.

117

Chapter 17

Gwen Jackson lent Bud three live traps and gave him instruction on their use. Gwen, the town vet, kept traps like these handy behind her office, just in case. Lured by a radish, the groundhogs stood no chance, and, by Saturday night, we'd trapped seven, three of them cubs. Gwen had informed us that a young groundhog is a cub or a kit, rather than a pup.

Moosey was happy to take one of the cubs home and begin its training as part of Moosey's Menagerie. Gwen took the other six and promised us that they'd be relocated. I called Harm Pooter and told him that he was free to camp out at the house and take care of whatever groundhogs were left. He was agreeable and promised a groundhog-free zone by Monday morning.

* * *

Kent called me on Saturday.

"Whatever the poison was that killed the women, it wasn't succinylcholine," he said.

"Yeah, that'd be too easy," I said.

"It really would have been. You can only get succinylcholine if you're licensed to practice medicine. They keep track of that stuff."

"But, alas," I said.

"Alas," repeated Kent. "I don't know if it makes any difference, but Crystal had leukemia. I just got the blood work back this morning. Early stages. She might not have even been aware of the diagnosis yet."

* * *

"Dr. Alison Jaeger is lying," said Nancy. We were meeting at Holy Grounds coffee shop for an afternoon espresso and update. "You told me she said that she only knew one of the victims."

"Crystal Latimore. She indicated that Crystal had been a patient a few years ago, but she hadn't seen her for a while."

"I went by the three houses like you asked and picked up the mail. If you're going to lie, you should probably make sure your billing department doesn't send out monthly statements."

Nancy handed me two envelopes, one addressed to Darla Kildair, and one addressed to Amy Ventura. The one addressed to Darla had her old address showing through the clear window of the envelope. There was a yellow, forwarding address sticker slapped catty-cornered over the window sending the envelope to Darla's new address underneath the Gun Emporium. They had been opened by Nancy. I took out the one addressed to Amy and saw that she had a balance of one hundred twenty-three dollars. There was no itemizing, just a balance due. Probably a copay or part of her deductible. Darla's statement was itemized for a flu shot and blood work, but she only owed ninety-six dollars.

Nancy said, "I looked at the picture I took of the contents of her medicine chest and guess what?"

"Alison Jaeger is the prescribing physician on the bottle of Premarin."

"Exactly right," Nancy said. "Why would she lie about knowing them?"

I ran the conversation back through my head, then said, "She might not have. She said she knew Crystal Latimore, then asked me for the other two names. She never actually said she didn't know them."

"She didn't say that she did," said Nancy.

"True enough," I said. "I assumed that she didn't know them."

"Either way something's not right."

"I have that same feeling," I said. "Like we're missing something."

119

Chapter 18

The dead make good clients; I mean they rarely complain; they don't drink your gin; they don't try to sell you Mary Kay Pore Minimizing Lotion to make their monthly nut; they're quiet for the most part except when the gas escapes — and really, who hasn't that happened to — no, as a whole, your graveyard stiff is just about the ideal mark. The problem is getting paid.

"Found 'em," said Pedro, as he finished rifling through Anne Dante's purse. "Six credit cards. That should keep us going through the weekend anyway."

"Holly Tosis is going to try to scuttle the St. Groundlemas movement," I said. "I don't know whose side we're on here."

"If Anne Dante came to you for help, and she was after the whistle-pig's paws, I'd put her on the side of the St. Groundleites."

"Yeah," I agreed. "I got no pig in this fight, whistling, flying, or otherwise, but you don't plug a dame in my office and think you're getting away with it."

* * *

I woke on Sunday morning to the smell of coffee. It was early, and Meg wasn't beside me in the bed, but Meg was usually up before me anyway, the weekends being no exception. I trundled into the kitchen, filled my mug with coffee and looked out the window at a foot of snow on the ground. That's the thing about snow: it sneaks up on you, not like a big thunderstorm that announces its presence every few minutes, but like a thief in the night.

Baxter, lying on his belly in front of the cold fireplace in the adjacent room, looked up at me as if he wanted to go outside, then seemed to think better of it and hid his muzzle under one big paw. Meg came in through the kitchen door with a load of firewood in her arms.

"Good morning!" she said brightly when she saw me. "Here, give me a hand, will you?"

I unburdened her and took the split oak over to the fireplace. It didn't take a minute to push a lit piece of pine fatwood underneath the oak and watch the fire blaze into being.

"I certainly didn't expect snow," she said. "The forecast was for a cold and clear weekend."

"Well, they were half right. It's cold."

"Can we make it into church this morning?" Meg asked.

"Oh, sure. That's no problem. The roads should be clear in an hour or so, and the four-wheel drive will take that truck just about anywhere."

"Hmm," said Meg. "It seems to me you've been stuck a few times, though."

"A few," I admitted, "but never in a foot of snow."

"Archimedes took off when I came out of the bedroom. I didn't even have a chance to give him one of those chipmunks."

I poured myself a mug of coffee. "He'll probably find his own breakfast this morning. All those rabbit and mouse tracks will be easy to spot."

We spent a leisurely couple of hours warming by the fire, watching the news, and getting dressed for church, then at 9:35 we bundled into the old truck and pointed it toward town. The ten miles usually took twenty minutes or so, but watching for ice and taking our time, we were there just in time to head up to the choir loft to prepare for the service.

As announced, Father Dressler had changed the service to Rite I, a formal service, but not as formal as he *could* go. I'd done a little research on Anglo-Catholics. Sometimes they went totally "off-book" and adopted the *Anglican Missal* as the prayer book of choice. I hadn't seen a copy of the *Missal* for a while, but a little research showed that it contained three versions of the Eucharistic prayers: the one from the 1928 *Book of Common Prayer*, the 1549 Canon as translated by Thomas Cranmer, and an English translation of the Roman Catholic Canon. For now, though — Rite I. We'd used Rite I in the past during Lent so it wasn't unfamiliar, but Mother Rosemary Pepperpot-Cohosh hadn't liked Rite I and it had been several years since it had made an appearance in our liturgy.

I was already at the organ when the first of the choir members made their way up the steps and found their seats. Our usual plan was to put on our robes in the vesting room by the sacristy, then head up to the loft, warm up, go quickly through the music, hit some trouble spots if there were any, and then relax and get ready for the prelude. In the days before Mother P, the choir would go down the stairs and process with the crucifer, acolytes, and priest during the opening hymn, make their way around the sides of the sanctuary and back up the stairs to the loft, leaving the clergy and extras at the front to perform their tasks. Since Mother P despised ceremony, she had done away with the processional, the cross had remained stationary in the front, candles were lighted before the service started, and the clergy casually walked to the front during the hymn, stopping to chat and shake hands as they walked. Many of the choir didn't even bother to put robes on. Today was different.

They all had managed to find their robes and we'd already gone through the Psalm and the anthem when Father Dressler appeared at the top of the stairs, dressed in his long black cassock with red band cincture, and a biretta with a red ball on top. I saw him come up, but was in the middle of giving directions as to a particular musical phrase when ...

"A-*HEM*," he said, not discreetly at all. I stopped speaking and all heads turned to look at him.

"As you know," he said, "we're going to be processing this morning. I've already given instructions to the acolytes and the crucifer. Sadly, we won't be having incense, but that will soon change."

The choir looked at him but didn't say anything.

"The acolytes and the crucifer will be adults this morning, since I haven't had time to train any young people, but that will change as well."

No comment.

"I'd like the choir to genuflect as they approach the altar. Does everyone know what I'm speaking of?"

"Sure," said Mark Wells. "Stop, give a quick nod, and move on."

"No," said Father Dressler. "Absolutely not. Stop, *go to one knee*, bow your head, cross yourself, then rise and continue in procession. If you need help kneeling or rising, there will be an usher there to assist. Kimberly Walnut and I shall remain kneeling in prayer for approximately thirty seconds. Then I shall ascend to the altar and offer the opening sentences."

The choir looked at him in stunned silence.

"That's probably going to take an extra four or five minutes," I said.

"Yes. That's why you need to plan your hymn interludes accordingly."

"Ah," I said. "It's a good thing you gave me a little warning."

He ignored the comment. "Everything else should be straightforward. I don't want to change too much of the service right away. We'll let the congregation adjust." He disappeared down the stairs to don his liturgical finery.

The entire choir looked over at Marjorie in expectation. She'd been a member of the St. Barnabas choir for almost sixty years and had seen a lot. She wasn't shy about expressing her opinion.

"We did some of that stuff back in the fifties," she said. "I had enough of it then! I'll tell you what: I'll walk down the aisle, give a wink to the acolyte, and smack the first usher that lays a hand on me."

"I'm walking behind Marjorie," said Georgia.

"Me, too," said Rhiza, followed by general hubbub in the choir. Meg looked at me with desperation in her eyes. I gave a halfhearted smile and shrugged.

"Just a moment," Meg said loudly, getting everyone's attention, then lowered her voice. "We might as well do what he wants and see how it goes. As your president, I'm calling on you to do your duty as choir members."

"Give 'em an inch and they'll take a mile," said Marjorie. "First thing you know, we'll be 'Hail Mary-ing' all over the church. Hail Mary, full-of-grace, Hail Mary, fair-of-face, something something placenta."

"Placenta?" asked Goldi Fawn. "What on earth are you talking about?"

I interrupted the discussion. "Anyone who doesn't want to genuflect can stay up here," I said, "but if you decide to go, that means you don't have a problem with kneeling in front of the altar as you process."

"It's not that I have a problem with kneeling," said Elaine. "I have a problem with getting back up."

"Ushers will be there to help," Meg said, but Elaine shook her head doubtfully.

"I don't know about this, either," said Mark Wells, "but I'll try anything once. I've got this new hip, though, so if I go down and don't come back up, tell Jane I love her and that I spent the insurance money on beer."

* * *

The service, including a nine-minute processional hymn, thanks to a lengthy improvisation between stanzas three and four, went fairly well. Since I was busy playing, I couldn't tell how many of the choir members needed help getting up after genuflecting. Meg indicated that not as many needed help as thought they would.

The congregation seemed to enjoy hearing the Psalm sung by the choir, and if they were put off by the somewhat unfamiliar *Trisagion, Sanctus,* and *Agnus Dei,* they didn't show it. Our two anthems went well, the other three hymns were fairly familiar, and John Wesley would have been happy to hear them sung "lustily and with good courage."

However, during the announcements, which Father Dressler made just before the Passing of the Peace, I was surprised to hear the following:

"I'd like to announce our Candlemas Service a week from Wednesday at five o'clock. This will include a Solemn Evensong and Benediction which the choir will sing and we hope that all of you will be in attendance for this important Feast Day."

"Huh?" said Goldi Fawn, somewhat alarmed, and many others looked up like startled deer. "We're singing what?"

"For those of you who aren't familiar with Candlemas," continued Father Dressler, "the date is established as forty days after Christmas. Under Mosaic law, as found in the Torah, a mother who had given birth to a man-child was considered unclean for seven days: moreover she was to remain for three and thirty days 'in the blood of her purification.' Candlemas therefore corresponds to the day on which Mary, according to Jewish law, would have attended a ceremony of ritual purification according to the twelfth book of Leviticus. The Gospel of Luke relates that Mary was purified according to the religious law, followed by Jesus' presentation in the Jerusalem temple. Forty days after the Nativity is February 2nd and it is on this day that we shall celebrate our first Solemn Evensong together."

"What?" said Martha. "February 2nd is Groundhog Day. I've never heard of Candlemas."

"That's because you didn't spend three and thirty days in the blood of your purification," said Randy, sarcastically. "You sure know all about Mother's Day, though."

"You bought me a *bowling ball*," snarled Martha. "A bowling ball for Mother's Day!"

"You're lucky I got you anything," said Randy, throwing up his hands and beginning the argument anew. "You're not *my* mother!"

"I'm the mother of your children! That should count for more than a bowling ball."

"It was on sale," Randy said, explaining his position to Steve DeMoss. "I thought she might like to take up bowling. She's always saying she never gets out."

"You're preaching to the choir," Steve said. "I got Sheila a chainsaw one year for her birthday and never heard the end of it."

"Did you hear *that*?" said Sheila. "A chainsaw! I'd take a bowling ball any day. Or even a toaster."

"I got a toaster one year for Christmas," said Elaine in disgust. "An engraved toaster. 'To Elaine from Billy,' it said. The next year I got a set of steak knives."

Meg sidled up to me and gave me a kiss on the cheek. "The peace of the Lord be with you," she cooed. "I hope you're taking notes."

* * *

Everyone was coming out of the church having been "refreshed in the faith" at the coffee fellowship that concluded the morning's activities. Meg and I were thinking seriously about lunch, our choices being limited if we were determined to stay in town, but boundless if we decided to venture out from our little burg. We chose the latter, walked across Sterling Park to the police station where we'd left the truck, and had started to climb in when Moosey and Bernadette puttered up in the golf cart. With a top speed of twenty miles per hour, the golf cart driving around town wasn't a big worry. Bud McCollough had been driving into town since he had been old enough to reach the pedals of the family truck —

125

probably twelve or so. This sort of thing happened a lot in the hills and we turned a blind eye. We checked on him when we saw him in town, warned him to be careful, but never stopped him. His family needed him to drive and he did.

"Good morning, Moosey," said Meg. "Bernadette. I didn't see you two in church today."

Moosey looked sheepish. Bernadette tossed her golden locks, flashed Meg her smile, recently enhanced by braces, and said, "Good morning, Miz Konig. I've decided to go by 'Bernie' from now on."

"Bernie," said Meg and clapped her hands. "That's just *lovely!*"

"We were too busy today for church," explained Bernie. "We'll be there next week, though. We're going to be acolytes."

"Excellent!" Meg said. "I'm sure you will do a fine job."

"Does Kimberly Walnut know about this?" I asked.

"Dunno," said Moosey.

"Father asked us," said Bernie.

"Father?" said Meg. "Your father?"

Bernie giggled. "No, not *Daddy*. Father. That's what the new priest said we should call him. Just 'Father.' Anyway, we have a new job!"

"We're ambulance drivers!" said Moosey. "Well, when we're not being acolytes or delivering wine."

"That's right," added Bernie. "Dr. Jackson says we can be the ambulance for sick animals around town. That way people won't have to wait to bring them in. We can only do it on weekends and after school till the summer. Then we're full-time."

I noticed that there was a medium sized animal crate in the bed of the cart.

"What about when you're in church?" I asked. "You know ... acolyting."

Moosey and Bernie looked at each other and shrugged at the same time.

"I guess we'll have to leave," said Moosey. "If it's an emergency, I mean."

"Of course we will!" said Bernie. "We took an oath."

"You did?" said Meg. "An oath?"

"Well ... no ... but Dr. Jackson said that lives depended on us. It's the same thing. I'm going to be a vet when I grow up, just like her. I love animals!"

126

"I love 'em, too," said Moosey, "but I'm going to be an ambulance driver when I grow up. We just got back from taking Miss Hannah's big ol' fat cat to the hospital. Dr. Jackson said he was okay, just a hairball or something, but she's gonna keep him overnight. Lookee here! We got pagers!"

He held out a pocket pager for us to see and Bernie held out hers as well, fishing it from the pocket of her coat.

Moosey said, "If there's a pick-up we're s'posed to make, Dr. Jackson's nurse sends us a page. Cool, huh?"

"*And* we get paid!" crowed Bernie. "Three dollars apiece for every delivery."

"You two are living the dream," I said. "Be careful and don't get in any wrecks."

"We won't, 'cause *I'm* the driver," Moosey said, looking sternly at Bernadette.

"For now," Bernie replied sweetly, in that way that pre-women have of knowing they'll get their way sooner or later. "You're the driver *for now* ..."

Chapter 19

The city resembled nothing so much as the nose of a giant woodchuck in excellent health: cold, black, and wet. We decided that Pedro would go undercover. A cantor of his standing would be as welcome as flowers in spring, tra-la.

"These crinolines are bunching up," he said, chomping on a stogy, "and this lace is sticking to me like feathers to a freshly-tarred heretic."

"Quit complaining!" I barked, not like a groundhog bark, although I probably could have managed it, which would have seemed very clever, this being a groundhog story and all, but, quite frankly, I didn't think about it until later, so the bark came out more like a medium-sized dog bark: maybe an Affenpinscher or even a pensive seal.

"Easy for you to say," said Pedro, not barking. "I've got nowhere to stash my heater."

"Stick it in your tunicle."

"Yeah," agreed Pedro.

I said, "Maybe we're looking at this from the wrong end."

"Could be," agreed Pedro. "What's the wrong end of a groundhog?"

It was a question for the ages.

* * *

My cell phone rang on Monday morning. I'd just arrived at the police station, having made my way down the mountains in good time. There was still some snow, to be sure, but yesterday's sunshine had cleared the roads nicely. I answered the call.

"Hayden Konig."

"Hayden? This is Alison Jaeger. From the Bookworms."

"Good morning, Doctor. How may I help you?"

"Well," she said, "I wasn't entirely honest with you when we had lunch. I did know all three of the victims. They were all patients of mine. I didn't want to say anything, because I didn't feel the rest of the Bookworms needed to be aware of that fact."

"That's perfectly understandable," I said. "How about the rest of it? Is it true that you hadn't seen Crystal Latimore for a few years?"

"No, that wasn't true. I saw her three weeks ago. She had been complaining about feeling very tired and had a low-grade fever that she couldn't shake, so she came in. It was time for her yearly physical anyway. Her blood work showed that she was in the early stages of leukemia. Specifically, chronic lymphocytic leukemia. It progresses slowly."

"Had you told her?"

"Oh, yes. The last time I saw her was when I told her. I prefer to give news like that face to face. She was going to make an appointment with a cancer specialist I recommended in Greensboro, but I never heard from her after that."

"Okay," I said. "How about Amy Ventura?"

"She's been a patient of mine for six years. General good health. Comes in regularly for an exam and occasionally when she gets sick. I treated her once for a sprained back, once for strep throat, and a few times when she had the flu. A year and a half ago she came in with TMJ. I prescribed some pain medication and referred her. Basically, though, a clean bill of health."

"Darla Kildair?"

"Darla didn't have any specific complaints. Just general aches and pains associated with middle age."

"Any medications?" I asked.

I heard the rustling of some papers, then, "Premarin — that's an estrogen replacement — and Lisinopril for high blood pressure."

"Did these three women know each other? That you know of?"

"Not that I know of."

I thought for a moment. "How about your waiting room? Were they ever all scheduled for an appointment within, say, an hour of each other?"

"I don't know. I'll have to check with my office manager and get back to you."

"Would you do that?"

"I'd be happy to. I'm sorry for the deception. You understand."

"I do. Thanks for calling, Doctor."

I told Nancy about Alison Jaeger's call when she came in.

"Humph," she sniffed. "Pretty convenient."

* * *

Dave had just come in from the donut run when the door to the station banged open and Kimberly Walnut appeared. Her shoulder-length, mouse-brown hair was an un-coiffed mess and her makeup had been applied with far less care than usual. She was a nut, but usually a well-put-together nut.

"I just heard!" she screeched. "I called Bun in the Oven to order some pastries for this morning's staff meeting, and Diana Evarts told me that I'm probably next on the list!"

"What list?" asked Dave. He was standing behind the counter perusing his box of donuts.

"The death list!" shrieked Kimberly Walnut. "A lawyer, a hair dresser, a publicist, and a *woman priest*."

"A minister, actually," said Nancy, choosing a donut of the chocolate cake variety.

"I'm the only one!"

"Well, the only one in St. Germaine," I said. "I'm sure there are more than a few others in the surrounding towns. Keep in mind that two of the women were from other communities."

"I want police protection!" demanded Kimberly Walnut.

"We can have Dave move in with you for a week or two," said Nancy. "Do you have an extra bedroom?"

Dave's eyes got big and he tried to say something, but his mouth was occupied with Bavarian cream.

"No police protection," I said. "If you were an intended victim, you'd probably be dead by now."

"You don't know that," said Kimberly Walnut, her screeching turning to a whine.

"Maybe you could take a sabbatical, like Hayden," suggested Nancy. "Go to New Zealand or somewhere."

"There's a staff meeting in a half hour," Kimberly Walnut said, now glaring at me. "Nine o'clock sharp."

"And this has to do with me?"

"Father Dressler said you should be there." She spun on her heel and banged out the door.

"Wow," said Dave, finally swallowing. "She's in a snit. Are you going to go to the staff meeting?"

I sighed. "I guess. There's now a Candlemas Evensong looming on the horizon. If I have to preside over another rehearsal, I should probably at least give the choir the correct music."

* * *

There are few things more exasperating than a Monday morning church staff meeting, and Father Gallus Dressler didn't do anything to take the edge off.

"I prefer Monday mornings for staff meetings," he announced, walking in five minutes late, the tails of his cassock flapping behind him. "It gives us all a chance to think about the service yesterday and discuss it while it's fresh in our minds." He came flouncing in with a stack of file folders in one hand and a large wooden box that he carried by its handle in the other. The folders were placed in front of him, the box disappeared beside his chair.

Seated at the conference table where our staff meetings were generally held was: Marilyn, there to take notes; Kimberly Walnut; Joyce Cooper, the church treasurer; Carol Sterling, the head of the Altar Guild; and Bev Greene, currently head of the Worship Committee. Bev had been appointed by the vestry at the beginning of the year, at my suggestion, after the last rector had departed. Before Bev, Kimberly Walnut had been acting as the Worship Committee all by herself — with the help of her disciple, Heather Frampton. Beverly had put the committee back together, but she was the only one of them present this morning.

Usually these meetings were preceded and accompanied by coffee. No such luck this morning, although there were some pastries on a glass tray in the center of the table. Five pastries. I stood, reached to the center of the table and took one. Father Dressler followed my example a moment later. None of the ladies bothered.

"Now, then," the priest said, placing both hands on the top of his folders. "I have an announcement to make."

"Shouldn't we begin with a prayer?" Bev asked sweetly.

"Yes, yes," muttered Father Dressler. "Absolutely. Hayden, would you be so kind?" He closed his eyes and bowed his head.

Bev caught my eye and gave me a smirk.

I had nothing handy, so I went with the *Chorister's Prayer*. I had several good graces for blessing food, some sentences for funerals, and more than a few collects committed to memory, but this one seemed right for the occasion:

Bless, O Lord, us Thy servants who minister in Thy temple. Grant that what we sing with our lips, we may believe in our hearts, and what we believe in our hearts, we may show forth in our lives. Through Jesus Christ our Lord. Amen.

"Amen," everyone echoed, then Father Dressler said, "As I indicated before I was interrupted ..."

"By our opening prayer," said Bev.

The priest ignored her. "I'd like to announce that I will be handing in my formal application to the vestry for the position of rector of St. Barnabas. I feel God's leading in this decision and, with my application on file, the hiring process may be quite a bit shorter than originally thought. If all goes well, St. Barnabas may have a new full-time rector within a month."

"You've only been here a little over a week," said Bev.

"Yes, but I'm quite capable of assessing the essence of a congregation very quickly. It's one of my gifts. I feel that this church would be a fine match for my particular skill set."

"And that skill set is ...?" said Bev. Bev was the only one weighing in on this announcement. I didn't particularly care whether he turned in his application or not. The others probably feared for their jobs.

"I think that's a conversation better left to the vestry and the search committee," he said with a smarmy smile, probably not realizing that Bev was a member of both. "Now, to business. As you know, I've announced a Candlemas Evensong on February 2nd, a week from Wednesday at five o'clock,. Hayden, you will rehearse the music *this* Wednesday, but the Chevalier will be here on Saturday, so you may feel free to continue your sabbatical after your rehearsal."

I smiled at him.

"The Chevalier?" said Carol.

"He will be our musician for the foreseeable future."

"Six months, anyway," I said.

"Indeed," said the priest with a small smile.

"Does he have a name?" asked Joyce.

"The Chevalier Lance Fleagle. He has a master's degree from Oberlin."

"Oooh," said Bev. "Wow."

If the priest noticed her sarcasm, he didn't acknowledge it. "He and I are both members of the Order of St. Clementine. He chooses to use the honorary title of 'Chevalier.' You will all respect that, please."

"Sure," said Bev. "What's the order of St. Clementine?"

"It's not like the Elks," I said. "Not one bit."

"The Order of St. Clementine is inspired by the statutes defined by Ladislaus the Posthumous in 1441. We are pledged to the chivalric virtues."

"Oh," said Bev.

Father Dressler continued. "I have gotten the names of two young people whom I have been told will make fine acolytes. I shall begin their training this Wednesday evening." He ruffled through a couple of sheets of paper, then came up with the names. "Bernie Kenton and Mossy McCollough."

"That's 'Moosey,' I believe," said Carol.

"Moosey?" said Father Dressler, making a note on his pad. "That's an odd name."

"A nickname," I said.

"Oh, that explains it."

"Yes," I continued, "his given name is Moosehead Rheingold McCollough."

Father Dressler looked up at me, decided I was joking and went back to his note taking. "Anyway," he said, "if there are no objections, I'll take these two and a couple of others into training. They will make their first acolyture this Sunday, but they will be installed at the Evensong. Make no mistake, this will be the solemnest of services! I think we should probably make an announcement that babies and small children should not be in attendance. Now, do we have a nursery available on Wednesdays?"

All of us looked at Kimberly Walnut, not just for affirmation of the nursery, but for some objection or comment as to the suitability of Moosey and Bernie as acolytes. I had no problem with either of them, but they were two of Kimberly Walnut's arch-nemeses, having been thorns in her side since she met them during the first Bible School she put on three years earlier when she was hired as our Director of Christian Formation. Kimberly Walnut was pale and chewing on the inside of her lip, but she didn't say anything except, "Yes, we'll have a nursery available."

"We will have a service of Evensong *and* Benediction of the Blessed Sacrament," Father Dressler said. "I'm sure you're well acquainted with the service ..."

"Actually, we're not," I said. "We've done Evensong, but we haven't followed it with Benediction."

"It's quite straight forward, really," said Father Dressler. "It's simply a blessing of the congregation with the Eucharist at the end of a period of adoration. The consecrated host is placed in a monstrance set upon the altar. We shall have a reasonable time for reflection as the choir sings the *Tantum Ergo*. I will bless the people with the monstrance. Then we will repeat the *Laudes Divinae* — the *Divine Praises* — and the Blessed Sacrament will be returned to the aumbry as the choir sings Psalm 117."

"What the heck is a monstrance?" asked Carol.

"This," said Father Dressler, reaching beside his chair and , with some effort, lifting the wooden box onto the table. The box was two feet tall and eighteen inches wide and was unassuming — stained a dark brown with a coating of polyurethane. He released two clasps and opened the case, revealing a traditional "solar" style monstrance. This was a vehicle of adoration that had more roots in Catholicism than anything the Anglican community had to offer. Twenty inches tall, the gold-plated sunburst sat atop a candlestick-like base that was about six inches in diameter. The spiked rays of the sunburst were of varying lengths and surrounded a large glass eye set in the center of the crown of the monstrance. The eye was designed to enclose the Eucharistic host and display it to the worshipers as they were blessed by the priest.

"Wow," said Joyce. "Is that yours?"

"Yes," said Father Dressler. "Obviously."

"So," I said, "am I to understand that the choir needs to prepare the Psalm for the day, the *Preces and Responses*, an evening setting of a *Magnificat* and *Nunc Dimittis*, an anthem, a *Tantum Ergo*, and a setting of Psalm 117? As well as the music for this Sunday?"

"Yes," said Father Dressler. "Also, if you could have the choir chant the *Angelus* at the end of the service, it would be most meaningful. If you'd like, you can substitute an *O Salutaris Hostia* in place of the *Tantum Ergo*."

"Ah," I said with a nod. "Good to know."

"If you're not up to the task, maybe I can call the Chevalier and see if he can come earlier."

"Oh, I'll take care of it."

* * *

Kimberly Walnut pigeonholed me in the church kitchen as I was getting a cup of coffee. The church always kept a pot of Community Coffee brewed and sitting on the Bunn coffee maker.

"You've got to help me!" she whispered. "I'm in real trouble!"

"Kimberly Walnut, in the three years you've been working here, I can't remember any time you've *not* been in trouble."

"This is different."

"Is it the murderer? Has he contacted you?"

She squinted at me and pursed her lips. "No. It's Father Dressler. You know he hates me, right?"

"I'm sure he doesn't."

"If he gets hired as the new rector, I'll be the first one to go — and you'll be the second. He seems to really love this Chevalier."

"I'm not worried."

"Of course you're not," said Kimberly Walnut, tears welling in her eyes. "You're rich. You have another job. People like you."

"Well..."

"I've done a terrible thing," she blurted, "and I don't know what to do."

"What?"

"You know the St. Germaine Garden Club?"

"Sure." I didn't know all the members by name, but I knew they existed as a group. "What do they have to do with you?"

"I told the Garden Club that I would preside over a service they want to have at St. Barnabas."

"Okay. That shouldn't be a problem. Just clear it with Father Dressler and Joyce."

"That's the problem. It's part of their Winter Festival and it's scheduled for Wednesday, February 2nd, at five o'clock."

Oh," I said. "Same time as the Evensong. Was your service on the church calendar?"

"No. I forgot to put it down. Now the Garden Club has already advertised and sold raffle tickets. The festival is in Sterling Park

135

right across the street from the church. I didn't know that the priest was going to have a Candlemas Evensong. Who's even heard of Candlemas?"

"It's a very important day in the Anglo-Catholic year."

"Apparently. So now I have to either tell Father Dressler that we have something else scheduled that I forgot about, or tell the Garden Club that they can't use the church and that I can't do their service. They were counting on me."

"It's a tough spot," I agreed.

"I'm going to get fired, for sure. I need this job. It's all right for you, but I'm fifty years old and I've got nothing else."

"Well, you'd better say something soon," I said, knowing that she probably wouldn't. If there was ever a procrastinator who avoided any hint of conflict, it was Kimberly Walnut. "I don't think there's any way you can combine the Garden Club thingy with a Solemn Evensong. What kind of service are you doing anyway?"

"It's a Service of Blessing," she said, bursting into tears. "The Blessing of the Groundhog."

* * *

Dr. Alison Jaeger called me back that afternoon.

"The three women didn't meet in the waiting room," she said. "At least not that I know of. They never had appointments on the same day. Not even close."

Chapter 20

The rising sun squirmed its way through the smog and slithered across the squalid cityscape into every nook and cranny like hot grease on a Waffle House griddle in the Sunday morning rush. I pondered the St. Groundlemas question. We were looking at the problem from the groundhog perspective, but what if we turned that pig around and peered prudently into the pitchy panoply of a proxy presumption?

"Alliteration is not your friend," snorked Pedro derisively.

"Maybe not," I said as flinty as a Presbyterian minister at an eHarmony speed mixer, "but I can use a simile quicker than a romance writer on diet pills."

Pedro fluffed the petticoats under his cassock. "I'm off to the basilica," he said. "St. Gertrude the Pretty Good. They're so high church the priests carry incense snuff boxes. We're singing the Ockeghem 'Missa Caput' with extended antiphons for twelve deviant voices." He looked down at his watch. "We should be out of church by three o'clock. We'll run out of candles by then."

Suddenly it hit me — hit me like one of those anvils dropped on a cartoon character after he already fell off a cliff because he forgot the first law of cartoon physics, "Gravity doesn't work until you look down," flattening him like a Shrove Tuesday pancake. It wasn't the groundhog. It was the candles.

* * *

I walked the two blocks from downtown to Bud's new house to check on the progress and things were moving quickly. Roberto and his crew had gutted the interior and were bustling inside, putting up new walls and running the electric wires. We had several inspections scheduled and the first one was tomorrow. I had no concerns. Roberto Gonzales was a topnotch contractor. Bud wasn't there, but had gone to Asheville to meet with a supplier.

The septic problem had been resolved and the groundhog infestation dealt with. I hadn't seen Moosey for the past few days, but I presumed he was thrilled with his new pet. The yard had been put back together, but still looked forlorn in the dreary doldrums of January. The big maple tree in the front yard was bare, the Indian hawthorn hedges, brown and sere. The grass was now mostly mud, thanks to the tramping of the workers, supplies set in the yard, the large dumpster, and Harmonious Pooter's backhoe.

Bud had been toying with names for his shop for a number of months. He had decided on The Wine Press since he was also planning an on-line newsletter that would carry the same title. He'd registered the business with the North Carolina Secretary of State as a partnership.

I headed back down the sidewalk toward town and saw Nancy coming toward me. We met in front of Holy Grounds and went inside to warm up.

"What can I get you?" said Kylie Moffit, the owner and barista. Holy Grounds was not busy. Not at this time of the day.

"Coffee," I said.

"How about an *espresso corretto al cognac*? It's a cold day outside and it's five o'clock somewhere."

"There's cognac involved?"

"Well, sure, but if you'd rather ..."

"I'll take it," I said.

"Me, too," said Nancy. "Put it on his bill."

We got our coffees and found a table. "Anything going on?" I asked.

"Glad you asked," Nancy said. "Kent just called. That's why I came to find you. He's identified the poison."

"Excellent. What is it?"

Nancy pulled out her pad and read. "Aconitum, otherwise known as aconite. It's the Queen of Poisons."

"Monkshood?"

"Exactly," said Nancy. "How did you know?"

"My brain contains a vast store of irritating and useless knowledge."

"Oh, yeah, I forgot. F.Y.I., it's also known as wolfsbane, leopard's bane, and blue rocket. Since there were no gastrointestinal effects apparent — no vomiting, etcetera — Kent thinks the toxin was absorbed through the skin. If the poison is absorbed rather than ingested, tingling will start at the point of absorption and extend to the arms and shoulders, after which the heart will start to be affected. Heart failure is imminent and will usually occur within the hour."

"Great. So where does that leave us?"

"Well, Kent says the strange thing is that the point of absorption was probably the soft palate, since that was where the lesions occurred. Also, that's where he discovered the traces of the poison."

"Why is that strange?"

"Well, if the poison was in the women's mouths, it makes more sense for it to have been swallowed. But it wasn't."

"Huh," I said. "That is odd, isn't it?"

"How about the book club?" said Nancy. "Anyone look to you like a poisoner?"

"Or maybe a gardener," I said. "Rachel Barstow gardens and sells at the farmer's market, if I recall correctly. You have your list?"

"Sure," said Nancy, and went to the other breast pocket. She pulled out her list of Bookworms.

- Rachel Barstow – home gardener, herbalist, sells at the Farmer's Market; has quite a *Pinterest* following; favorites include historical mysteries, political satire, and existentialist fiction.

"Historical mysteries would include murder by monkshood most certainly," I said. "What's her *Pinterest* following concern?"

Nancy pulled out her phone and spent a moment connecting with the Holy Grounds WiFi, then said, "Herb gardening mostly. Nothing here about monkshood, though … hang on." She scrolled her finger across the small screen of her iPhone. "Hang on …" she said again, then, "nothing about monkshood, but here's an entry about wolfsbane. There's a poem: a medieval charm used when harvesting the plant for medicinal purposes." She passed me the phone.

O one berie, who planted you?
Our Ladie with her five fingers trewe,
thru all her miht and power,
She brought you hyd to flower,
hwæt I shall have my healthe.

I passed it back. "Motive?" I asked, taking a sip of coffee and considering one of the muffins I'd seen lurking in the glass case beneath the cash register.

"Usually either money, sex, or revenge," said Nancy. "Some criminologists throw in fear and rage, but those tend to be impulsive. If the homicide is planned, and this one certainly was, I'd go with one of the first three."

"How about 'accidental?' As an herbalist, maybe Rachel was using the monkshood as some sort of remedy and made a mistake on the dosage, then remembered the book and used the coincidence in careers to cover it up."

"That's a stretch," said Nancy. "Possible, though."

"I agree. Let's go with the first three. So which is it? Rachel Barstow admitted knowing Amy and Darla. Did she know Crystal as well? Also, remember, it was Rachel who recommended *See Your Shadow* to the Bookworms in the first place."

"Seems kinda easy when you put all the pieces together," Nancy said with a grin.

I stood up. "I'm getting a banana nut muffin. You want one?"

"Sure. A celebratory muffin."

"We still need a motive," I said, "and actual evidence."

"We'll get it," said Nancy.

Chapter 21

It took the better part of Wednesday afternoon to put all the music together for Father Dressler's Candlemas Evensong. I decided that the *Tantum Ergo* would do double duty and we'd sing it Sunday during communion, as well as next Wednesday for the service. I chose a *Tantum Ergo* by Anton Bruckner because we'd sung it before. It was straightforward and something we could put together easily. The *Preces and Responses* were Richard Shephard's and so were the evening canticles — the *Magnificat* and *Nunc dimittis*. The canticles were easy: a unison treble line with a four-part *Gloria* at the end of each. We had learned those pieces for Advent and I hoped they had stuck. The Psalm appointed for Candlemas was Psalm 84: *How Lovely Is Your Dwelling Place.* Psalm 117, which was to be sung at the end of the service, is only two verses long and I had a lovely little Baroque Charpentier setting that would be just fine. We would also use this one on Sunday for the offertory anthem.

I cleared all the music with the priest and was feeling good about the whole thing, so I took a break for supper and met Meg at the Bear and Brew. Now we were back in the choir loft waiting for the crowd to arrive.

Marjorie was first. She was always first. I surmised the reason was to retrieve her flask from behind one of the organ pipes before everyone showed up. No one ever asked what was in the flask, and she kept it hidden unless she was in the choir loft, in which case it was in the hymnal rack in front of her.

"Good evening," she said sweetly, putting her purse down on her chair and making a beeline for the organ case. "I trust you are both well."

"Great," said Meg. "And how are you, Marjorie?"

"Terrible!" barked Marjorie, her mood suddenly turning. "Where's my flask?"

"I haven't seen it," I said.

"I didn't take it," said Meg.

"Well, it's gone! The last time it disappeared, it was that drunken sexton who took it. The one that Ardine killed."

"Ardine didn't kill him," I said. "That's just rumor. Rumor and scuttlebutt."

"Of course, you couldn't prove it," said Marjorie. "That's the beauty of Oleander tea. But that's neither here nor there. I want to know who swiped my flask!"

"Maybe you misplaced it," I said, knowing it was a vain hope. Someone had found Marjorie's flask and I had a good idea who.

"It's that nosey little priest, isn't it?" said Marjorie, venom in her voice.

"Take it easy. I'm sure it was just misplaced."

"Misplaced, my Aunt Millie's butt!" Marjorie was already across the choir loft and jimmying open the door to the bell tower. It was supposedly kept locked, but anyone could get in by using the old nail that was left sticking into the door casing for just such emergencies. The door opened and she disappeared into the bell tower for a minute, then reappeared holding another flask in her hand. She pulled the door shut behind her.

"He didn't find this one," she said. "It's a good thing, too."

"How many of those do you have up here?" asked Meg.

"Not as many as you might think," Marjorie replied. "The trick is to keep them moving."

Sheila DeMoss was the next one up the stairs, followed by Bev, Rhiza, and Elaine.

"Ah," said Sheila, picking up her music, "the newest installment." I had copied my latest effort onto the back of Psalm 84. It seemed appropriate.

* * *

"Follow the money." That's the third rule in the Detective Handbook right after "Don't put your tongue in the jar of mustard at a dinner party" and "If there are clowns involved, do not take the case."

I snuck into the back of St. G's and squinted through the bluish-gray haze. One thing about the Anglo-Catholics at St. Gertrude the Pretty Good: when they smoked the place up they didn't mince around with a couple of swinging smoke pots, but went ahead and hooked their incense machine up to the exhaust fan. The atmosphere was Los Angeles on Labor Day, not that it was full of glitz and glam, although it was, and unseasonably warm, which

142

it also was, but rather that LA is known for its poor air quality despite the prevalence of electric cars and "alternative energy" nuts, and therefore the metaphor is apt, so don't send me any emails.

There were bells going off every few seconds, priests twirling like manatees in the aisles, rampant nuns genuflecting to every guy with a beard, and Pedro at the front, wearing his night-vision goggles so he could see the music, canting for all he was worth. The place was lit by candles, hundreds of 'em, maybe millions, and though I couldn't see much, I saw right through this little scam.

* * *

"Okay, I'm really getting into this story," said Sheila. "Priests twirling like manatees, rampant nuns ... so descriptive."

"I don't get it," said Marjorie.

"I don't get it, either," said Meg, "and I'm married to him."

The rest of the choir climbed the stairs to the loft and were finding their seats with varying degrees of comments.

"I heard we had to learn about three hours of music for this evensong," said Phil.

"Not quite," I said, "Just a couple of extra anthems we need to rehearse for this one."

"Hey," said Mark Wells, appearing at the top of the stairs. "Sorry I'm late. I had a Jehovah's Witness knock on the door just as I was getting ready to leave. Nice young fella."

"I had one show up yesterday afternoon," said Phil. "Did you give him the heave ho?"

"Nope. I decided to do the Christian thing and invite him in. I told him to come on in and sit down. So he did."

"And?" said Phil.

"And I asked him what he wanted to talk about. He says, 'Beats me. I've never gotten this far before.'"

The choir broke out in laughter. A good start.

* * *

If the Fraternity of Insane Bishops managed to merge Groundhog Day with Candlemas, the Anglo-Catholics were done for, not because they couldn't bear the merger — although tying their rosaries to a rodent that predicted the weather wasn't their idea of parochial correctness — but because their entire funding came from the Liturgical Candle franchise. They ran the biggest candle recycling program in the country and supplied everybody with their bougies - from those little white taperinos that congregations pass around on Christmas Eve, to those hundred-pound Paschal mega-wicks all tarted up like Tammy Faye with more lilies, crosses, and solid-gold Chi Rho symbols than a Trinity Broadcasting stage set. And the Queen Mother of all Holy Days in the world of glimmer-glow was ... Candlemas.

I figured that, with Candlemas out of the liturgical calendar, the Anglo-Catholics would be ten million in the red by Pentecost. Sure, they'd get some graft from the wedding planners, a little swag from the "Silent Night" crowd, but without Candlemas most of their boodle would go up in smoke. They'd dry up quicker than Betty White in the hot sun.

Suddenly I felt someone poking me in the back, not the gentle poke of "Excuse me mister, you're standing on my guinea pig," or even "Hey buddy, sit down, I can't see the stripper," but rather the insistent poke of a couple of 38s and I don't mean the good kind.

"Ja, ja," Klingle sprinkled. "It's time we took a walk."

* * *

Dr. Ian Burch, PhD, was the last to arrive. He was preceded by his nose, which was abnormally long, red, and honking, and his attitude, which was, as usual, haughty and not a little overbearing. He couldn't help it. His allergies accounted for his sounding like a goose in heat and his PhD in music history (Specialty: The French Chanson 1413-1467) accounted for his attitude. He'd tried to garner

144

numerous teaching positions over the years, but this hadn't worked out for him. As a certified Medievalist he was fluent in Latin and Old French and proficient on a number of instruments, none of which anyone wanted to hear: the rauschpfeife, the racket, the cornemuse, and several unpronounceable bladder instruments. Now he made his living as the owner of the Appalachian Music Shoppe, specializing in selling reproductions of these instruments to other delusional folks. Almost all of his business was done via the internet.

All that being said, he was a marvelous countertenor and held down the alto section brilliantly. He did have an unrequited crush on Tiff St. James. She'd told Meg his ears reminded her of a Volkswagen Beetle with the doors open.

"Glad you're back, Ian," I said. "How was the tour?"

"Brilliant!" He grinned ear to ear and it startled everyone. No one had ever seen him smile before. He made a beeline for Tiff, took the seat next to her and, ignoring everyone else in the choir, leaned over and whispered in a loud tone, "I heard we are getting a new organist. A *Chevalier*!"

"The concert venues were good?" I asked, knowing that Ian had expressed some concern about the Appalachian Rauschpfeife Consort's bookings. Ian had found a shady Italian concert/travel agent online and each member of the consort had paid several thousand dollars to go on this tour. The group hadn't received an itinerary before they departed, but were hoping to get one when the plane landed in Paris.

"We played in train stations mostly," said Ian, "but the crowds were most appreciative."

"Any reviews?" asked Marjorie. "I love reading bad reviews."

Ian sniffed. "None that you could read, dear. They were all in French."

"Oh, I read French all right," said Marjorie. "I was a nurse's aid back in WWII. I spent several happy months in Amiens with this good-looking *soldat* named Henri. I nursed him back to health after he caught a dose of the Spanish Pox. The rest of the unit moved on, but I hid in the supply closet so I could stay and look after him." She looked wistful for a moment. "Oh, the fun we had ..."

"That explains a lot," said Bob Solomon.

"Hang on," said Meg. "How old were you?"

145

"Sixteen," said Marjorie, "I ran away and enlisted with my sister's birth certificate. I was very mature for my age."

"Sounds like it," said Bob.

"Let's get started," I said. "We have a lot to cover."

* * *

We went through all the music and there seemed to be no major problems. I explained again to the choir that the Chevalier would be arriving shortly and I extolled his many virtues. When we got to the anthem that we'd be doing on Wednesday, there was general hilarity.

"You did this on purpose," Meg said.

"I cannot confirm or deny that statement. All music has been approved by Father Dressler."

"That's because he hasn't read your detective story," said Georgia. "He probably doesn't even realize that Candlemas is also Groundhog Day."

"This anthem has nothing to do with Groundhog Day. It's a beautiful expression of love from the Old Testament. It's perfect for a Candlemas Evensong, especially accompanied by the service of Benediction."

"Really?" said Rebecca Watts, her sarcasm apparent.

"Sure. Look at the text."

"We're looking at it," said Steve.

What they were looking at was Edward Bairstow's setting of the text from the Song of Solomon.

I sat down under his shadow with great delight.

"We can't sing this with a straight face," said Marty, from the alto section. The rest of the altos nodded their agreement.

"Alas," I said, "it's already been approved and has probably gone to the printer." I wasn't sure about that last part, but it sounded good. "It's a beautiful piece and you all will sing it just fine. Now let's have a prayer and dismiss."

* * *

After choir was over and folks were dispersing, Georgia came up to the organ console, leaned over and said softly, "I'm in the St. Germaine Garden Club, you know."

"Oh?" I feigned ignorance of what was coming next.

"You haven't told the priest about the Blessing, have you?"

"Blessing? What blessing?"

Georgia growled at me.

"Umm ... well ... Kimberly Walnut did mention something about a groundhog being blessed, but I told her she should take care of it. Either tell the Garden Club or tell Father Dressler, but one of them is going to be very upset."

"You know she won't. She avoids confrontation like you avoid writing classes. She'll try to figure out some way to make everyone happy. Or at least not to make anyone too mad."

"That's hardly my fault."

"You should say something," said Georgia, with an evil smile. "You will have a lot to answer for on Judgement Day."

"Maybe," I said. "But, *technically*, I'm still on sabbatical."

Chapter 22

The Chevalier Lance Fleagle arrived on Thursday morning. I know this because Georgia walked into the Slab Café, stomped up to the table, put both hands on her hips and announced it.

"The Chevalier Lance Fleagle is here. He's moving into your office." Georgia hadn't bothered to remove her coat, hat, or mittens. "Kimberly Walnut is running around like a chicken with its head cut off, saying she's going to be murdered and left in a closet. The whole place is in an uproar."

My eyebrows went up. Pete, sitting at the table with me, guffawed. Cynthia turned from the table she was waiting on and said, in a small voice, "Oh, my." I was waiting for Dave and Nancy to come over for our weekly staff meeting (otherwise known as "free breakfast") and was enjoying my second cup of coffee.

"Moving into my office, you say?"

"Yes," said Georgia. "Father Dressler told him he could box up your things and stack them in the storage closet down the hall, so that's what he's doing. He also requested the password for your computer so he can use it since it contains the music library database. *And* Kimberly Walnut has gone crazy!"

My eyes narrowed. "*Moving into my office?*"

"Yes," said Georgia. "He has quite a number of boxes. I believe he brought all manner of books, encyclopedias, and music with him in his van. Also, vestments and several cartons of other religious paraphernalia, including his own *prie-dieu* and small Mary altar. Did you hear me about Kimberly Walnut?"

I took a deep breath and relaxed. "A kneeler, eh? Well, that's certainly reasonable. *Beati possidentes*: Blessed are those who possess. Don't worry about Kimberly Walnut. She's not going to be murdered. At least, not this week."

"Quite frankly, it'd be a relief if she were." She waggled a finger at me. "Back to the Chevalier. He's screwed his nameplate to the door." Georgia pulled out a piece of paper and read, "It says *Le Chevalier Lancelot Fleagle, KStY, A.A., B.M., M.M. Master of the Musik,* and he spelled 'Musik' with a 'k.' What do you think of *that*? It's your office, for heaven's sake!"

"All I can say is *Date et dabitur vobis*: Give and it shall be given unto you. Please tell *Le Chevalier* that the computer doesn't have a password and to use it with my compliments."

"*E pluribus unum*," sputtered Georgia. "Are you listening to me?"

"I am," I replied, "but like the holy men of yore, I have found my spiritual center. I shan't be tousled upon this stormy sea."

"Oh, my," said Cynthia again. "This isn't going to end well, is it?"

I smiled and slurped my coffee.

"How come you never put all those letters after your name?" Pete asked.

"Too many," I replied. "It'd be like alphabet soup. There just wouldn't be room for anything else on my new door nameplate."

"Okay, smart guy," said Georgia through gritted teeth. "How about this, then? Father Dressler has applied for the full-time position. I have his formal letter of application on my desk and so does the rest of the vestry."

"He did tell us that he was applying," I said in my nicest voice, "and he indicated that it shouldn't be too long before we had a new permanent rector."

Georgia growled — a deep growl, bear-like, low in her throat. I'd never heard a woman growl like that before. Pete looked startled. Cynthia's eyes grew wide.

I said, "Never fear. I shall come over and greet the Master of the Musik as soon as I check with Nancy and Dave on a couple of things and maybe have a little breakfast."

"You do that," snarled Georgia, then turned on her heel and marched toward the door. Dave and Nancy met her as they were coming in and held the door. She didn't acknowledge the gesture, as all well-bred Southerners do, but stomped right past them into the frosty air, muttering beneath her breath.

"Wow," said Dave, pulling out his chair and sitting. "She's steamed."

"She's the Senior Warden," I said. "This is all on her plate now."

"I wonder," said Pete, "how long it will really take to appoint the new rector."

"Father Dressler is probably correct," I said. "I don't think it will take too long. These things tend to work themselves out." I changed the subject. "Anything new on the murder front?"

"Nope," said Nancy.

"Nope," said Dave.

"Well, that's it for our staff meeting, then. Let's order breakfast."

After our delicious repast that included Pete's new menu item — Belgian waffles stuffed with cream cheese and covered with blackberries — Nancy and Dave went back to the office to detect some stuff, and I walked across Sterling Park to St. Barnabas. The park was desolate, as it is every January. The trees were bare, the grass was brown, and the sounds of the park heard before Christmas — laughter, people talking and walking their dogs, music made by itinerant buskers, late-season squirrels and birds — were all gone and wouldn't reappear until spring. Even the leaves had vanished, thanks to Billy Hixon and his crew of landscapers. It was a desolate park in January, with snow scrambled in the roots of the tall maples and oaks. I crossed the street, bypassed the two red front doors of the church, and walked around the side to the entrance of the offices. I found the door locked, pulled out my keys, then opened the door and walked down the hallway to Marilyn's office. She was sitting at her desk, rifling through papers with a look of consternation on her face.

"Why is the door locked?" I asked her, in a quiet voice, figuring that Father Dressler probably had his ear to the door.

"He's out," said Marilyn. "He told us to keep the church door locked in case of vagrants wandering in and asking for a handout."

"When was the last time that happened?"

"The day he got here. I took care of it like I always do. I took the woman back to the food pantry and loaded her up. She had two little kids with her."

"And?"

"And Father Dressler doesn't want to deal with that sort of thing, so now everyone has to be buzzed in. If they're after a handout — that's what he called it, a handout — they're to first check in with the Bartholomew Center and their counselors will refer them to the appropriate agency. If they decide that we're the ones to help, they'll make an appointment. He's set all this up with the Center. He doesn't have time to deal with everyone on a one-on-one basis. Besides, he says that certain people work the system. That's why everyone has to be buzzed in."

The Bartholomew Center was a nonprofit agency outside of town that dealt with families in trouble. They did good work, but I knew they had their hands full as it was. Marilyn had always dealt with walk-ins who needed help. She was happy to do it. She *liked* doing it and she'd told the vestry so on more than one occasion.

"I didn't even know that we had a buzzer," I said.

"Well," said Marilyn sadly, "we do."

"How about the front doors?" I asked.

"Locked."

"Are you kidding?" Never in my experience had the front doors of St. Barnabas been locked during the day. Old Henry Landers, the sexton, usually didn't lock the doors till eleven and had them open again by eight. It wasn't unusual to find people sitting in the church at all hours.

"I'm not kidding," Marilyn hissed softly.

I sighed heavily and said, "Is the Chevalier in? I thought I'd say hello."

"He is. Shall I announce you?"

My eyebrows went up for the second time this morning, something they didn't do often.

"I like it when your eyebrows go up," said Marilyn, finally giving me a small smile. "They go up and then stuff happens." She picked up her phone, punched in three numbers and said, "Chevalier Fleagle? The Chief is here to see you." Silence, then, "No, not Father Dressler. The *Police* Chief. Chief Hayden Konig. Yes ... yes ... I'll send him right down." She hung up the phone and rolled her eyes, then pointed down the hall to my ex-office.

"The Chevalier will see you now," she said.

"What's that extension, anyway?" I asked. "I never bothered to use it."

"Six six six," said Marilyn.

* * *

"*Entrez vous*," called the Chevalier when I knocked on the door. I glanced at the new nameplate as I turned the door handle and walked in. Gold with engraved script. Lancelot Fleagle was busy putting his hardcover, twenty-nine volume set of the *New Grove Dictionary of Music and Musicians* on one of the shelves directly behind where his head would be if he were sitting in my expensive, leather desk chair. I didn't own those particular volumes any longer. I'd given mine to the St. Germaine library. Since the

151

Grove Dictionary went online, I much preferred to pay the subscription fee and have everything available at my fingertips and easily searchable. Wading through more than 22,000 articles was a daunting task and one suited to graduate students. I had done my time in the days before personal computers and I wasn't going back.

The other shelves contained equally scholarly tomes, some I recognized: *The Study of Counterpoint* by Johann Joseph Fux, first published in 1725, and *French Baroque Music* by James Anthony — the definitive text on the subject. Some I didn't recognize and had no desire to read. It was clear that the Chevalier had boxed up my entire hardbound collection of Peanuts comics.

Another wall of shelves was full of books of organ music. A few were unmistakable, even from across the room, and I recognized the spines right away: the Bach complete organ works, Mendelssohn, Handel, Durufle. Standard stuff.

On the desk was a small sword stuck into an acrylic stone. Applied to the stone, a golden plaque proclaimed his knighthood into the Order of St. Clementine. There was also a framed scroll on the wall, in Latin, advertising the same thing. At least I thought it must. I recognized the words "ST. CLEMENTINE" in bold, Gothic lettering. The desk also had a copy of Sunday's printed bulletin (Marilyn had been busy this morning) and a working copy of the Evensong bulletin. It wasn't hard to figure these two out, even seeing them upside down. The computer was on, the monitor pointed inexplicably toward the door, and had a new screensaver: the Chevalier being knighted by an even grander knight, presumably the head of the order. To the right of Lance Fleagle was Father Gallus Dressler, dressed in his long, clerical garb, but with a heraldic overlay. There were other knights present as well, and the venue was a good replication of one of the Great Halls in England, complete with banners, shields, huge oaken beams holding up a vaulted ceiling, and stone walls and floors. It was a portrait worthy of a Pre-Raphaelite.

"Please have a seat," Lance said, pointing to the small, plastic office chair he'd pilfered from the conference room. He let himself down easily in the leather chair behind the desk. *My* leather chair, bought by *me*, for *my* office, covered with the hides of unborn Nubian goats, hand-stitched, rubbed and dyed by beautiful Alpine *ledermädchens*, and stuffed with the downy pinions of Danish snow geese — or so I'd been told. Knowing what I'd paid for it, I didn't doubt the veracity of the provenance. I took a deep breath and sat down. *Bis vincit qui se vincit*: He conquers twice who conquers himself.

"I'm Lancelot Fleagle, *Chevalier.*"

"Hayden Konig, Chief of Police. Pleased to meet you." I extended my hand across the desk, but he didn't reach to meet it.

"Forgive me. I don't shake hands. You understand."

"Nope," I said, looking him in the eye. "I don't. Why don't you explain it to me?"

He was medium height and build, fleshy, and a little pudgy. His hair was receding and he had it cut short and spiked with some sort of goop that gave him the look of a fat, little hedgehog. He sported round, tortoise-shell eyeglasses and a sparse goatee that did little to cover up the fact that he had no chin to speak of. He was wearing a long, black cassock just like Father Dressler, but without the red cincture. His band cincture was black and he wasn't wearing a priest's dog collar.

"I must keep my fingers unimpaired," he snuffled. "I once had an ugly incident shaking hands with a lumberjack. I had a very bad bruise for almost a week." He wiggled his digits at me. "These are my instrument, as you well know."

"Are you ordained?" I asked, gesturing toward his dress.

"I've almost finished the discernment process."

"So, the answer is 'no.' You really haven't even started."

"Not yet, but the bishop says it's academic," he said, and waved his hand as though it were nothing, then changed the subject. "I've been going over the specs for the organ. It seems to be quite adequate for our use." He frowned and pouted his lips. "It's not really a concert instrument though, is it? Who is the designer?"

"It's a Baum-Boltoph, built here in North Carolina. Thirty-two stops and thirty-eight ranks across three manuals and pedal. Trompette en chamade, zimbelstern, and a nachtigall."

"Ridiculous," said the Chevalier, dismissively. "Who ever uses a nachtigall?"

A "nachtigall" was one of the toy stops that Baroque organs used to have in abundance. This one was made up of two small pipes, mounted upside down, blowing into a jar filled with water. It was meant to sound like a toy bird, or translated, a "nightingale." I didn't say that it was a delightful gift from Michael Baum, the organ builder, and I was happy to use it when I could. No, I didn't say that. I didn't say anything. I just smiled.

"Father Dressler told me there was quite a bit of money in St. Barnabas' coffers. Perhaps we can use some of that to upgrade the instrument and make it ... shall we say ... more inclined toward the French literature. I know a wonderful organ builder in Ontario who could make this organ playable in no time."

"That's always a possibility," I said, "but you know, my sabbatical is over at the end of June."

He ignored that comment and said, "I've looked over Sunday's music and it all seems to be in order. Thank you for preparing the choir. I wonder about your choice of hymns, though. They seem a bit pedantic. One might even say 'sententious.'" He managed a mild sneer in my direction.

"Yes, one might say that, if he didn't know what 'sententious' meant. Taking your meaning, I might agree with you, but since the hymns were chosen by Father Dressler, it really wasn't my place to say anything. I *am* on sabbatical, you know."

"Well, if Father chose them, I'm sure they're just fine." He held up the bulletin and seemed to peruse it in more detail, then said, "In fact, now that I look at the flow of the service closely, I can see where he's going with all this. Yes! Yes, this will be excellent for my first Sunday. Perfect, really. I shall improvise on the last hymn for my postlude!"

"Great," I said.

"I know the Bruckner *Tonto Ergum*, of course, but I don't know this offertory anthem."

"You mean *Tantum Ergo*? I believe that Tonto Ergum was the Lone Ranger's sidekick."

He reddened at his misspeak. Easy enough to do, and, Lord knows, I'm the worst offender, but he was starting to irritate me.

"You remember," I said, smiling, "*Tonto ergum kemosabe.*"

He ignored the barb. "Is the anthem accompanied?"

"It is. It's a little three-part Charpentier setting of Psalm 117. All the music is up on the console. Since we didn't have much rehearsal time, I thought it would be good to have something that could do double duty this Sunday morning and next Wednesday for the Evensong."

The Chevalier nodded his head thoughtfully, back in control. "That's a good, safe plan. Not what I would have done, but you know the choir better than I do right now." He leaned back in my chair and looked at the ceiling, his pudgy hands clasped over his belly. "Back when I was doing my study year in England, my mentor and dear friend, Sir David Willcocks, always said to me ..."

I stood up to leave and interrupted him. "If you have any questions about the organ, just have Marilyn give me a call. She has my cell number."

"Oh!" he said, brightly. "Why don't you give it to me as well?"

"It's a police number," I said. "I don't give it out."

* * *

I went and retrieved my gun from its hiding place under the organ bench. No sense in tempting fate.

Chapter 23

Rachel Barstow's house was positioned to take advantage of one of the loveliest gorge views I'd seen, and I'd seen a lot. Coming up the walk, Nancy and I had paused when the view came into sight, then made a slight detour around the house to admire the panorama. It stretched for miles and I could pick out Grandfather Mountain and several other well-known landmarks. Clouds bunched beneath us and crowded into the sides of the mountains. It was stunning.

"Wow!" said Nancy. "So this is how you rich folk live."

We made our way back to the front walkway and wandered through a number of gardens, both flower and herb, by the look of them, although they were now fallow. There was a greenhouse visible in the side yard and a number of fruit trees and arbors with bare vines.

The house was a large, two-story structure that owed its design to the Arts and Crafts look of the late 1920s. The wooden, Dutch lap siding was painted a greenish-gray to blend beautifully with the landscape. The accent paint was a creamy off-white, and the ceiling of the porch was painted in the old Southern tradition of powder or "haint" blue. This, according to whichever theory you chose to believe, was either to confuse the insects into thinking the ceiling was the sky, to scare away the evil spirits (haints), to extend the feeling of daylight, or just to bring good luck.

Stonework accentuated the house and included a flagstone walk, retaining walls, flower beds and porch pillars. It was quintessential Appalachian architecture, something out of a Thomas Kincaid painting. It looked as if it had been here for decades.

In reality, once one looked closely, it was obvious that it had been constructed in the past few years. The siding was cement board, the stonework showed not a crack, and the masonry was still well-pointed. The porch on which we were standing was constructed of some kind of PVC product designed to look like painted wood. Not that it didn't look good. It did. This was, as they said in the real estate biz, a high-end property. I knew that the view alone was probably worth a couple of million bucks.

We'd called and made an appointment. Nancy rang the doorbell and Rachel opened the door a few moments later and invited us in.

The inside of the house was what you might expect after having seen the view. We walked into a huge living room with vaulted, paneled ceilings, crisscrossed with gigantic timbers probably from the Pacific Northwest — at least, I'd never seen trees that large here in the southern part of the United States. The room was tastefully appointed in "mountain chic." The kitchen was open, featured a granite island that was larger than my first apartment and appointed with the latest in polished, stainless steel appliances, including a Wolf six burner gas range with a double oven and a huge subzero refrigerator. I knew this because I had the same models.

Rachel ushered us into the sitting area and we admired the view from a wall of plate glass that looked out over the gorge. A gas log fire blazed in the oversized fireplace. All the comforts of home at the click of a button.

"How may I help?" asked Rachel. "You said you had some questions."

"Just a few," I said. "We were looking at your *Pinterest* page and wondered about the wolfsbane."

Rachel nodded and repeated the poem.

O one berie, who planted you?
Our Ladie with her five fingers trewe,
thru all her miht and power,
She brought you hyd to flower,
hwæt I shall have my healthe.

She pronounced hyd "here," and hwæt "that."

"It's an ancient charm I found," she continued. "Probably medieval. It's supposed to protect you when harvesting it. They needed protection. Just picking the plant can be fatal."

"But you use it?" Nancy said.

"Don't be ridiculous! Didn't you hear me? Even *picking* the plant will kill you. I put it on the *Pinterest* page with a warning. In Europe it has been well-known since Roman times to be a potent and dangerous poison. They used wolfsbane to kill panthers, wolves, bears … whatever. The Roman naturalist

Plinius describes it as 'plant arsenic.' It's deadly in almost all its forms."

"*Debitum naturae*," I said. "Debt of nature."

"Exactly."

"Then why was it used as a medicine?" I asked. "Like the charm says."

"Because medieval people were much more ignorant than the Romans. In Chinese and Arabic folk medicine, its roots were used for the treatment of various diseases. Later on, Plinius wrote about its application in ophthalmology. As the healing dose was very difficult to determine, most patients died. In the eighteenth century, it was introduced to medicine by a Viennese physician — I can't remember his name — but even after that, no one used it. Too dangerous. Then, in the sixties, when hippies were trying everything, they decided that maybe smoking it would be a good high. It wasn't."

"So you don't use it in your practice as an herbalist?" I asked.

"No, I do *not!*"

"Do you grow it?"

"Absolutely not. I've got three kids in elementary school. That would be absurd!"

I asked, "Well, have you seen it growing around here? It would be easy to spot."

"Sure," said Rachel. "It grows wild. You can see it in the late spring and summer all over the place. It's quite a beautiful flower. Now, if I may ask, why all the questions?"

I said, "It seems the three women were killed by the aconite. The Queen of Poisons."

"Wolfsbane," said Rachel with a nod.

"Or monkshood," said Nancy. "It was found in all the women's systems. It caused all three heart attacks."

"That's *terrible!* You suspect me?"

"You're an herbalist," I said. "You have quite a working knowledge of wolfsbane."

"I have quite a working knowledge of hundreds, maybe *thousands,* of herbs and plants. I have a master's degree in botany from the University of Florida specializing in the flora of the Blue Ridge region. I worked for the Forest Service for six years. I make my living giving talks on the properties of plants."

"Pretty good living," said Nancy, looking around.

Rachel harumphed. "My ex-husband is the North American CEO of Mitsubishi. After twenty-six years he decided he'd rather have some arm candy, so he married a college sophomore. Her name is Taffi. With an i."

Nancy gave a small snort, not a laugh, but close.

Rachel raised her eyebrows and smiled for the first time since we'd sat down. "However," she said, "I and my children shall be comfortable for the rest of our lives."

"Well, you see why we had to ask," I said. "Besides the wolfsbane being on your *Pinterest* page, it was you who recommended reading *See Your Shadow*, and, according to the rest of the book club, you were the only one to read it before the murders happened."

"I suppose that's true," said Rachel, seeming to think about the possibility. "Boy, that was a stupid thing to do. I just hope that choosing that book didn't set all this into motion." She looked at me with an expression of real concern. "I trust you don't still suspect one of the Bookworms."

I got to my feet without answering and was followed by Nancy. "Thanks for your time," I said. We went to the front door, said goodbye, then walked onto the front porch and down the walk toward my truck.

"What do you think?" Nancy asked.

"She didn't do it," I said, shaking my head. "Can't see it. Of course, that's just my gut yacking."

"I agree with your gut," said Nancy. "So where does that leave us?"

"Driving back to town."

* * *

We rattled back to St. Germaine, "rattled" being the operative word because no matter how I tried to get the old 1962 Chevy tightened up, everything was jiggling loose. After almost fifty years, the old girl seemed to have finally had enough. The only thing I'd done to her was put in a good sound system. Other than that, she was all original and untouched.

"You know," said Nancy, "I have a friend who does auto restorations. This rattletrap would be like new. Better even."

"It may be time," I said. "Meg wants me to get one of those new fancy trucks. A Tundra, or maybe a Chevy diesel, but I keep putting it off. What do you think a restoration would cost?"

"Probably about the same as one of those, but you'd have your truck back and another twenty years to drive it. You could be buried in this thing."

"It's a comforting thought," I said. "Let's do it. Will you give him a call?"

"Sure will!"

We pulled up in front of Bud's new house. He wasn't there, but Roberto's crew was swarming like ants over the property. It had been just over a week since the construction workers began the renovation, and it looked to me as if they'd be finished in another few days.

"Nah," said Roberto. "Sure, we're done with the big stuff ...walls, electric, drywall, cabinets, plumbing and junk like that. It's the finish work that takes the time. We've got all the shelves to build, more trim to put up, painting. We're redoing these hardwoods." He looked around, then continued, "Light fixtures, security system, cameras ... "

"I get it, I get it," I said. "How long do you think?"

"Another two weeks, give or take."

"That's great! When you have a definite date, let us know and we'll set up our Grand Opening."

"Will do," said Roberto.

Chapter 24

"I've made you breakfast," said Meg, "and in return, it is your duty to come to church and introduce the new organist to the choir. I'm the choir president, and I insist."

"You insist, eh?" It was tough to argue with Meg when she insisted, especially when she was dressed to the nines for church.

"Yes, I do. It's the least you can do for the choir since you're abandoning us ... to *him*." Meg had already met the Chevalier.

"I'm on sabbatical."

"So you've said."

"Yet I shall do as you bid, m'lady, and come and introduce everyone." Truth be told, I was planning on going to church anyway. Call it professional curiosity.

Meg said, "He's called for the choir to be robed and ready at ten o'clock. An hour before the service."

"He probably wants a little rehearsal time to get a feel for the group. I know I would."

"Yes, probably," said Meg, glumly. "You might as well take the rest of your detective story. It'll be the last bit of fun we'll ever have."

"I don't think so. From what I know of the Chevalier, he wouldn't appreciate it. Anyway, it's not quite finished. I've been busy for the last couple of days. I'll get it finished by next week and you can smuggle it in if you want."

On the way into town, we listened to some Renaissance motets being sung by a fine octet of voices, and I told Meg about Nancy's idea to restore the old pickup. If we had needed to rely on the four-wheel drive this morning, we would have been in the old Chevy truck, but there was no need on a day like this, still cold, but with the sun shining and the roads clear. We were in Meg's Lexus, which was a much more comfortable ride.

"Would there be new shock absorbers?" she asked.

"A whole new suspension. New seats, upholstery, a rebuilt engine, transmission, paint, everything."

"It sounds like a good plan," she said. "How long will it take?"

"I haven't gotten that far. I haven't even talked to the guy. He's a friend of Nancy's. I suspect it will take at least a month or so. Maybe a little longer."

"Do it," said Meg. "You can go and rent something while your truck is in the shop. Get something fun — like a convertible."

"It's twenty-eight degrees out," I said. "How much use do you think we'll get out of a convertible?"

"Hmm," said Meg. "Okay, how about a minivan?"

"How about a four-wheel drive Suburban? We still have two months of winter to worry about."

"Only if the groundhog sees his shadow," said Meg.

I looked at her warily. "How did you know about the groundhog?"

"What?" she said. "Groundhog Day? Everyone knows about Groundhog Day. It's not a secret. If the groundhog sees his shadow, six more weeks of winter." She looked at me sideways. "What's going on? Something's up."

"Nothing's up," I said. "That's what I meant. Groundhog Day."

Meg looked at me, but didn't say anything.

* * *

At ten o'clock sharp, I walked up the stairs to join the choir. It was strangely quiet and I wondered if any of the singers had bothered to show up except Meg, whom I knew was here. We had arrived at church at 9:45 and I had headed for the coffee pot in the kitchen, while Meg decided to go on upstairs and get settled. By the time I'd coffeed up and climbed the stairs to the choir loft, I was met with quite a sight — eighteen choir members struggling to fasten ruffs to the collars of their choir robes. The Chevalier hadn't waited for my introduction.

A choir ruff is a conservative fashion statement to say the least and has its roots firmly in the Elizabethan era. In the late nineteen and twentieth centuries ruffs had been relegated to church choirs, then finally, choristers: that is, boys and girls. I had never seen an adult choir wearing ruffs and I'd seen my share of choirs. That didn't mean there weren't any. I just hadn't seen them. Now I had.

Shakespearean ruffs could be twelve inches wide or even larger, but those fashion monstrosities, luckily, had been outlawed by Philip IV of Spain in 1643, or, no doubt, the Master of the Musik would have gone with something even larger than the eight-inch collar jutting from under the chins of the unfortunate singers. As it was, the choir looked as though their heads were all resting on giant, pleated, supper plates. Had it been possible to hot-glue some vegetables around the edges, the choir could have auditioned for the Entrée Chorus in *Donner Party — the Musical*. Mark Wells turned to me with terror in his eyes. His graying beard scraggled across the top of the ruff like an old rat trying to escape down the front of his choir robe, held by its hind legs in a pitiless snare. "Help us," Mark silently mouthed.

I wanted to laugh. I might have laughed. Then Meg caught my eye and the laugh turned to ice in my throat. I'd seen that look before, so I stifled my mirth and sputtered, "Nice ruffs." The choir was absolutely silent, and those who had managed to attach their own collars were helping those less fortunate. It was like watching a war movie where they all knew they were about to die, but bravely accepted their fate and donned their uniforms for the last charge. There was nothing to be said. No final goodbyes, no speeches. Just the mute camaraderie that certain doom creates.

"Nice ruffs, indeed," said the Chevalier Lancelot Fleagle, his gelled and spiked hair standing at attention. He adjusted his glasses. "These are my personal crinoline ruffs handmade in Holland. I carry them with me. Thirty of them."

Steve DeMoss, standing next to me, made a small, pitiful mewing sound.

"It's very difficult to find ruffs that will fit an adult choir," said the Chevalier. "It's especially difficult to find craftsmanship like this. This is handwoven Dutch crinoline — horsehair and linen. The horsehair gives them extra stiffness. They don't even need to be starched, but I have it done anyway."

"They are something special," I said. "Truly."

The choir, one by one, fastened their ruffs and sat down in their chairs, gingerly, because now they had no vision below their chins no matter how they tilted their heads. They used their hands to find their seats, then lowered themselves gently onto the cushions.

"There are two advantages to the choir ruff," announced the Chevalier. "First, of course, is the obvious: wearing a ruff, the choir considers itself to be professional and therefore conducts itself accordingly. Secondly, the singers are forced to hold their music at the correct angle and therefore keep the organist in their field of vision. Marjorie managed a guttural, "Gaaack," as she tried to croak out a rebuttal.

"Now, let's sing."

The Chevalier played a five-note scale and ascended by half-steps as the choir tried to follow his lead. He changed the pattern every few minutes with no explanation, and the choir struggled to keep up. I had to take the blame for this. I usually warmed up the choir using a chorale that we all knew or had been working on. At Christmastime, *Lo, How a Rose*, in Lent, *O Sacred Head*, F. Melius Christiansen's *Lamb of God*, that sort of thing. We'd do it in different keys and work the vowel sounds. There was no one way to do a choral warmup — other directors went up and down the scale and got beautiful results, but the choir just wasn't used to it. The Chevalier had no patience with them and, after about five minutes of ear-tearing scales, decided that the group would probably sound better if they *didn't* warm up.

"Choir," he said, using a tone that implied that he had their confidence, "we *really* have some work to do."

"Gaaack," managed Marjorie.

"I'll need you all to come for a rehearsal tomorrow evening. I know it's Monday, but we have a major performance on Wednesday and I'm busy on Tuesday, so Monday will have to do. Seven o'clock. It shouldn't take more than two hours. You there ..." He pointed at Marjorie sitting at the end of the tenor row. "You really don't need to attend. You're excused."

"Hang on!" said Meg. "You can't just ..."

"*I thought I made it clear,*" barked the new director. "*No talking!*"

He glared across the choir, but his stare was less than intimidating. Still, Meg's mouth clamped shut.

"Now to the anthem," he said. "*Laudate Dominum* by Charpentier." He played the introduction, then stopped abruptly and said, "Dr. Burch?"

Dr. Ian Burch, PhD, stood up and recited, "Marc-Antoine Charpentier, born 1643, died 1704. A French composer of the Baroque era, Charpentier was a prolific and versatile composer, producing music of the highest quality in several genres, including works for the stage in collaboration with Molière. His mastery in the composition of sacred vocal music was recognized and acknowledged by his contemporaries. If you'd like to learn more, please visit my website: www.ianburch.phd.com."

Ian sat down and offered Tiff St. James a greasy grin. Green teeth. I watched her shudder.

"What a wonderful asset to the choir," said the Chevalier, clapping his pudgy hands together in delight. "A true music historian. I bow my head to you, Dr. Burch." Then he did just that with the fingers of one hand extended in a twirl of affected elegance.

A moment later, and without warning, he started the introduction again. The choir had been stunned to silence, but managed to come in when the time came. Badly, and not all at the same time, but who could blame them? The Chevalier didn't stop and regroup, now hearing what he'd expected to hear in the first place. He plowed straight through the piece throwing in Baroque ornamentation here and there, giving the little anthem a bit of pizzaz. He was a good organist, no doubt about that.

Father Dressler appeared beside me, beaming. "He's brilliant, isn't he?"

"He's a fine player," I agreed.

"I've never heard better," declared Father Dressler. "He and I are of one mind when it comes to the art of liturgy. We act as one."

The choir finished miserably, mangled the cutoff, and ground to a halt a few beats after the Chevalier had finished playing. He signed audibly and sarcastically and said, "Yes, choir, we certainly do have a *lot* of work to do."

Father Dressler said loudly, "We want to welcome the Chevalier here to St. Barnabas." He started applauding wildly, and one by one, most the members of the choir halfheartedly joined him. Some didn't. "Now, remember," said the priest, once he'd finished his ovation, "we will all genuflect this morning. Not only during the procession like last Sunday, but also when you come down for communion, which all of you forgot to do last week. Remember, you set the tone for the congregation. They will follow your lead. Stop, go to one knee, wait three beats, then rise and continue. If you need help, an usher will assist you. During the processional hymn, the Chevalier will be improvising between the verses and it may be mesmerizing to you. I implore you, don't stop to listen! Please keep the procession moving."

The choir had no comment. I turned, walked back down the steps, chose a seat in the back of the sanctuary, and waited for the service to begin.

* * *

165

In my opinion, the highlight of the service, as it was whenever he took part, was Benny Dawkins' display of the thurifutic arts. As a two-time world champion thurifer, he had complete command over his medium, and his medium was smoke. Benny carried his own thurible, and this incense pot was platinum, rather than the traditional gold. It hung from matching Figaro chains and was set with polished obsidian from Mount Vesuvius. This hand-made thurible had been presented to Benny by the Archbishop of Naples after he had brought the man to tears during an Epiphany service in which he had created a remarkably lifelike rendering of Botticelli's *Adoration of the Magi* during the censing of the scriptures.

Most of the thurifer's display took place at the beginning of the service during the processional, for it was here that the smoke-slinger could really shine, but Benny didn't stop there. Yes, the processional was something to behold, and on this particular frigid morning on the last Sunday of January Benny came down the aisle using his now-famous maneuver, St. Sebastian's Revenge: arrows of smoke darting into the space between the congregants and leaping into the air before dissipating into nothingness. Then, when he had ascended the steps of the chancel and was standing before the altar, the thurible became a blur in his hands, and before us, hanging in the space between heaven and earth, was a traditional Shinto garden scene. Monochromatic waters moved gently across a serene lake, a waterfall tumbled in the distance, trees swayed in the peaceful breeze, then, suddenly, two cranes leapt from the rushes with beating wings and ascended into the rafters. From where I was sitting, the intake of collective breaths from the congregation was audible, even over the music. A few moments later the smoke dropped away, leaving the priest standing behind the altar, his hands raised in prayer, as if he had appeared by magic. The effect was breathtaking and we felt as though we were in the presence of holiness.

This was Benny's entrance and most thurifers' bread and butter, but even more impressive was the censing of the altar during the Great Thanksgiving, that part of the service that leads us into communion. Most priests at this point will take the pot from the thurifer and swing it clumsily at the Eucharistic elements like they are trying to douse them with lighter fluid. To his credit, Father Dressler allowed Benny to do it.

"In the name of the Father, Son, and Holy Ghost," Father Dressler said, as two smoke signals rose slowly from the cloud surrounding the altar, looking like nothing much until they were ten feet above everyone's heads, then morphing into two characters: the Alpha and the Omega. Then the Alpha character became a dove that swooped through the middle of the Omega and winged its way heavenward.

"Holy smokes!" I muttered, then smiled at my own joke. "Holy smokes ..."

* * *

Moosey and Bernie performed admirably in their acolyting debut, nothing being set afire that wasn't supposed to be. The choir wasn't atrocious, although most of them found that kneeling and getting back up with a stiff choir ruff on was totally different from performing the same feat unruffled. Almost all of them needed help from the two ushers stationed on either side of the center aisle. Despite each member of the choir genuflecting, none of the congregation, including me, followed suit.

The communion anthem was worse than the offertory anthem, neither of them being particularly good, and the Psalm wasn't their best effort either. The Chevalier didn't bother to conduct with either a head-nod, a look, or the occasional free hand. The choir would be able to handle his style eventually, but not at first blush.

And, as was expected, Meg was fit to be tied.

Chapter 25

Pete, Meg, Cynthia, and I were sitting in the Slab on Monday morning having a cup of coffee. Meg was waiting for Bev to come in then they were going down to Asheville to meet with some other investment folks about opening a branch of their nonprofit down in the big city. Pete was taking a break from cooking, and Cynthia wasn't working tables this morning since it was her morning over at the courthouse.

"Who hired this guy, anyway?" asked Cynthia. "The priest, I mean. He sounds singularly awful."

"I was not on that committee," said Meg. "I don't remember who all it was, but Bev was on it, that's for sure."

"Joyce Cooper, Mark Wells, Bob Solomon, Georgia, and me," said Bev, appearing at the table. She pulled up a chair from an adjoining table and squeezed in. "Also, Fred May and Francis Passaglio. We're all meeting on Thursday. It's the first time we can get together. An emergency meeting."

"I guess you all should start looking for a full-time rector sometime soon," I said. "Like, maybe immediately."

"I guess," said Bev, "but you know that Father Dressler has already been marshaling his minions: the dispossessed, disenfranchised, the unappreciated, the poor in spirit. He's been at St. Barnabas two weeks and already has a claque. He's garnering support for his application even before it's been accepted. He's told several people privately that they'll be on the vestry within the year and then they can help him affect the changes that need to happen."

"How do you know that?" Meg asked.

"Because Goldi Fawn Birtwhistle can't keep her trap shut, bless her little blabbermouthing heart. We've got to do something soon or it will be too late."

Meg and Bev both glared across the table and gave me the stinkeye.

"Don't look at me," I said. "I'm on sabbatical."

"You're the whole reason we're in this mess," said Bev. "If you were still in the choir loft, at least there would be some semblance of normality. You could ride herd till this guy blew out of here."

"You're not blaming this on me," I said. "This one's on you."

Bev sighed. "I know. Can't I just pretend it's someone else's fault?"

"You can blame Pete," I offered.

"Sure," said Pete. "Why not?"

"I'm so mad I could just spit," said Meg. "You know, he just came right out and fired Marjorie. She's been in the choir since Abraham was in knee pants!"

Cynthia laughed. "What did you just say?"

Meg put her head down on the table. "I know! I'm so upset, I'm using my mother's expressions!"

"There's a big rehearsal tonight," I said to Pete and Cynthia. "It could even get worse."

"I'm sure it will," moaned Meg.

"I'm thinking about not going," said Bev. "Maybe it's time we *all* took sabbaticals."

"You could," I said, "but that's probably what the Chevalier wants. Then he'll go over to the university, hire a bunch of ringers using the music fund money, and run the rest of you volunteers out of there."

"*What?*" said Bev. "Over my dead body! This is *our* choir!"

"You want something to eat?" Noylene asked, putting down a clean place setting and coffee cup in front of Bev. "Or are you just taking up space like the rest of 'em?"

"Just taking up space, thanks," said Bev, "but I would like some coffee."

"'Course you would," grumbled Noylene.

"What's wrong, honey?" Meg said to her. "You are way out of sorts this morning."

"It's Hog," she said. "He's making me crazy. I gotta go over to Boone and get him some medicine. And, according to His Majesty, I gotta go this morning. It can't wait till tomorrow!"

"Nothing serious, I hope," said Meg.

"Not as far as I'm concerned. He saw on TV that he's got reptile dysfunction."

"Huh?" said Cynthia. "What on earth is that?"

"Reptile dysfunction," said Noylene. "I guess that means his reptile don't work."

"Ohhh," said Cynthia, then laughed. Meg joined her.

"It ain't funny!" snarled Noylene. "Those pills are ten bucks a piece. I'll tell you this much. They sure ain't worth ten bucks to *me*. I wouldn't give you a plugged nickel!"

The cowbell jangled against the glass door and I saw Nancy come in. She shed her coat, hung it on the wall and wandered through the maze of tables to where we were sitting in the back. She pulled up yet another chair and we all scooched closer to make room.

"I thought of something," she said. "You remember when that article came out in the *Tattler*? The one about the victims?"

"Sure," I said.

"Do we still have a copy somewhere?"

I shook my head. "I don't."

Everyone else at the table also answered in the negative.

"Gimme a minute," said Noylene. "Lemme look in the back. I've got a stack of those things that I save for wrapping old, used color foils. Which week you looking for?"

"Two Fridays ago," said Nancy, and Noylene disappeared into the kitchen.

"What are you thinking?" I asked.

"Something Helen said to Annette. It's been bothering me for two weeks and I finally figured out what it was."

"Well, don't keep us in suspense," said Cynthia. "What was it?"

"Hang on," said Nancy. "I just need to read the article again."

Noylene walked out of the kitchen and handed Nancy a copy of the *Tattler*. The headline read "Foreclosed Properties Cloak Gristly Murders."

"That's the one," said Nancy. "Gristly Murders. Thanks."

She pulled out her pen and started reading the article silently to herself, then stopped, circled a sentence and said, in her best law enforcement voice, "A-ha!"

"Aha?" I said.

"A-ha! I have solved it!"

"Solved the murders?" Pete said.

"Practically."

"Let's hear it, then," I said.

Nancy laid the newspaper on the table and spread it out so we could see where she drew her circle in blue ink, then read, "The detectives at the scene acknowledged that all the women were found in the same circumstances. It is not known whether the missing earring was common to all three victims."

"Well, that's true enough," said Meg.

"Sure it is," said Nancy. "Here's the thing: Helen snuck into the room with us just after we found the body. Then she got queasy and went into the hall. When she was outside the bedroom, I checked and pointed out the missing earring to Hayden. But Helen didn't ever see that. She wasn't there. *That's what we were missing.*"

Meg said, "Maybe she heard you talking about it."

I shook my head. "Nope. I remember exactly what happened. Nancy never uttered a word because Helen was in the hall. She pulled Crystal's hair back off her shoulders, checked her earrings, then put her hair back."

Nancy nodded. "So Helen had no way of knowing at that point that Crystal was missing an earring. She came back into the room, but we were already standing back up."

"Couldn't she have heard it from one of the Bookworms?" asked Cynthia. "You told them, didn't you?"

"Not until after the paper came out on the next Friday. We didn't tell anyone. Kent knew, Dave, and us. You or Pete didn't tell anyone, did you?"

"Not me," said Cynthia, looking over at Pete. He shook his head. "Nope."

"How about Mom?" said Meg. "She was the one who discovered the similarities to the book."

"Didn't tell her," I said, shaking my head again. "She read *See Your Shadow*, but we never said anything about the missing earrings to her."

"There it is," said Nancy triumphantly. "Another case solved."

"Dadgummit!" I said. "I should have caught it. That's the kind of detective stuff I'm really good at."

Meg leaned over and kissed me on the cheek. "I'm sure you would have figured it out eventually, sweetie."

"That Helen Pigeon!" said Nancy in disgust. "I knew I should have arrested her straight away."

"No harm done," I said. "Why don't we have another cup of coffee and then go and get her?"

We would have done just that, but at that exact moment, who should come into the Slab but Helen Pigeon and Monica Jones? They took a table next to the large front window and positioned themselves so they could watch the snow, which was beginning to fall again. It was a pretty snow, light and sparkly in the half-sunshine. Looking closely, you could make out the individual snowflakes as they drifted in, big as quarters. Noylene, who had been privy to our conversation, eyed the couple warily, not sure whether to go over to the table or not. I nodded to her. Let Helen have her last cup of coffee, I thought. She won't be getting anything this good in the big house.

We finished at a leisurely pace, chatting about the weather, St. Barnabas politics, and Meg and Bev's new project in Asheville. Then Nancy and I excused ourselves and walked over to Helen Pigeon's table.

"Helen," I said. "We'd really like to speak with you."

"Can it wait?" said Helen. "Monica and I are on our way into Boone."

Monica said, "Maybe we should postpone our trip, Helen. The snow is really coming down." She gestured toward the window and we could see she was right. "I don't want to go down the mountain in a snowstorm."

"You're right," said Helen. "I hate to miss the sale at the Mast General Store, though. I guess I took a personal day for nothing."

"You're skipping school?" asked Nancy.

"I have four months left before I retire and about three years in personal leave built up. At this point I can afford to take a day here and there."

"That's great," I said. "We'd appreciate it if you'd come with us to the station. We have a few questions for you. It's about the evening we found Crystal Latimore in your house. We need to rely on your memory for a couple of things."

"Have you discovered something?" said Helen, excitement evident in her voice. "Can I help with the investigation?"

"You certainly can and will," I said, helping Helen to her feet. Nancy had her coat and handed it to her.

"You'll excuse us," I said to Monica, who, unlike Helen, seemed to know something was amiss. Monica nodded and watched us warily.

We walked out into the weather and down the sidewalk toward the police station, the snow muffling our footsteps. We didn't say anything to Helen and I sensed that she was beginning to feel uncomfortable. One block later we walked into the station. Dave was sitting at his desk behind the counter, working on his laptop, and looked up as we entered. I ushered Helen into my office and offered her a chair. I took the one behind my desk. Nancy stood. Dave listened in from his desk.

"Helen," I said. "We have a problem." Good cop.

Helen now looked scared.

"Remember back when we were in your house and Nancy told you to stay on the porch?"

Helen nodded mutely.

"You didn't stay on the porch. You came into the house, followed us to the back bedroom and walked in on the body of Crystal Latimore. Remember that?"

She nodded again, her eyes widening and her lower lip beginning to quiver.

"You got a little queasy and went into the hall, then came back into the bedroom while we were working the crime scene. Do you remember the last thing I told you before you left?"

"Do I need a lawyer?" asked Helen in a quavery, little voice.

"You're damn right you need a lawyer!" barked Nancy. Bad cop. Helen's head snapped around and she looked with horror at Lieutenant Nancy Parsky, one hand on her gun, glowering, now all business.

Helen broke down in sobs. "All right. I admit it. I'm so sorry ..." She buried her head in her hands.

"You have the right to remain silent," said Nancy. "That means no crying."

Chapter 26

"Everything you say can be used against you in a court of law," continued Nancy. "You have the right to an attorney."

"*Wahhhhh,*" wailed Helen, no longer able to contain her anguish.

I interrupted. "Helen," I said, "why did you do it?"

"I didn't mean to," she blubbered. "No one was supposed to find out!"

"How could you think no one would find out?" said Nancy. "Of course we're going to find out."

Helen tried to get hold of herself, failed, and then sobbed, "She told me no one would know."

"Who told you that?" I said.

"Annette."

"Annette Passaglio?" I asked.

"She said no one would know it was me who talked to her for the newspaper article. She said I'd be a confidential source! Confidential! I should have known she'd give me up!"

"Oh, for heaven's sake," said Nancy. "We're not talking about the stupid article. We're talking about killing those three women."

"What?" said Helen. "You think I killed them?"

"Yeah, we do," growled Nancy. "You killed them and put them in the closets."

"I never did!" exclaimed Helen, the tears gone as fast as they appeared. "I could never kill anyone." She paused, then shrugged and said, almost to herself, "Well, maybe that Pat Strother." She looked at me and glared. "Did you know that she took my parking spot twice last week? That's *my* spot over by the library! I'm a volunteer. I came by the police station and told Dave, but *oh, nooo,* he's too busy! The police are always *sooo* busy!"

"Helen," I said. "Back to the point. The story in the newspaper said that Crystal Latimore had a missing earring."

"She did, didn't she?"

"Yes, but how did you know that?"

"Everyone knows that," said Helen. "It's common knowledge."

"It is now," said Nancy, "but it wasn't then."

Confusion clouded Helen's face. "Huh? I don't understand."

"When the story came out," I explained, "there was no way you could have known about the earring. But you did. You knew that Crystal only had one earring."

"Oh, my *God!*" said Helen, her eyes growing big as saucers. She lowered her voice to a trembling whisper. "Do you think I really might have killed them? Like one of those dual personality killers, or maybe homicidal somnambulism like in that movie that was just on HBO?"

"Oh, brother," said Nancy. She looked at me and rolled her eyes skyward.

"How exciting," said Helen. "I'll have to use the sleepwalking defense." She wrinkled her nose in thought. "I wonder if I can sleepwalk over to Pat Strother's house. I'll give her a surprise, I can tell you."

"Go on home, Helen," I said, sighing. "We'll call you if we need you."

"And don't leave town," Nancy added in disgust.

* * *

"Well, that was two hours I'll never get back," huffed Meg when she climbed into the truck.

"I take it you did not enjoy the emergency Monday night rehearsal."

"No one enjoyed the rehearsal. It was like pulling teeth. Pulling them, then putting them back in and pulling them again."

"Ouch."

"We bludgeoned the Anglican Chant for forty-five minutes, working on 'shading,' and *still* didn't finish. I'll tell you this much: that man is a walking advertisement for gun control."

"How so?" I asked.

"If anyone in the choir had been packing heat, he'd be stuffed under the organ right now."

I chuckled and pulled out of my parking space at the police station. I'd brought Meg to choir practice in the truck, then spent my time at the station doing some after-hours work. It had started snowing midmorning and had continued off and on all day. The roads were still fine, but four-wheel drive was a better option once we got off the main thoroughfares. The truck might be old, but the heater worked like a champ.

175

"He gave the solos in the *Mag* and *Nunc* to Ian," said Meg.

"That might be interesting. Ian's a good countertenor."

"It's *not* interesting. They fawned over each other until I thought I would vomit." She raised her voice in theatrical exaggeration. "*Ohhh*, Dr. Burch, how do you think this mordent should be executed? *Ohhh, Monsieur Chevalier*, we should approach the embellishing note from above in the way of Michel de Fromage in his treatise of 1432. *Ohhh*, Dr. Burch, I kiss your feet. How lucky we are to have your expertise!"

It was a good imitation of both men and I laughed in appreciation. "How about Marjorie? Was she there?"

Meg shook her head sadly.

"I'll go by and talk to her," I said. "Does the choir have a plan?"

Meg sighed. "I talked to a few members as we were walking out and told them about him hiring a new choir from scratch using the music fund money. They agreed that we'll stand it as long as we can, just to keep that from happening. Once he's ensconced, we may never get him out."

"That does happen," I agreed. "I've seen it more than a few times. How about Georgia? She's the Senior Warden. Was she there tonight?"

"She wasn't there. She didn't sing yesterday, either. Maybe she's under the weather."

"Maybe she threw up her hands and she and Dwain went on a cruise. It's about that time of year."

"Maybe," said Meg, then changed the subject. "How much is in that music fund? If he does hire a new choir, how long can he keep going?"

"Depends, but it could be a long time. I've been putting my salary into the fund since I got rich. We've used a lot of it over the years, but I think there's probably close to two."

"Two thousand?" said Meg.

"No, dear. Two *hundred* thousand."

"Kripes!" Meg said. "It's been years since I was Senior Warden and I never worried about the fund because you were in charge, so tell me again. The church musician has complete discretion over the money?"

"Yep. Sweet, huh?"

"The priest can't get at it? The vestry either?"

"Nope. Sole discretion of the church musician. He does need to be transparent and everything must go through the vestry to keep all the spending above board, but the funds are at his disposal for the musical needs of the church."

"How about an *interim* church musician?" she asked.

"Sure," I said. "An interim needs to hire instrumentalists, buy music, stuff like that."

"How about a *sabbatical replacement* musician?"

"Same deal. If the Chevalier wants to hire twenty choral singers tomorrow and pay them each a thousand dollars a month, he can do it. At least until the money runs out."

"Oh, my," said Meg. "Does he know this?"

"All he has to do is read the guidelines set down for the music fund."

"I'm sure he's already done that," said Meg.

"Pretty sure he has."

"He probably thinks he's died and gone to church musician heaven."

"It is a sweetheart deal," I said. "Of course, since he's drawing a salary ..."

"*Your* salary," said Meg.

"Yes, my salary, there won't be anything added to the fund. There's not even a music line item in the budget because we didn't need one. Anyway, don't worry about it. I'll be back in June."

"I am worried," said Meg. "What if those two take over?"

"I don't see it happening," I said.

"Do *you* have a plan?"

"Um ... no. Not really. But these things tend to work out."

Chapter 27

Gliding silently through the gloaming of a nameless Mesozoic sea, the giant mosasaur was blissfully unaware of the trilobites clicking ravenously in the primordial slime far below, trilobites that due to their easily fossilized exoskeleton would become part of the strata and eventually find their way through the rock crusher at the Mercury Concrete Factory and into the sidewalk where we now stood. Sixty-eight million years later, Klingle looked at me with a cold, fishy eye.

"What's it gonna be, Klingle?" I asked. "Is it the big sleep for me?"

"Ja, ja. Der grosse Schlaf."

"Mind telling me what you've got to do with the St. Groundlemas merger?"

"I have nothing to do with it."

"Then why not pack those 38s back in your dirndl and call it a day?"

"I'm afraid I can't do that. You are bound to discover the truth."

I waited for her to unburden her soul. They all unburdened their souls just about now. They couldn't just shoot and shut up about it. They had to tell me a tale. It was what separated me and Pedro from the mosasaurs.

"I murdered Anne Dante," Klingle pringled. "I had to. She was responsible for my father being eaten by snow tigers in Mexico after the expedition was lost in an avalanche."

I nodded knowingly. "Deus ex Machina, eh? I should have seen it coming."

"Huh?" ringled Klingle. "Don't you want to hear the rest of my story? I think you'll find it fascinating and then I can shoot you knowing that at least you will have some appreciation, however brief, of the ignominy that I've suffered. What has Deus ex Machina got to do with anything?"

Bang! went Pedro's gat, bang! bang!

"Deus ex Machina," repeated Pedro after he'd calmly put three dingles into Klingle's shingle. "A rather debatable

178

and often criticized form of literary device whereby an implausible concept or character is brought into the story in order to make the conflict in the story resolve and to bring about a pleasing solution."

"Glad you shook loose of the cantoring," I said. "I thought it was curtains, for sure."

"Nah. Not curtains. Petticoats," said Pedro, adjusting his crinolines. "I gotta get back. They're just now getting to the Credo and I have a reputation to protect."

* * *

"Another dead end," said Nancy. We were sitting in the police station, puzzling over our dilemma. Dave was out, hopefully writing some traffic tickets.

"I agree," I said. "Helen Pigeon didn't do it. We're missing something. We need to find out what the three women had in common."

"Do we revisit Dr. Jaeger? They were all her patients. So far that's all we have."

I nodded. "I guess so. I can't see that she was involved in this, though. Do you still have that photo of Darla's medicine cabinet on your phone?"

"Yep. I'll shoot it to the desktop."

A few seconds later, she opened the photo up on the large monitor on Dave's desk, then pointed to the bottle of pills. "Premarin," she said. "The prescription date is last November. Dr. Alison Jaeger, prescribing physician. Filled at the CVS in Boone. No automatic refills."

"Nothing special," I said, looking over her shoulder. "How about the drug store?"

"Maybe," said Nancy, "but almost everyone I know uses that CVS."

"The pharmacist?" I said. "A pharmacist would certainly be well versed in aconite. As well as every other poison, for that matter. Jed Pierce works down in Boone. Is he at the CVS?"

"I don't know. I can find out real quick," said Nancy, pulling her phone out. "You think Jed has a connection with the three victims?"

"He lives in town," I answered. "He would have known Darla for sure. Maybe he saw Crystal on television. There were lots of people around town who knew Amy. It's not that much of a stretch."

Nancy's cell phone connected and she asked a couple of questions of the person on the other end.

"Jed Pierce doesn't work at CVS. The pharmacist knows him, but she says he works at the Walmart pharmacy."

I looked back at the photo on the computer screen. "TMJ disorder," I said.

"TMJ? I don't get it." Nancy looked hard at the monitor.

"Alison Jaeger said that Amy Ventura came in complaining about TMJ."

"Okay," said Nancy. "What's TMJ?"

"It's a jaw thing," I said. "I know, because it's a complaint among singers. I've known several people who had it. Look it up on Google."

Nancy opened a browser window, typed the info into the search engine and clicked on a link.

"TMJ," she read aloud. "More properly called temporo-mandibular joint disorder. The temporomandibular joint is the hinge joint that connects the lower jaw to the temporal bone of the skull, which is immediately in front of the ear on each side of your head. The disorder occurs as a result of problems with the jaw, mandibular joint, bite, or surrounding facial muscles. Very painful." She looked away from the monitor and up at me. "You think this has anything to do with the murders?"

I shrugged. "Maybe. Dr. Jaeger said that she prescribed some pain medication and referred her."

"Referred her to who?" asked Nancy.

"That's the question, isn't it?" I said, then tapped the picture, still visible in the corner of the screen, with the eraser end of a pencil. "Look here." Behind the bottle of Premarin was a black case made of hard plastic. "Remember this?"

"A retainer," said Nancy, a slow smile creeping across her face. "You think the referral was made to an orthodontist?"

"Maybe not at first," I said, "but read this." I tapped back on the article.

Nancy read, "Problems of TMJ are often aggravated by the lower jaw being positioned too far back so that the blood vessels and nerves of the TMJ are compressed. In phase two of TMJ treatment, neuromuscular orthodontics can relieve this pressure and reduce and pain by moving your teeth to stabilize your jaws in a new, more comfortable position. This movement of teeth can be easily and effectively accomplished by dental braces or other standard orthodontic devices."

"There," I said. "Do we have an orthodontist on our radar?"

"We do, indeed," said Nancy. She used Google again and had a phone number in a matter of seconds.

"This is Lieutenant Nancy Parsky of the St. Germaine Police Department," she said into the phone. "Oh, hi, Robin. I didn't know you were working over there. Listen, we're investigating those three murders you might have heard about. Yes ... yes ... I get it. We just need to know if Darla Kildair, Crystal Latimore, or Amy Ventura were patients. I can get a warrant if you need one, but it's really not confidential information. Yes, I'll wait."

She looked around the room and tapped her fingers impatiently on the desk. In a minute or so, she was back on the phone.

"Uh, huh ... uh, huh ... okay, sure. No problem. Thanks, Robin. Thanks very much."

Nancy clicked her phone off and grinned at me like the cat that ate the canary. A cat with very good teeth, like he'd been wearing braces.

"All three of them," she said, "were patients of Dr. Francis Passaglio."

* * *

An hour later we met Kent Murphee at his office and handed him the black plastic case containing Darla Kildair's retainer. We had stopped by her place since Nancy still had the key and retrieved it.

"Don't touch it," I said. "Not if aconite can be absorbed through the skin. We're fairly sure it's on the retainer plate. The part that fits against the roof of the mouth. I think it's what caused the lesions on the soft palate."

"Wow," said Kent. "That's a new one. Give me a couple of minutes and I can let you know for sure." He took the case and walked out of his office. Nancy and I sat down and waited.

"What are the chances?" she asked.

"I'm thinking maybe sixty-five percent," I said.

Nancy shook her head. "Seventy-five and going up all the time."

Ten minutes later Kent reappeared and said, "Yep. You were exactly right. The poison was dried, probably at a very high temperature, but then reactivated with the moisture from the victims' mouths. Reactivation might take about an hour, give or take. The retainer probably wouldn't hurt you to touch it, but once in your mouth, it's 'Goodbye, Sally!' Who did it, do you think?"

"Orthodontist," I said, "but keep it under your hat."

"Francis? Really?"

"We're going over to have a chat with him now," I said. "All three victims were his patients."

"The autoclave would work," said Kent. "For drying out the poison, I mean. He'd have one there on the premises. Smear the retainer with the stuff, pop it in the autoclave, and *voilà*!"

"Thanks," I said.

"Let me know how it goes," said Kent. "I'm writing a book."

* * *

"Do you have an appointment?" asked Robin, looking very worried when she saw Nancy and me walk into the office of Dr. Francis Passaglio, DDS. The waiting room was full, mostly moms with adolescents and young teenagers in tow. Two grown women sat against the far wall reading old *National Geographic* magazines.

"We do not," I said, "but we'd like to speak with Dr. Passaglio if it's not too much trouble."

"He's very busy as you can see." Robin gestured around the room. She lowered her voice to a whisper. "May I ask what this is in regard to?"

I whispered back, "This is in regard to three murders. Now we can wait for the warrant which will show up in a half hour or so, in which case, I'll make a rude announcement and send everyone home for the day. Or we can just talk to the good doctor for a few minutes and he might be able to clear all this up."

"I'll see if he can spare some time," Robin said, then disappeared through a door on the back wall.

A minute later she reappeared and motioned us back. We went through the door into the hallway and followed her to Francis' office. It was nicely appointed: leather furniture including a sofa and two comfortable side chairs; bookshelves containing leather-bound tomes, most of which had never been cracked; several teeth-related art prints and diplomas on the walls; and a monolithic walnut desk. Opulence. The office of a successful orthodontist pitching a twenty-thousand dollar product to a prospective customer. Francis was sitting behind the desk, his hands folded and resting on the blotter.

He was a handsome man — movie star handsome, with medium length salt-and-pepper hair, startling blue eyes, and a killer smile. He was in his early fifties and very fit; not just the kind of fit from eating right, but the kind of fit that comes from working out six days a week. I knew that he was a runner as well. I'd seen him burning up the streets of St. Germaine every summer for years.

"How may I help you, Hayden?" he said, focusing on me. He ignored Nancy.

"You know about our three murders?" I said.

"Sure. Everyone knows about them. Three women found in closets. Three foreclosed houses. You know, I bid on one of those. I would have gotten it, except for that woman from Banner Elk. I made her an offer on the house a week later. A fair offer. She would have made ten thousand and walked away. She wouldn't take it." He shook his head, as if disgusted by her stupidity. "What a silly cow."

"Why did you want that house so badly?" I asked.

"Good neighborhood. I could rent it out or even turn around and sell it in a year or two. It was a good property."

"The Cemetery Cottage."

"That's what they call it," he said, his gaze narrowing almost imperceptibly.

"Do you have any interest in the cemetery part of the property?" I asked. "Or just the house?"

His mouth came open for a moment, then closed, then his shoulders slumped slightly and he said, "Fine. The cemetery is a Civil War burial ground. I could have gotten state money to move those bodies over to Fayetteville or another Civil War memorial."

"How much?" I asked.

"I don't know exactly — sixty or seventy thousand. The house would have been gravy."

"Who else knew about the cemetery deal?" Nancy asked, and Francis looked at her as if she'd just come into the room.

"No one around here. A friend of mine from Hendersonville told me about the program. He just did the same thing. An old cemetery was on some property he'd bought, so he called the V.A. and they put him onto this relocation program. You know, honoring our fallen heros. He made a lot more, but he had a lot more graves."

"Huh," I said, not sure what to make of this information. Then I said, "You know why we're here?"

He nodded. "The three women that were killed. Robin told me."

"They were all patients of yours," I said. "You didn't think that was pertinent information you might have volunteered? You didn't think that we would like to know that connection?"

"I can't see how that is possibly relevant to the investigation," Francis said, splaying his hands upward. He was nervous. I could see it.

"Hmm," I said. "What I wonder is whether you were having affairs with those three women."

Francis went pale as a ghost, sputtered for a couple of seconds, then jumped to his feet and said through clenched teeth, "*How dare you!*"

"Judging by your reaction, Francis, I think we've hit the molar on the crown."

"You have no right … you … you … you get out of here this instant!"

"Tell him about Crystal's diary," said Nancy. "The one we found under her mattress."

"*What?*" said Francis, panic now in his voice. "Diary? Crystal kept a diary?"

"More like a journal," I said, waving it off. "But never mind about that. Tell you what. Dave is getting a search warrant and we have good cause to believe that this office is where the murders took place. So, if you wouldn't mind waiting outside, we're just going to clear everyone out and wait for Dave to show up."

"You can't just paw through everything," said Francis, losing his color again. "Patient records are confidential!"

"Never fear. We won't infringe upon anyone's rights."

"You'll regret this," said Francis, but there were no teeth in his threat.

"Did you kill these women, Francis?" I asked. "Some sort of lover's pique?"

"Don't be an idiot!"

"But you did have affairs with all three." It was a statement, not a question.

"That's not a crime," said Francis, then, "I want to call my lawyer."

"Just one more question," said Nancy, showing him her teeth. "Do you think I need braces? I've got this slight overbite."

Chapter 28

We executed the search warrant and came up empty. The warrant specified that we were granted access to the entire office, but only to the records of the three murdered women. Nancy went through them in Robin's receptionist cubicle while Dave and I searched the rest of the building. Kent was right about the autoclave. There was one in the workroom, along with molds, dental plaster, and various other tools of the trade. In the corner was a large box strapped to a refrigerator dolly, shipping straps still in place. On the outside of the box was a label from Ross Orthodontic Supply and the words "Wehmer's Pro Vacuum Mixer," and "No Forks," and "This End Up." The walls of the office were lined with different machines, presumably all with an orthodontic purpose. We didn't find any poison.

The victims' records indicated that they all had retainers, although the only one we'd found was Darla's. As far as definite proof of Francis' guilt, though, there was nothing. He as much as admitted the affairs, but he was right about one thing: that wasn't a crime. Everything else we had was circumstantial. A competent lawyer would argue that anyone might have access to Darla's retainer.

"Found something," said Nancy, walking into the workroom where Dave and I were finishing up. She had a sheet of paper in her hand. "Darla, Crystal, and Amy all had appointments on January 10th. That was a Monday. Darla's was at eleven o'clock. Crystal and Amy were back-to-back at 2:30 and 2:45."

"Those appointments are close together," I said.

"That's the way they're scheduled. Every fifteen minutes."

"What did they come in for?" I asked.

"It just says 'adjustment' in the calendar. There isn't anything in any of their records."

"They all showed up?"

"Looks like it," Nancy said. "They're checked off and I found the sign-in sheet. There's a problem, though."

"What?" I asked.

"According to the same calendar, Francis was in Raleigh on the 10th through the 12th at some orthodontic conference.

"You're kidding."

"I wish I were," said Nancy. "Easy enough to check."

"Well, I doubt that Francis is going to be talking to us anyway. Let's keep looking. Maybe we'll find the poison in the bottom drawer of his desk."

But we didn't.

* * *

Evensongs at St. Barnabas are rare. During my twenty year tenure, we might have averaged one a year depending on the priest in charge. When Gaylen Weatherall was our rector, and before she went away to be a bishop, we did a few more — one in Advent, one in Lent, maybe another — but these were just standard fare. A Solemn Candlemas Evensong and Benediction would be something to see. This was my thought, as well as the thought of many of the parishioners. There was a good crowd in Sterling Park across the street, most of whom I thought were planning to attend. Father Dressler and the Chevalier had put up posters advertising the service around the downtown area — nice posters, printed at OfficeMax in full color and featuring the Virgin Mary looking down from heaven in her holiness upon St. Barnabas.

The principal reason for the gathering across the street was the Garden Club's Winter Festival. This wasn't really a festival, but an excuse for the club to get everyone in town together and celebrate Groundhog Day by selling raffle tickets for bulbs, bare fruit trees, and lawn services to be used when spring had finally sprung. The money raised by the Garden Club would be used to beautify the downtown area. They had put up flower boxes in all the windows a few years earlier. They were responsible for the baskets bursting with color that hung from the lampposts every summer. They maintained the gardens in Sterling Park. The club consisted of a dedicated group of gardeners who took their mission seriously.

There were colorful, striped tents set up all across the park: the Girl Scouts selling hot chocolate; a food tent; some vendors hawking mountain crafts. Dr. Ian Burch, PhD, had his display of replicated Renaissance instruments. Noylene was advertising the Dip-n-Tan, even though it was much too cold to do such a thing outside. She was pointing patrons into the Beautifery to get their bronze on. The Blue Hill Bookworms were selling used books, and

186

with every book came a certificate for a free cupcake from Bun in the Oven. Patrons were going in and out of the bakery like ants.

The main feature of the Winter Festival was the groundhog. The "official" groundhog, Punxsutawney Phil, had already predicted six more weeks of winter, but we had a groundhog of our own, so why would we listen to some Yankee groundhog? Our groundhog lived in a box in Penny Trice's bedroom so seeing *his* shadow was a matter of turning on the lights. At 4:30 the sun was just beginning to dip behind the mountains. It was a brisk and beautiful, late winter afternoon.

I was at the central tent — the one selling raffle tickets. I didn't buy any since where I live I have no need of free gardening. I did donate a hundred bucks to the cause and Georgia was happy to take my check.

"How come you've been skipping choir?" I asked her. "Meg says you missed Sunday, as well as the Monday night rehearsal."

"Cold," croaked Georgia. "I can't sing a lick. This happens to me every January. From what I hear about the rehearsal Monday, I didn't miss much. I'll come to the service, though." She gave me a wink and a smile. "I wouldn't miss it."

"I take it by your evil grin that Kimberly Walnut didn't explain her predicament to Father Dressler."

"She did not. She did talk to me about it. She seems to have come to the conclusion that it's always better to ask for forgiveness than for permission. That's what Rosemary Pepperpot-Cohosh impressed upon her."

"That was Rosemary's mantra, sure enough," I said. "But I wonder why Kimberly Walnut would think that playing the forgiveness card was the best approach with this particular priest."

"I'm sure I don't know," said Georgia with a shrug, then pointed toward the front doors of the church. "There she is. Why don't you ask her?"

"Nah. How's she going to get the groundhog inside the church?"

"Probably she'll have it smuggled into the front row in a baby blanket. Not that I would know anything about that."

"Of course not. Probably we're speaking of Penny Trice's little groundhog."

"Oh, probably," said Georgia. "I believe his name is Pig Whistle. Where's Meg, anyway?"

"They were required to show up at four o'clock. They have to get their choir ruffs on."

Georgia laughed, but, thanks to her cold, it came out more like a bark. "Choir ruffs?"

"Yeah," I said, "and they look ridiculous." Then I asked, "How have you, or rather the Garden Club, managed to keep all this from Father Dressler?"

"He doesn't really talk to anyone," said Georgia. "I mean, he talks, but he doesn't listen. It's like he's in his own little world."

"I understand."

"Not that anyone would want to talk to him anyway. I think the Garden Club just assumes he's good with it. I'm the only member of the club in the choir and so Kimberly Walnut has been our only contact, not Father Gallus Dressler. Since she's doing the opening sentences, it *might* have been suggested to her that she motion for Penny to bring Pig Whistle up during this time, then get a quick blessing before Father Dressler knows what's going on. Penny and Pig Whistle exit, the Solemn Evensong continues, and everyone is happy."

"This all *might* have been suggested?" I said.

"Yes, it just might have," said Georgia.

"I'm getting a front row seat," I said.

"Save one for me," said Georgia.

* * *

I was right about the crowd. When five o'clock rolled around and the Blessing of the Groundhog was imminent, almost everyone in the park headed for the church. It was getting cold, the sun now gone, although, there was still plenty of daylight left. The festival-goers probably thought this was going to be a quick service of blessing, as it had been in the past. A wave of the priestly hand over the rodent, a few words of wisdom about the folly of trying to predict God's ways, a blessing on the upcoming season of growth, and home in time for drinks.

As the hour drew nigh, the church became packed. Many were St. Barnabas parishioners, but many weren't. People were chatting amongst themselves, as was common at one of these events. I looked at the bulletin I'd picked up on my way in. At the top, in bold print, was the announcement: *Let us keep silence in preparation of the worship of Almighty God.* I had a feeling that the priest wasn't going to appreciate all the good-natured visiting. I couldn't tell for sure. I was in the front pew and I knew that Father Dressler would be in the back arranging the processional.

Sitting on the altar was the unveiled monstrance. The altar cloth had been changed, probably chosen from the priest's private collection. It was beautiful — intricate gold overlay on a white embroidered satin background. I knew that the priest's vestments would match the altar cloth. He probably had a second set for Kimberly Walnut as well. The monstrance looked stunning. One of the spotlights at the top of the nave had been adjusted so that light glittered off the golden sunburst and flashed on the crystal eye of the icon. The eye was empty, waiting for the priest to insert the host and present it to the congregation for veneration.

The Chevalier Lance Fleagle had repositioned the anthem I'd rehearsed, moving it to the beginning of the service and using it as an introit.

"*Ahem!*" boomed Father Dressler's voice, coming over the loudspeaker from the back of the church. He had figured out the crowd wasn't going to respect his rubric at the top of the bulletin and so went to the next best thing: a welcoming announcement.

"Ahem," he said again. "Welcome to this Candlemas Service of Solemn Evensong and Benediction. Please be aware that during a Solemn Evensong, it is customary to keep silence for a few moments before the service begins."

The crowd was silent, but Father Dressler pushed his "few moments" to about four minutes, and the chattering started back. Then the organ gave some pitches and the choir sang:

I sat down under his shadow with great delight,
and his fruit was sweet to my taste.
He brought me to the banqueting house,
and his banner over me was love.

I smiled and I heard some titters as the first line was sung by the choir. Then the beautiful choral sounds filled the church and the congregation stilled. The final chords of the introit faded and the processional began.

This processional wasn't a hymn, as was usual at St. Barnabas, but rather a couple of movements from *Hommage à Frescobaldi* by Jean Langlais. Written in the 1950s, I thought, although I didn't know the work. The *Offertoire* began with a kind of brooding dance on the manuals with a chant tune in the pedals. It was the type of piece I hated to hear in concert, the type of piece most organists loved, the type of piece that generally made the congregation's teeth hurt. But it did add to the atmosphere of holy mystery, so I decided to appreciate it for what it was.

First in was Benny Dawkins, his thurible smoking like a 1969 Volkswagen van. At his side was Addie Buss, his young *protégé*, but instead of being relegated to sideboat duty, she now had a pot of her own. She matched Benny step for step and when he began his first "adoration" it was clear that we were seeing something special. Benny's thurible spun on its chains, seeming to defy the laws of physics. Addie's smaller pot, on shorter chains, was no less spectacular, twisting and turning inside the arc of the larger pot's orbit. We watched as wonderfully intricate Celtic knots appeared and disappeared, tied and untied, Addie's intertwining with Benny's, and vice-versa. Never did the pots touch, never did the artists falter, step after measured step until they reached the chancel steps. Several non-parishioners applauded spontaneously, but were quickly shushed.

Following the two thurifers was the crucifer, Robert, one of Moosey's friends, who carried the cross proudly. He'd obviously been well coached. Moosey and Bernie, now official acolytes, followed carrying the torches. It would be their job to light all the candles, and there were plenty of them. They went around the thurifers, who had paused at the steps, and got to their task.

The choir was next, processing with their heads sitting atop ruffled crinoline platters, hands pressed in a prayerful pose, teeth gritted, eyes straight ahead. Genuflecting was still the order of the day. The two ushers were there to help everyone back to their feet, but most of the choir just grabbed the side of the pew and hoisted themselves back up. As the choir split, made their turns, and headed back down the side aisles toward the narthex steps, Benny and Addie stood side by side at the chancel and their smoke now billowed like a scene from *The Ten Commandments*. They mounted the steps and stood on either side of the altar, and the smoke rose in pillars of glory.

Kimberly Walnut and Father Dressler were last in line and they ascended the steps with all due dignity. They were wearing matching copes, golden capes obviously from the Dressler catalog of liturgical finery, since they also matched the altar cloth. Father Dressler went to his chair, but remained standing, Kimberly Walnut made her way behind the altar, raised her hands and waited for her moment.

The choir had wended its way up to the loft, Moosey and Bernie had finished lighting the dozens of candles that the priest had positioned around the chancel, Robert had placed the cross in its stand and withdrawn, and Benny Dawkins and Addie continued their magic, censing the altar with a cloud never before witnessed in St. Barnabas Episcopal Church. We could no longer see the altar, but beheld smoky visions of the Presentation of Jesus in the Temple. We saw the two sacrificial turtle doves soar into the eaves. We beheld Simeon, the old man, rejoicing in his blessing. We envisaged Anna, the elderly prophetess, giving thanks to God. Finally, there was the Holy Family. It was breathtaking. No applause this time, though. It would have been like applauding the Mona Lisa.

The organ prelude wheezed to a halt. The thurifers finished their exaltation and the smoke around the altar cleared slightly, revealing Kimberly Walnut still standing with arms extended, blinking smoke out of her eyes like an owl with Tourette's Syndrome.

According to the bulletin, after the Collect for Candlemas, spoken by Kimberly Walnut, she would then have a prayer for the Blessing of Candles. According to my sources, Penny Trice would quickly ascend to the altar after the opening sentences, but before the Candle Blessing, to get an extra blessing tossed in on Pig Whistle. Then Penny would carry the blessed groundhog down the center aisle and out the front door. With all the smoke, I thought, Kimberly Walnut might just get away with it.

"Almighty and Everlasting God," she started, reading out of her playbook. We had a very good sound system at St. Barnabas, complete with those black Star Trek microphones that wrapped around the priests' faces and made them look like part of the Borg, or maybe auctioneers. The controlling sound board was in the choir loft, off to the side and in the back, out of the way. Terry Shager was working the sound this evening. He was an electrician by trade, but, as a new member of St. Barnabas, had discovered his calling as a sound engineer thanks to a class taught by Mother P last fall called "Discovering Your God-given Gift." That Terry was totally deaf in one ear and had only thirty percent of his hearing left in the other one was just more evidence of God's grace. His hearing loss was due to an electrical accident which had also left Terry with hair on only one side of his head. This made the one headphone he used fit particularly well.

Terry always wore his professional ensemble to church — faded blue bib overalls, a long-sleeved white shirt with a tie, and heavy, rubber-soled work boots. Bob Solomon, sitting in the bass section, generally kept the sound at a reasonable level when Terry was working by giving him a thumbs up or thumbs down, depending on the situation. This evening, though, Bob seemed to be as disgusted as the rest of the choir and Terry was on his own. Thus, Kimberly Walnut's voice was clear and strong and more than just a tad loud.

"We humbly beseech Thy Majesty that as Thine only begotten Son was this day presented in the temple in the substance of our flesh ..."

Penny was sitting on the front row at the end of the aisle nearest the right transept. I saw her pick up her bundle and start to walk toward the steps leading up to the altar.

"So too Thou wouldst grant us," continued Kimberly Walnut, "to be presented unto Thee with purified souls and bring us into your presence ..."

I looked up at Father Dressler. He was motionless, a small smile on his lips, his eyes closed in devotion.

"Through the same Christ our Lord. Amen," finished Kimberly Walnut.

"Amen," echoed the congregation.

Penny was at the altar and held Pig Whistle up at arm's length, her hands under his arms, with his hindquarters dangling. He wasn't as small as he looked when cradled against Penny's chest. He was a good-sized groundhog. "Eatin' size," as we say in these mountains.

Kimberly Walnut chanced a quick glance back at the priest, but he was still in his adorific pose, waiting for the Candle Blessing. So far, so good.

Kimberly reached a hand across the altar, fingers splayed, and held it over Pig Whistle's head.

"God our Father," she said, lowering her voice as if this would help disguise the blessing that was about to be delivered. Terry, recognizing the drop in decibels, gave the system a boost, and her voice now bellowed over the system, "Creator of all good things, bless now your humble rodent, Pig Whistle, ..."

Father Dressler's eyes flew open, his head snapped around, and his mouth formed a perfect "O."

"... your gentle groundhog who reminds us of the changing of the seasons according to your Word."

A sound was coming out of Father Dressler's mouth now. Not a shout: more like a cry of anguish. Terry heard it and dutifully turned up Father Dressler's mic. Kimberly Walnut heard it, too, recognized it for what it was, and began to hyperventilate, forgetting her carefully-worded blessing.

"Uh ... uh ..." she stammered, gulping air. "Uh ... Bless the groundhog ... Let him see his shadow ... or not ... according to Thy will be done in earthasitisinheavenamen." She spat out the last part in a stampede of verbiage, then looked back at the priest who was now turning red with rage and on the verge of apoplexy.

"Oh, my *Jesus!*" Kimberly Walnut cried in terror, obviously forgetting where she was.

Penny was waiting for the signal from Kimberly Walnut that Pig Whistle had been dutifully blessed and she was to head back down the aisle when the groundhog started coughing. She was still holding him aloft, but now turned sideways to the congregation. She spun Pig Whistle in her hands and looked him in the face. Another hack — sort of a wheezy bark — produced a puff of smoke that exited his lungs like he'd been lighting up in the vestibule. Three more smoky, little coughs and Pig Whistle went limp.

A gasp went up from the congregation. Kimberly Walnut's hands went to her mouth and her face registered panic. Benny and Addie, standing on either side of the altar, their pots still producing quite a fog, looked alarmed as well.

"Pig Whistle!" shrieked Penny. "*Pig Whistle!*" She turned back to the altar and screamed, "*He's dying!*"

Kimberly Walnut froze for a split second, then looked at Father Dressler. She saw what was registered on his face — something between demonic rage and imminent clergycide — hiked up her liturgical skirts, and ran for the sacristy door.

Penny followed her as far as she was able, still holding the limp groundhog aloft. She got as far as the altar, but was blocked from going further. "*Save him!*" she wailed at the departing Kimberly Walnut. "*Save Pig Whistle!*"

Father Dressler almost danced up to the altar in his fury. "What the hell? *What the hell?*" he managed, his amplified voice echoing through the church. "What *is* that thing?"

"My groundhog," sobbed Penny. "*He's dying! Wahhhhh.*"

"It's the smoke," said Benny. He'd hung up his pot in a flash and now he pushed the monstrance aside, took the groundhog from Penny, and laid the little form, face up, on the altar. Addie stood frozen, a look of terror on her face.

"Does anyone know CPR?" Benny shouted to the congregation, but it was difficult to make out what he was saying over Penny's screams.

"*Wahhhhh,*" wailed Penny.

"What?" some people shouted back. "We can't hear you!"

"Does anyone know CPR?" Benny shouted again, this time into Father Dressler's mic.

"I know it, of course," said Father Dressler, in an enraged daze. "What are you talking about? Who needs CPR?"

"Here!" said Benny, stretching Pig Whistle's little arms out and starting to push rhythmically on his chest with three of his fingers. "Give him mouth to snout resuscitation."

"*What?!*" yelped Father Dressler, not at all sure he'd heard Benny correctly. "Do *what?!*"

"Mouth to snout resuscitation!" Benny let go of the groundhog, grabbed the priest by the edges of his cope and shook him like a terrier shaking a rat, accentuating each word. "*Mouth ... to ... snout ... resuscitation!*"

"*Hurry up!*" Penny's mother, Liz, screamed at the priest from the front row. "You killed him! Now you bring him back!"

"Hurry!" shouted someone else from the front row and close enough to see what was going on. "Mouth to snout!"

"I saw it on the Nature Channel," hissed Benny, Father Dressler's mic still picking up all the action. "Just hold his jaws shut, put your mouth over his snout, and breathe."

"I will *not!*"

Penny howled again. "*Wahhhhh!*"

"*Do it!*" commanded Benny. He resumed pushing on Pig Whistle's chest.

"*Do it!*" shouted Penny's mother angrily, now coming around the side of the pew.

Father Dressler looked as though he was ready to come apart at the seams, but then did as he was told, held Pig Whistle's mouth shut and breathed into the groundhog's snout: once, twice, three times, and the little fella twitched, coughed again, then flipped onto his stomach and gasped for breath.

"Oh, Pig Whistle!" cried Penny in relief. "You're *alive!*"

It was at this moment that the back doors of the church flew open and a gas-powered golf cart came barreling down the center aisle, engine roaring, headlights blazing, and the two occupants' white acolyte robes whipping behind them like banners of salvation. I'd known about the golf cart, and of Moosey and Bernadette's new venture, but I hadn't known about the addition of the siren. I didn't know where they had gotten it, or who had installed it for them, but it was quite effective — not an emergency siren exactly, but more like a car alarm.

Whoomp! whoomp! whoomp! blared the siren. People screamed and shrank from the center aisle as the cart tore through the nave with only a foot of clearance on either side. Moosey was either lucky or being supernaturally guided by the Holy Spirit, and, knowing Moosey, it was both. He made it to the front with minor scrapes, the only casualties being the ends of a few pews.

That Moosey and Bernadette had darted out of the side door the moment they'd recognized the crisis was a credit to their new profession as veterinary rescue agents. That the golf cart obviously had no problem climbing steps in front of the church was a credit to the four-wheel drive transmission and independent suspension.

Whoomp! whoomp! went the siren. "Get out of the way!" yelled Moosey, driving with one hand and waving people back with the other. "Pet ambulance! Clear out!"

Worshippers in the front pews scattered as the cart screeched to a halt on the flagstone floor.

"Get in!" Bernie hollered excitedly. "We already called Dr. Jackson! She'll meet us at the office. *Hurry!*"

Moosey was already reversing and executing a tight three-point turn when Penny clambered into the back, clutching a quivering Pig Whistle. He slammed the cart into a forward gear, and, siren still trumpeting, tore out of the church, leaving stunned clergy and congregants in his wake. We heard the golf cart bang down the front steps and scream away into the evening.

It took a good five minutes for everyone to get back into their seat, and another two or three to settle down. Father Dressler stood behind the altar. He had the monstrance cradled in his arms and was rocking it back and forth, like he would a baby. He didn't say anything, he just stood there, staring down at the marble top of the altar where the groundhog had recently lain. The congregation finally quieted, then total silence enveloped the church. The priest stood there another minute, then two, rocking, rocking. He didn't look up. The Chevalier, not knowing what to do, decided to take it from the top. He whispered some hasty directions, then gave pitches from the organ.

I sat down under his shadow ...

* * *

I waited for Meg out in the park where the Winter Festival was just now winding down. She came out of the church with Elaine and Bev, then found Georgia and me over by the hot chocolate tent.

"Well, that was really something," said Meg, as she walked up. "I don't believe we've ever seen the like."

It hadn't been a long church service, maybe fifteen more minutes. Father Dressler had simply wandered off without a word, clutching the monstrance to his breast. The choir sang the *Mag* and *Nunc* back to back, then called it a night. Kimberly Walnut was nowhere to be found.

"You guys sounded good," I said.

"No thanks to the numbskull," said Bev. "We finally ignored him and just sang everything like we knew how."

Elaine added, "When we were finished singing, he said, 'See what one good rehearsal with a master musician can accomplish?'" She snorted in derision. "I'm gonna quit. I've already had enough."

"You may not have to," I said. "Father Dressler did not look at all well."

"Wait a second," said Meg, her eyes narrowing. "Did you plan this whole thing?"

"You did, didn't you?" said Elaine.

196

"Holy cow!" added Bev. "That's why you weren't worried."

"How could I possibly have planned all that?" I asked. "Anyway, it wasn't me. It was Georgia."

"It was not!" said Georgia. "No one could have known what would happen."

"Of course you knew," said Meg, with a smirk. "You both knew. This is St. Barnabas, after all."

Chapter 29

Buxtehooters was bouncing by the time I'd pigeon-holed the new hatcheck girl, bought her a couple of Peppermint Squirts, and told her my life's story. Her name, she informed me, was Taffi -- with an i.

"I don't get it," Taffi tittered buxomly. "How did Anne Dante get shot by Klingle without you seeing it? And didn't Pedro have a smoking gun in his shorts?"

"Deus ex Machina," I said smugly.

"And why was Anne Dante in the obituaries before she was even killed? That seemed like a good clue, but you didn't go anywhere with it."

"Deus ex Machina."

"How about Claire Annette Reed? I really thought she'd have something to do with this. I mean, she'd just broken up with Pedro and, suddenly — blam — there he was implicated in a murder he didn't commit. You can't just throw in a character for no good reason."

"Deus ex Machina," I said again.

"What happened to Holly Tosis? Did he solve his case? And Ginger! She was foreshadowed back in Chapter Eleven as Anne Dante's long lost sister. Is it the same Ginger - Ginger Vitas - that was the sister of Holly? And if so, wouldn't Anne also be Holly's sister?"

She paused and thought for a moment, then said, "So Holly Tosis was actually involved in trying to solve his own sister's murder, although he didn't yet understand the relationship? Oh, the irony!"

"Deus ex Machina," I grumbled.

"What about the St. Groundlemas merger?" she queried. "Ecclesiastica Rodentia? And the candle franchise? There just seem to be a lot of loose ends."

This dame was beginning to get on my nerves. I didn't mind a few questions from a good-looking sheila, but the ones I expected from Taffi-with-an-i were more along the lines of "What's your sign?", "Is that a shotgun in your pocket?", and "How far is it to your place, handsome?" ... these and other pertinent interrogatives accompanied by a giggle and a playful grobble under the table.

"You know," she said with an air of disdain, "the use of Deus ex Machina is seen to be the mark of so poor a plot that the writer needs to resort to random, insupportable and unbelievable twists and turns to reach the end of the story."

"Listen Taffi-with-an-i," I said as I stuffed my hat onto my head. "You spell your name with an i, so don't be giving me no literary advice."

"And what about Jimmy the Snip?" Taffi-with-an-i answered, priggishly flapping her eyebrows and draining the last drops of her Peppermint Squirt.

I chomped my stogy glumly and left her to argue the merits of White Womanhood and Interracial Kinship in the 20th Century Clerical Detective Genre with some Doctor of Ministry from the University of Life Long Learning.

* * *

"I don't think that Francis Passaglio's going to admit to the murders," Nancy said. "He's lawyered up."

"You're right," I agreed. "He's still denying it, but he knows something."

"You think?" asked Dave, managing his third bear claw of the morning.

"I do," I said. "Let's go over what we know."

Nancy opened her pad and summarized: "The three women were all killed by a dose of aconite, absorbed through the membranes of their soft palates. Darla, for sure, had the poison administered by way of her retainer, a retainer made by Dr. Francis Passaglio. We don't know if the other women were poisoned through their retainers as well because we haven't found them, but it seems reasonable to assume as much. We know that they all had appointments on Monday, January 10th, and that Francis wasn't in the office on the 10th. We also know, but can't prove, that Francis was having an affair, in the past or currently, with each of them."

"Probably not admissible," said Dave, "unless you can come up with a connection and proof."

"What's bothering me," I said, "is the other stuff — the clues we quit looking at after we found the retainer. We figured the retainer was the Holy Grail."

"Like what?" said Dave.

"Like, how did Helen Pigeon know about the missing earring? Like, why were the women dressed up like characters in *See Your Shadow*? Like, what do the Bookworms have to do with all this?" Like, why would Francis put a dead body in a house that he was trying to buy? Even stranger, why put bodies in all three houses when he was only interested in the one?"

"Who knew he was only interested in the one?" asked Dave.

"According to him," said Nancy, "no one."

"Hang on," I said. "Be real quiet for a second."

There was a vague memory bouncing around in my cortex like a crazed, flying squirrel, jumping on the furniture, climbing the curtains, almost within reach, then gone again.

"Almost ..." I closed my eyes and concentrated, my hands slowly reaching out. "Careful ..." The squirrel stayed put for just a moment, looked at me with his big Bambi eyes and blinked, then ...

"Gotcha!" I said.

"Huh?" said Dave. "What are you doing?"

"Catching the squirrel," I said triumphantly. "The answer has been there all along. This is what comes of getting old."

"What?" said Nancy.

"What?" said Dave.

"I know who the murderer is, obviously," I said. "I just should have realized it sooner."

"Are you kidding?" said Nancy. "Francis did it."

"Nope," I said.

"Dagnabbit!" said Nancy. "Okay, genius. Who did it?"

"Who else besides Helen was in the room with us when we found Crystal's body?"

"No one," said Nancy.

"Yet it was in the paper. It was part of the story."

"Yeah?" said Nancy, still confused. Then realization lit her face.

"I still don't get it," said Dave.

"If Helen didn't know about the missing earring," said Nancy, nodding, "but it was in the article, who else knew about it?"

"I guess whoever wrote the article," said Dave, then, after a pause, "Son of a gun!"

"Annette," said Nancy.

"I should have remembered," I said. "At the auction, when Helen complained that they couldn't look in the properties before buying them, Annette told me that she and Francis had already taken a peek inside the houses."

"If she'd done that, she had to have had the keys," said Dave. "You think she found out about the affairs and stuck the bodies where Francis would find them?"

"Or find at least one of them, then hear about the other two. Annette said he wanted to buy one of the houses for a rental property. She didn't know about the cemetery relocation deal he was working."

"She'd have to be crazy," Dave said.

"Certifiable," I agreed.

"What about the book club?" asked Nancy.

"She was spurned by the Bookworms, same as Ruby. I have no doubt she went onto the blog, read that trashy murder mystery and was struck by the similarities in the women's professions. Not exact, but close enough to make a comparison. I think reading the book probably triggered the whole plan. When we check with Robin at the office, I'll bet we find that all three victims came in to get their retainers cleaned on the 10th, and it was Annette who did it."

"She covered the retainers with poison," said Dave. "Then she sent the women home and picked up the bodies the next day."

"Maybe the next night," I said. "Francis was at a three-day conference."

Nancy continued the narrative. "She dressed them up, gave them all one earring, and counted on someone noticing."

"Implicating one of the Bookworms," I said. "That one was easy. Ruby said that it was Annette who told her about the Bookworms' blog. Annette would have known that Ruby would read that book, realize the similarities, and tell me about it. She is my mother-in-law, after all, and sharp as a tack."

Nancy squinted in thought. "How did she get them out of their houses and into the closets?"

"How about that refrigerator dolly we saw in the office workroom?" I said. "And Annette has that minivan."

"You realize," said Nancy, "that Francis has known all along who the murderer is."

"Of course he knows," I said, "but how could he turn in his own wife? Especially when it was his fault."

"Can we prove any of this in a court of law?" asked Nancy.

"We'll get a warrant and check Annette's minivan for trace evidence," I said. "She's been good so far, but I doubt she's *that* good."

"Francis is going to throw a right fit," said Dave. "He's best friends with Judge Adams."

I nodded. "*Fiat justitia ruat caelum.*"

"Let justice be done though the heavens fall," said Nancy.

"How did you know that?" I asked.

"You're not the only smartass in town," she said.

* * *

When we served Francis the warrant on the minivan, he crumpled.

"My God," he said. "Annette. I guess it's my fault."

"You're damn right it is!" snapped Nancy.

"We have to talk to her," I said. "If you want to bring her down to Boone with your lawyer and have her turn herself in, that's okay with us."

"She's not here. She took a trip to Paris."

I was skeptical. "Really? Paris?"

"I think it was Paris. Maybe Peru." He shrugged as if he didn't care. "Polynesia? Something with a 'P,' I think, but I wasn't really paying attention. I'm sure you can check on these things. She'll be back in a few weeks."

I snarled at him.

"She's been having some real trouble adjusting to her new medication. She's been suffering from major depression since last fall."

"No doubt being married to you," said Nancy.

Francis ignored her. "It started when Maggie left for college. She's our youngest. Empty nest syndrome they call it. I suppose you'll want to talk to her as soon as she returns."

"Sooner," I said, a real edge in my voice. "When did she leave?"

"Yesterday. It was a spur of the moment trip."

"I want you to get her on the next plane back to the States."

"I'm afraid I don't have a contact number for her," he said with a shrug. "Unfortunately, she left her cell phone here, but I'll tell her when she calls."

"I will have you up on obstruction charges," I growled. "I'm not kidding, Francis."

"You do what you have to do," he said sadly, a heaviness in his voice. He didn't look the dapper playboy we'd seen two days before. There were heavy lines in his face and his eyes had no sparkle in them. He looked older. Much older.

"Call my lawyer if you want to speak to me again," he said and closed the front door in our faces.

* * *

We searched the minivan and found exactly what we were looking for, although the van had been carefully cleaned. Some stray hairs that had found their way into the spare tire wheel well and another retainer wedged under the driver's seat, both of which, we thought, would end up tying Annette to the victims.

And we were right.

Postlude

Once we checked Annette Passaglio's passport record to see where she had gone, we discovered that she'd driven to Atlanta, flown to Qatar, from there to Bangkok, finally arriving at the airport in Vientiane, Laos, two days after she'd left St. Germaine. The passport agency told us that the Passaglios had been in Laos the previous year for two weeks — a business trip, according to Francis' tax return — and Annette, presumably, had decided Laos was her favorite non-extradition country. Her passport had been flagged, so if she decided she missed her children or her grandchildren enough to make a clandestine trip to any country that had an extradition treaty with the U.S., we'd be waiting for her.

Francis, meanwhile, had fired his receptionist, Robin, hired a new twenty-year-old assistant named Britni right out of Community College, gotten a facelift, some pectoral implants and a tummy tuck, had laser eye surgery so he would no longer have to wear contacts, and bought a vacation home in Myrtle Beach. In early May, he took Britni to an "orthodontic conference" in Costa Rica and was having the time of his life till he was bitten by a snake while on a zip-lining tour of the jungle. According to the report we heard, he mistook the twelve-foot poisonous bushmaster for a large vine — the final "tweaking" of his eye surgery scheduled for the week after he returned from his conference. He and his nubile assistant were in the middle of the rain forest with the guide and another couple and the nearest hospital was several hundred miles away. He died screaming. "Well," said Nancy, "karma's a bitch."

St. Barnabas got a registered letter on the Friday after Candlemas from Father Gallus Dressler. In the letter, he withdrew his application to be full-time rector and regretted to inform us that he'd accepted another full-time position in New Hampshire, effective immediately. Marilyn told me he didn't even come back to pack up his office. Two men appeared from Ackerman's Moving and Storage, boxed everything up, and walked it out to the truck. That was the last Marilyn saw of it.

The Chevalier, once Father Dressler had departed, didn't have much standing, and the vestry informed him that his sabbatical replacement status had been revoked. He smiled and produced a contract, signed by Father Dressler, hiring him until June, at which point, "further negotiations for full-time employment would be entered into." The church honored the contract, paid him for six months of service, and bade him depart immediately in the way he had come, taking his choir ruffs with him.

"That's my money, you know," I said to Georgia. "You gave him six months of *my* money."

"Money that would have gone into the choir fund anyway," said Georgia. "So quit your whining. You want me to call him back?"

"No, thanks," I said. "Meg would kill me."

"By the way," said Georgia, "the vestry cancelled your sabbatical."

"Fine with me," I said. "I was getting bored sitting at home on Sundays, anyway."

St. Barnabas Episcopal Church in St. Germaine, North Carolina, muddled through the next few months with supply priests, then finally hired a new rector. But that's another story.

Bud McCollough's grand opening was a success. The Wine Press was an instant internet phenomenon thanks mainly to his reputation among wine snobs across the world. Funded by Yours Truly, Bud had been holding forth at wine conventions, international competitions, and food fairs for the past couple of years in preparation for this day, and the combination of his youth, nose, and notoriety made him an overnight success. Not inconsequential were the thirty-three bottles of Chateau Petrus Pomerol 1998 that went up for auction in the first month. Different prices were realized, but no bottle sold for less than $7600. Toward the end, as the bottles were disappearing, the prices went up. The last four bottles, bought by a connoisseur in Rio de Janeiro, sold for $11,300 each. All told, the partnership pocketed $266,900. It was a good start, and the auction created "buzz," a crucial element, I was informed, to any internet site.

I rolled my earnings back into the company. Bud bought Annette Passaglio's Honda minivan for a song, had it professionally detailed, painted with the company's logo, and was a happy guy. He offered to buy his mother, Ardine, a new mobile home, but she declined. She still thought that her boy "just weren't quite right."

Moosey and Bernie delivered wine all summer long and occasionally helped out with an animal emergency. They made enough money in tips to buy themselves iPhones and pay, in advance, for two years of unlimited calls and texts.

My 1962 Chevy pickup got its makeover and, boy howdy, was it ever sweet! I didn't go for an original restoration — quite frankly I wanted a newer engine, a suspension that didn't rattle my fillings, and leather interior as opposed to the factory-issued vinyl. Even with all the upgrades, it sure *looked* original. It wouldn't win any car shows, though. The minute someone looked under the hood they'd notice the 5.3L V8 EcoTec3 engine, the fancy computer, and a wiring harness never dreamed of in the 1960s. The sound system now took advantage of satellite radio and mp3 technology. No more CDs for me. The truck's body had been totally redone, including new chrome, a two-tone blue and white paint job, and a lacquered oak truck bed. Meg would now have to give me half of the garage, but Nancy was right: I could drive this pickup for the next twenty years and then be buried in it.

Ruby and Meg were both invited into the Blue Hill Bookworms and, after mulling it over, decided that they would go ahead and join. There was an installation and, although I wasn't invited, I had it on good authority that part of the initiation involved a piglet, a flashlight, and five gallons of spaghetti sauce.

* * *

In late May, Meg and I stopped into Bun in the Oven bakery to buy some bread. Diana greeted us.

"Did you get into the book yet?" she asked Meg, wrapping up the loaf of tomato basil rye.

"I started it last night," said Meg. "It's a slow beginning."

"You're not lying," said Diana.

"What are you reading?" I asked.

"*Beyond Good and Evil,* by Friedrich Nietzsche," said Meg.

"Are you kidding?" I said with a laugh. "On purpose?"

Diana said, "No kidding. It starts out 'Supposing that Truth is a woman — what then?' After that, it becomes obtuse."

"Obtuse, you say?"

"Incredibly," agreed Meg. "Sara Black put it on the list. Why? I don't know. I believe that I may tough it out to the end of the prologue, then get the Cliff Notes."

"I already have the Cliff Notes," said Diana. "You can borrow them when I'm finished. It's my turn to pick the next book, by the way, and we're going to read *Bleak House*."

"Dickens," I said. "A good choice."

"Don't leave yet," said Diana, "I have some day-olds for Dave in the back."

"Would you also get me a lemon cannoli?" asked Meg. "I've really been dying for a lemon cannoli." She put a finger to her chin and said, "And asparagus. I've been craving asparagus, too."

"Sure. One cannoli coming up. I don't have any asparagus, though. You should check with Stephanie. She grows the stuff." Diana disappeared into the kitchen.

Meg gave me a strange look. "I guess this is as good a place as any," she said.

"As good a place for what?"

"To break the news."

"News?" I asked. "What news? Are you divorcing me?"

"And you call yourself a detective," Meg said. "Look around."

"We're buying a bakery?" I guessed.

Meg giggled. "No, silly. Cannoli and asparagus cravings ... Bun in the Oven ..."

My blood ran cold.

* * *

Marilyn was back on Tuesday from her National Literary Device Convention. We'd gotten Anne Dante out of the office and parked her on the back seat of a Greyhound with a month-long bus pass in her hand. Where she ended up was no concern of ours.

"Did you learn anything?" I asked Marilyn.

"Sure did," said Marilyn. "For instance, did you know that hyperbole is a literary device wherein the author uses specific words and phrases that exaggerate and overemphasize the basic crux of the statement in order to produce a grander, more noticeable effect?"

"I think that hyperbole is, without a doubt, the single greatest thing in the history of the entire universe," I said.

"Really?" said Marilyn, her eyes big as boiled eggs. "That's what I think, too!"

"Fix me a cup of java and let's discuss it," I said.

It's good to be a detective.

About the Author

Mark Schweizer lives in the foothills of the Blue Ridge where he writes mystery books and works in the parochialesoteric branch of church music. He tends to make up words on a daily basis.

Other books

The Alto Wore Tweed
Independent Mystery Booksellers Association "Killer Books" selection, 2004

The Baritone Wore Chiffon

The Tenor Wore Tapshoes
IMBA 2006 Dilys Award nominee

The Soprano Wore Falsettos
Southern Independent Booksellers Alliance 2007 Book Award Nominee

The Bass Wore Scales

The Mezzo Wore Mink

The Diva Wore Diamonds

The Organist Wore Pumps

The Countertenor Wore Garlic

The Christmas Cantata
(Okay - it's not a mystery, but you should read it anyway.)

The Treble Wore Trouble

The Cantor Wore Crinolines

Dear Priscilla
A 1940s comic noir thriller!

Just A Note

If you've enjoyed this book—or any of the other mysteries in this series — please drop me a line. My e-mail address is mark@sjmp.com.

Also, don't forget to visit the website (www.sjmpbooks.com) for lots of fun stuff! You'll find the Hayden Konig blog, discounts on books, recordings, and "downloadable" music for many of the now-famous works mentioned in the Liturgical Mysteries including *The Pirate Eucharist, The Weasel Cantata, The Mouldy Cheese Madrigal, Elisha and the Two Bears, The Banjo Kyrie, Missa di Poli Woli Doodle,* and a lot more.

Cheers,
Mark